"A penny for
Joy said.

"Save your money."

He was back to short, cryptic answers. Joy grew fearful. Maybe their lovemaking hadn't meant a thing to him. Then he took her hand, holding it with surprising need.

"Is something wrong?" she asked.

The dimness of the night created shadows on Stephen's features. Joy lifted his hand to her lips, brushing it gently. "Stephen?" she whispered.

His hold had been tight enough to suggest he'd never let go, but suddenly he did, casting her adrift.

"I haven't been honest with you," he said. "I don't know how to tell you the truth."

His words caused panic in her heart. A faint light was edging up over the eastern horizon. Which did she want? The new day or the old? The passion they'd shared, or the dawn, suddenly filled with the unknown...?

Dear Reader,

Welcome to Silhouette **Special Edition** . . . welcome to romance. Each month, Silhouette **Special Edition** publishes six novels with you in mind—stories of love and life, tales that you can identify with—romance with that little "something special" added in.

May has some wonderful stories blossoming for you. Don't miss Debbie Macomber's continuing series, THOSE MANNING MEN. This month, we're pleased to present *Stand-in Wife,* Paul and Leah's story. And starting this month is Myrna Temte's new series, COWBOY COUNTRY. *For Pete's Sake* is set in Wyoming and should delight anyone who enjoys the classic ranch story.

Rounding out this month are more stories by some of your favorite authors: Lisa Jackson, Ruth Wind, Andrea Edwards. And say hello to Kari Sutherland. Her debut book, *Wish on the Moon,* is also coming your way this month.

In each Silhouette **Special Edition** novel, we're dedicated to bringing you the romances that you dream about—stories that will delight as well as bring a tear to the eye. And that's what Silhouette **Special Edition** is all about—special books by special authors for special readers!

I hope you enjoy this book and all of the stories to come!

Sincerely,

Tara Gavin
Senior Editor
Silhouette Books

ANDREA EDWARDS
Sweet Knight Times

Silhouette Special Edition

Published by Silhouette Books New York

America's Publisher of Contemporary Romance

SILHOUETTE BOOKS
300 East 42nd St., New York, N.Y. 10017

SWEET KNIGHT TIMES

ANDREA EDWARDS

is the pseudonym of Anne and Ed Kolaczyk, a husband-and-wife writing team that concentrates on women's fiction. "Andrea" is a former elementary schoolteacher, while "Edwards" is a refugee from corporate America, having spent almost twenty-five years selling computers before becoming a full-time writer. They have four children, two dogs and four cats, and they live in Indiana.

Chapter One

Stephen Van Horne dropped the two grocery bags onto the counter by the sink and breathed a sigh of relief.

He'd throw the food into the fridge, pop into his running duds and take a trot down along the shores of Lake Macatawa. His shower would be followed by some chicken stir-fry and, since it was Friday, that would be followed by a hot fudge sundae with lots of nuts, just like they used to have Friday nights when he was a kid. The grand finale of his evening would be a couple hours in his workshop out back.

He enjoyed his accounting business along with the extra-curricular activities of his budding political career, but after a week of meetings, luncheons and church dinners, he was more than ready to be alone. Sanding down that antique bureau, Stephen welcomed the silence and solitude, the physical activity rejuvenating his soul as he refinished the piece of furniture.

The front doorbell rang just as he was closing the refrigerator door. "Damn," he muttered.

He hoped that it wasn't somebody lobbying for chamber of commerce favors. It was easy to get things done in a small town like Holland, Michigan. Everyone was like family and the dividing line between work and play, home and business, was rather thin. That could be a problem though, for people felt no hesitation in dropping over to discuss issues. He jerked open the door.

"Yes?" He snapped out the question like a bullwhip.

But it wasn't a staid businessman who Stephen found standing on his porch. It was a young woman. Worn cutoff jeans clung to beautiful legs, while a Chicago Bulls T-shirt valiantly strove to contain her womanly curves. A Bruno's Pizza cap perched atop an unruly mop of light brown hair framing a face that traveled the road of life on the sunny side of the street.

Good Lord, Stephen thought. They're hiring them younger every day. This one looked barely old enough to have a driver's license.

"Yes?" he said again. This time there was no snap to his question. Just plain old Friday night tired.

"Pizza," the young woman sang out with a broad smile.

Stephen just shook his head.

"This is 1533 Harrison Avenue, isn't it?"

"Yes." Stephen thought that some of the little girl faded from her face as an adult hardness crept into her eyes.

"Well, sir." She stepped close and grabbed his arm. "Then you're our winner for tonight. Just give me fifteen dollars and eighty-six cents and you will be the proud owner of this delicious large pizza, covered with mushrooms, green peppers, broccoli and pineapple."

"Ugh." Stephen made a face. "I can't imagine eating hot pineapple."

"Then you shouldn't have ordered it, sweetie."

Her eyes sparkled, with the emphasis on *spark*.

"Come on, sweets." Her smile stayed bright but her voice was rapidly growing hard. "I'm sure you're hungry and Bruno has more goodies for me to deliver."

"I didn't order the pizza."

She put her free hand on her lovely hip and gave him a come-on-now look. His eyes took the scenic route down her side and along the one luscious leg. Various emotions bubbled within him and Stephen chose to focus on the smidgens of anger that threatened to surface.

"And besides not ordering that pizza," he said, "I'm not sweetie, sweets or sweet in any way."

"We all have our problems, hon." Her smile was definitely losing its wattage. "And what you're saying is that you're not paying for this pizza."

"Since I didn't order it, that is correct."

"But as long as I brought it all the way out here, I might as well leave it, right?"

He couldn't believe it. The little elf was accusing him of trying to stiff her. Stephen Van Horne, owner of Van Horne Financial Services and president of the chamber of commerce, trying to stiff some kid over a damn pizza. It was ludicrous. It was also easier now to concentrate on his anger.

"I didn't order it," he insisted.

"Right." She turned and hurried down the steps. "Better luck next time."

Angry words stood ready to fly off his tongue, but she was climbing into her beat-up old truck before he could draw a breath.

Just as well. He turned on his heel and shut the door. It wouldn't do any good for him to get into a shouting match with some kid, but he would have liked to have given her a piece of his mind.

Suddenly conscious that he hadn't heard her motor start, he turned to stare out the sidelights. Better watch and make sure she left without any further problems. As hot-tempered as that kid was, she'd be likely to throw the pizza on his lawn or worse. She'd be better off tracking down the right address instead of blaming him for her problems.

Stephen frowned. The truck was still there. What was she fooling around for? He opened the door to hear the melodious tune of a grinding automobile engine. Jeez! He stomped down the walk.

"You're running the engine down," he shouted.

"Well, excuse me."

Great. All he needed was another exchange of words with little Miss Big Mouth. Stephen stopped in mid-stride. There were two little kids in the car, each wearing a Bruno's Pizza cap.

"What are you doing?" Stephen asked. "Baby-sitting while you're making deliveries?"

"We're helping Mommy," the little girl announced.

Mommy? Stephen turned to the young woman, suddenly seeing tiny crinkly lines near her eyes even as the words came out of his mouth. "You can't be their mother. The boy looks like he's ten."

"Very good, sir." The boy sang out in a phony circus ringmaster tone of voice. "Give that man a giant see-gar."

Stephen glared at the kid while the woman glared at him, all the while grinding the motor. Annoyance at the sound finally won over all. He'd never been able to tolerate useless noises.

"Would you cut that out?" he snapped. "All you're doing is running down the battery."

The woman turned off the ignition and jumped out of the delivery truck.

"You got any better ideas, Mr. Know-it-all?"

"Sure. Close your mouth and open the hood."

"I don't need your help," she pointed out tersely, climbing back into the truck. "So just go back to your big old house and let me—"

"Hey, hey." Stephen made a T with his hands. "Time out."

The glare burned fiercely but she did keep quiet, staring down at the interior parts of her stranded vehicle.

"It looks like you're not into mechanical things, so let me point out a few essentials." He kept his voice calm and soothing. "This is the hood," he said, pointing to the front of the truck. The woman was leaning closer then. "And these are your lips. You shut these and unlock that."

"You—"

"You're getting them mixed up again."

"I'm going to come out there and mix up your teeth."

The truck door opened and the woman put one sandaled foot on the pavement. Stephen's heart did a backflip. It looked like in three seconds or less he was going to be brawling with a shapely little elf. That would sure perk up the eleven o'clock news.

"Hi," a voice called from behind them.

The heat and lightning disappeared as quickly as a summer storm on a windy day. They all turned to look at his sister Beth standing on the porch, yawning and rubbing her sleep-heavy eyes as she smiled at them all.

"When did you get in?" Stephen demanded.

His sister shrugged. "A few hours ago. You weren't home so I let myself in. And then I took a nap."

"I thought you didn't have a key," Stephen said.

Beth shrugged as she turned toward the delivery kid...woman. "You got my pizza?"

"Vegetarian with pineapple?"

"Uh-huh."

The young woman pulled out the box and, with a smirky little smile, sashayed past Stephen to hand it to Beth. "Fifteen eighty-six."

Beth turned toward him. "Stephen."

He clenched his teeth but pulled out his wallet. "I only have a twenty."

"Keep the change," Beth said, handing the woman the bill.

The smile became bright again as the woman profusely thanked Beth. Stephen wanted to point out that it was his money, but wasn't silence the better part of valor? Something like that.

"Beth," he said. "Why don't you take these kids into the house? This woman's pickup sounds sick."

"Are you going to make our truck all better?" the little girl asked as she stepped onto the sidewalk. "It don't feel good."

Before Stephen could reply, the boy butted in. "You don't look like no Mr. Goodwrench."

"I'm an accountant and financial planner," Stephen replied.

The boy just shook his head. "That means he can't fix nothin'."

Stephen glared after them as Beth promised them pizza and three different kinds of ice cream. The boy was really a charming little fellow. Certainly no doubt whose son he was.

"Well," a snippy little voice purred behind him.

He turned to look into the coolest pair of green eyes that he'd ever seen float on this earth.

"Can you do anything?" she asked.

Scores of neighborhood bullies had learned the answer to that question, but her challenge stirred other emotions within him. One thing for certain, taking up that challenge here in broad daylight, in the middle of Harrison Avenue would get him even more publicity than the knockdown brawl he'd almost stepped into.

Swallowing hard and forcing such errant ideas from his head, Stephen turned toward the truck. "Unlock the hood, please."

Surprisingly, she did as he told her and Stephen lifted it up. "Ugh."

The truck's innards were a mess. The ignition wires were pitted, the distributor cap appeared to have a crack in it, while rust and dirty grease covered everything else. Someone needed to take this little lady in hand on the topic of engine maintenance.

"What's with the 'ugh'?" she asked. "That your favorite word?"

Stephen clenched his teeth for a long moment. Perhaps "taking in hand" was the wrong way to put it. "That motor looks like a mess," he said. "Haven't you been taking care of it?"

"I've been giving it a lot of love."

Stephen continued staring at the motor. Family legend had it that they had a pirate for an ancestor, but Stephen hadn't believed that or any of his grandmother's tales. Until now, that is. For Stephen could feel the old reprobate on his shoulder, whispering all sorts of lascivious suggestions. Suggestions that the president of the Holland Chamber of Commerce and would-be governor had best ignore.

The woman sighed. "I guess you're going to tell me that love's not enough."

He kept his eyes down, in spite of urgings of his roguish genes. Love could be enough, should be more than enough if it was the right kind of love.

Stephen ignored the images dancing in his mind. It was her lilting voice that threatened to unnerve him. She could use his help with her transportation, and he'd give it willingly, but that would be all.

"You're not going to tell me it's a goner, are you?"

He looked up then, scowling at her. Her green eyes and dimpled cheeks were framed with worry, but Stephen wasn't moved. Well, not much. Maybe just a little.

"I don't know what it is, certainly nothing I can fix." He slammed the hood back into place. "It'll have to be towed to a service station. Can you handle that?"

She made a face, but nodded.

"Come on in," he said. "I'll call somebody and you can wait in the house."

"Did you know that Beth's daddy invented chocolate?" Katie asked.

Joy paused a moment to stare in semihorror at the huge concoction of ice cream, whipped cream, nuts, and cherries that Katie had before her. Then shaking her head, Joy answered. "No, I didn't know that. I hope he got a patent on it."

"That's not what she said," Robbie corrected his little sister, the words barely able to squeeze out around the ice cream he was stuffing into his mouth. "She said an ancestor. Somebody who's been dead a long time."

"Our daddy's been dead a long time," Katie said.

"Not that long," Joy said, though some days the ten months seemed like a lifetime. "But chocolate was around even before your daddy was born."

Beth padded over and put a generous bowl of chocolate ice cream in front of Joy. "Actually, I'm not too certain of that story. My grandmother only told it once. Right after the one about the ancestor who invented ice cream."

"Wow!" Katie breathed.

Robbie just stared dubiously at them, letting his eyes shout out his doubt.

"Actually, we've got some real ancestors that aren't bad, but Gram sometimes forgets who they are." She nudged the bowl of ice cream closer to Joy. "Don't you want any? I promise you it's not from the first batch my ancestor made."

Joy just shook her head. "I'm not really hungry. Thanks anyway."

"Where's Stevie?" Kate asked.

Stevie? Was that another ancestor or the man auditioning to be the next emperor of the civilized world?

"He's calling the gas station for your mom," Beth said. She sat down. "Come on, eat it before it melts."

"Why don't you save it for Caesar?"

Beth just burst out laughing. "That's very good. Fits, too. Don't know why no one ever thought of it before."

"I thought his name was Stevie," Katie said.

Joy leaned over to kiss Katie, savoring the tenderness brought on by her daughter's bewildered expression. Then she pulled the bowl of ice cream over. "What did his playmates call him?"

"Not Mister Van Horne, which is what you're probably thinking. No, he's always been Stephen," Beth replied. "Mom called all of us by our given names, but Stephen was never a nickname type. I mean, even Mom used to laugh about how serious he was and how he always had to run things."

"Can we go watch for the tow truck?" Robbie asked, interrupting them.

"Sure," Joy said. "But stay on the porch."

"Okay." He turned to Katie. "Come on, Squirt."

Joy picked at her ice cream in silence as the patter of the kids' feet died away. Some of her tensions were melting away, enough so that she could admit to herself that her earlier annoyance hadn't really been at Stephen but at one Joy Marie Chapin. A grown woman who was letting someone take care of her again.

But Stephen calling the gas station for her wasn't the same as Paul having to deal with any repairman that came to the house. She hadn't had any auto repairs done since moving here four months ago and didn't have the faintest idea who to call. Letting Stephen do it wasn't letting someone run her life again, but using someone else's experience.

"Stephen was actually pretty cute as a kid," Beth said suddenly. "Gram said God made him cute so that people would listen when he bossed them around."

"Did it work?" It hadn't with her, or had it? She was in his kitchen, picking at his ice cream, while his garage was coming for her truck.

Beth chuckled. "I don't know if it was his looks, but he sure got away with bossing all us kids. Mom used to say that a house could only have one boss, and since Stephen was so good at it, it might as well be him."

"Oh." No wonder he was so sure of his right to the scepter; he'd bossed people around all his life.

Beth leaned forward to put her chin in her hands and her eyes took on a dreamy look. "Jane and Robert—they came right after Stephen and probably wouldn't agree—but I thought Stephen was really nice. I was three years younger than Robert, but Stephen always made sure I got included. Whenever something traumatic happened to me, I could always run to him. He was my knight in shining armor."

The perfect big brother who would grow up to be the perfect father. Joy thought of Paul, racing away on the fast-track evenings and weekends. He had thought he was their knight in shining armor by taking care of everything, but he'd left his business impossibly overextended, her with no idea of even when the mortgage payments were due, and the kids with precious few memories. That was the most tragic of all. They'd never run to him with their victories or their problems; he'd always been too tired, too busy, too far away, even though he'd been doing it all for them.

She had learned from it all though. To stay away from knights in shining armor. The armor was just there to hide secrets, but the shininess blinded you until it was too late. "Does Stephen have any children of his own?"

Beth paused a long moment, before shaking her head. "He was married for a while, but he and his wife were both into their careers. Donna, his ex, was a firstborn, too, and Gram says those things never work out."

Joy grunted noncommittally.

"Donna still lives in Chicago. Some kind of bigwig in a CPA firm. Stephen came back home after the divorce." Beth wrinkled her nose. "He's a small town kind of guy."

"The tow truck should be here any minute."

Joy had somehow known he was there, even before he had spoken. It was as if the air vibrated with his presence, giving emphasis to his words. Joy turned toward the door before she could stop herself. His shorts and T-shirt showed off his lean, athletic physique too nicely and she looked away. Better to concentrate on the last of the ice cream in her dish.

"You going running?" Beth asked him.

"Once I get Joy and her kids settled."

Joy pushed the bowl away. She wasn't so helpless that he had to rearrange his plans to watch over her. "You don't have to wait on my account," she said and got to her feet. "I can point out which vehicle is mine."

"And can you also get you and the kids back home?" he asked.

She paused a moment, then swept up her purse with an anger that she was too mature to turn on him. All right, so she was wrong. So she had to depend on him a little bit longer. She didn't have to listen to that mocking voice in her heart that asked if she could make it on her own.

"I think I'll go wait on the porch," she said. "The kids shouldn't be out there alone."

She was conscious of both Beth and Stephen following her, but chose not to think about it. She had done great in the ten months since Paul had died. She'd settled his estate, charted a new course for her and the kids' lives and set it in motion. Just because the truck's maintenance had slipped through the cracks, it didn't mean her parents were right. One little mistake wasn't proof that she and the kids should have moved in with them.

"Nobody's here yet, Mommy," Katie announced as Joy stepped out onto the wide, old-fashioned porch.

"They should be here shortly, honey," she said. "Mr. Van Horne called them."

"So what?" Robbie muttered. "Is he some kinda big cheese?"

Joy gave her son a stern look, ignoring the smothered snicker that escaped Beth.

"Here's the truck now," Stephen announced as he stepped out from behind them.

Joy could have sworn he spoke before the tow truck turned the corner. Was he psychic or was Robbie right? He was some kind of big cheese. Stephen spoke and the world seemed to obey.

Joy hurried down to meet the tow truck driver, feeling as if she was almost running in order to keep up with Stephen's longer stride.

"I'm not certain what's the matter with it," she told the man when she was still a good ten feet away. "It doesn't want to kick over."

"Yes'm, that's what Mr. Van Horne told me."

Joy stopped, arms akimbo, telling herself to be reasonable. He had to give the mechanic some idea what was wrong.

She watched in brooding silence as the man hooked up the battered old truck, real worry starting to shove her annoyance aside. She hoped it wasn't anything too serious, which would translate into too costly. She couldn't do without transportation, but she sure couldn't afford much in the way of repairs.

"Here's my card, ma'am," the mechanic said and handed her a card that listed the address and phone number of the station. "How about you give me a call late tomorrow morning?"

Joy nodded and started slowly back up to where the kids were waiting. Stephen was walking with the man over to the driver's seat, either telling the man more of what was wrong with her truck or how to drive his tow truck properly, but she just didn't care. She'd thought she had everything planned out so well, now this.

Her father would say he'd told her she didn't have enough money or experience to go off on her own and start a business, that she should have let him and her mother take care of the kids and if she wanted to keep busy, she should be a library volunteer. Right, and she could see him driving her the three blocks to the library and picking her up. It would be high school all over again.

"Get into the car," Stephen said. "I'll get my keys and be right with you."

He was gone before Joy could say anything, if there had been anything she'd wanted to say to him. Which there wasn't. She knew better than to try to justify herself to fathers, husbands or Caesars. She got the kids into the back seat of the plush Lincoln Towncar, then climbed in herself, waving goodbye to Beth as Stephen got into the driver's seat.

"Where to?" Stephen said as he backed down the drive.

The conversation was simple; she just gave him directions to Bruno's and in between told herself that her dreams weren't in jeopardy. It didn't matter if the whole rest of the world thought she was incompetent as long as she believed.

In what seemed like a few hours later, even though the lying dashboard clock said ten minutes, they were pulling into Bruno's parking lot.

"What's this?" Stephen asked with a frown as he stopped in front of Bruno's.

"Bruno's." Joy got out and opened the back door for the kids.

"I can see that," he snapped. "What are we doing here?"

The man was not only bossy, he was dense. "This is where I work." She pointed to the cap back on her head. "You see? B-R-U-N-O'S. Bruno's. The best pizza in town."

Her explanation didn't seem to have pleased him or brought enlightenment to the dark corners of his mind. In fact, it seemed to have spread those dark corners out to cover everything.

"You may work here, but the kids don't. I assumed I was taking you home."

"Well, you assumed wrong." There he went again, trying to run her life. Did she have a sign on her forehead that said "incompetent" or was it the genetic reaction all tall, blue-eyed men had to short, green-eyed women? She sent the kids up to the sidewalk running along the storefronts while she took a deep, steadying breath.

"I have another couple of hours to work," she told him quietly.

"The kids don't. They should be at home playing ball or watching TV. Or eating a real dinner."

She knew that. She knew it deep in her heart and didn't need some bossy know-it-all to tell her what was the right way to raise her kids. Sometimes a chosen road led through some brambles though, and you either plunged forward or turned around. She wasn't turning around.

"That's where they would be, too, if my baby-sitter hadn't gotten sick," she said as sweetly as she could manage. "Rather than leave them home alone, I brought them with me. And now, they'll play games in the employees' lounge until I get off. In the No-Smoking-Allowed Employees' Lounge, that is."

He had the grace to look mildly embarrassed. "You should have left them with Beth and me then," he said.

"Right. With two total strangers rather than with me. Sure. Thanks for the ride and all." She shut the door, not quite as hard as she wanted, but enough to satisfy her need to have the last word.

She didn't though. With the push of a button, he was lowering the front window.

"You should have—"

"Thanks for the ride, Stevie," Robbie called out from the restaurant doorway.

"Thank you for the ride, Uncle Stevie," Katie added.

Joy fought back a sudden urge to laugh and watched as his shoulders sagged. He turned to stare out the front window a moment. When he turned back, anger no longer vibrated in the air.

"Are you going to be all right now?" he asked.

"Just fine, Stevie," Joy replied.

She couldn't help herself, and watched with delight as the storm clouds rolled back into his eyes. She just smiled and stepped back from the car. He pulled out of the lot.

"We should always say thank you, shouldn't we, Mommy?"

"Yes, Katie. We should."

"It makes everybody feel good."

Joy savored the image of the scowling Mr. Van Horne. "It certainly does, honey. It certainly does."

Chapter Two

"I really would appreciate it if you'd give me some warning whenever you decide to move in for a spell," Stephen said, looking up from the Saturday morning paper to frown at his sister.

Beth just made a face and pulled a box of oat bran cereal off the shelf. "Mom said we should all look on this house as our home."

Stephen turned his attention back to the high school baseball scores. He knew their mother had said that when he'd taken over the old family home a few years back, but she hadn't meant to saddle him with permanent boarders. Well, really it was only Beth, the family gypsy, a free spirit. All the others had homes and families of their own.

A dark cloud drifted over the words before him. He had the house, but no family, putting him somewhere between Beth and the others. Stephen wondered what that made him? Certainly not a gypsy, but what then?

"You doing anything today?"

"What?"

Beth was eating a handful of dry cereal right from the box. "I just wondered if you were doing anything today."

"Why?" he asked, tightening his eyelids to slits.

"Yuck, this cereal tastes like it's been here for years. I bet even the squirrels would gag on it." Beth put the cereal back in the cabinet and poured herself some orange juice. "My creative writing group is having a picnic on Ottawa Beach this afternoon."

Stephen hunched forward and concentrated on the sports stories before him. He knew better than to get involved in anything with his sister.

"I'm going to be busy," he growled.

"The whole day?"

"My whole life."

"We have this new woman who's started coming a few weeks ago. She's from the Detroit area."

"In fact, I'll be tied up for all of eternity."

His sister drained her glass. "She's real nice."

"Beth." Stephen ground his teeth. "I don't intrude on your life. So I would appreciate it if you'd return the favor."

"Oh, for heaven's sake," Beth exploded. "I'm just trying to put a little fun in your life."

"I can take care of myself."

"Right, just like you did with that pizza lady."

Stephen's jaw dropped, but Beth had stomped out of the room before he could get it closed and reloaded for a retort. He turned his attention back to the sports page, for the umpteenth time.

What the hell was his sister talking about? That woman had come to his house, ran into some car trouble, and he took care of things. One, two, three. Like he had when Jane had fallen from her high chair, or when Beth's bracket came loose from her braces or when the hospital needed a new pediatric wing.

He turned the page to see a picture of a high school baseball player crossing home plate. The kid wore a grin as wide as the ocean, inviting him to share in the excitement, but Stephen just turned the page. He wasn't going to look closer at that photo. He was not going to squint at the kid's features, trying to see if he had Van Horne eyes or a Van Horne chin. It was a stupid waste of time. His kid was probably a Californian. Every second person in the United States was.

Stephen slapped the paper onto the table as he stood up. "I'm running some errands," he called upstairs to Beth, then hurried outside before the ghosts in the kitchen could lure his thoughts back.

He needed to keep busier, that was his problem. The past could only steal you away from the present if you let it. He backed out of the drive and made a mental list of the errands that needed doing. The first was to get some gas.

"Hey, what's happening, Mr. V?" Lou, the station owner, came ambling over to the self-service pump as Stephen got out of the car.

"Not too much, Lou," Stephen replied. He concentrated on getting the nozzle in place before he glanced very casually at the battered Toyota pickup truck parked along the back fence. "Get that truck fixed?"

"Your lady friend's?"

Stephen gave Lou a good example of Van Horne haughty. "She was just delivering pizza to my house. I'd never met her before."

Lou's grin warmed in a most disgusting manner. "You mean that sweet young thing with the two little kids?"

"I mean that truck," Stephen said. Lou was as bad as Beth in some ways. "Driven by a pizza deliveryperson."

The service station owner took a moment to scratch his jaw. "Now your brother, he wouldn't be letting a chance like this slip away. Used to say he was a descendant of some great lover and had a reputation to uphold."

"Since he's been happily married for ten years now, I would hope his days as a ladies' man were over," Stephen muttered. "Now, about the truck..."

Lou sighed. "Made a start on it," he admitted.

"Need a lot of work?"

"It's been neglected. Lady looks to be a little squeezed for funds right now." Lou paused a moment to glance at Stephen. "I got the important stuff fixed up. We worked out a payment plan."

"Oh."

Lou nodded. "Forty bucks a month for the next four months."

"Good." Stephen cleared his throat. "You going to run the truck over to her place?"

"Randy's off sick today." Lou shrugged. "She's got some kind of art shop down on Fourth Street. Said she'd walk over after lunch."

"Thanks for coming out so quickly."

"Service is our motto," Lou replied with a broad grin as he started to amble off to take care of a customer. "Same as yours."

"Wonderful," Stephen replied. Lucky for Lou, the older man had moved a little faster than usual.

In a few more minutes Stephen was back out on the road, but somehow his list of chores had vanished, replaced with memories of a green-eyed lady. A mellow spring breeze danced in the sunshine, refusing to retreat before Stephhen's darkening mood.

He shook his head. People were so careless about their future. They didn't plan or prepare themselves, then they not only brought woes onto their heads but onto their children's as well.

Stephen's foot hit the brake as he passed a scrollwork sign advertising arts and crafts products. He would stop in and give them all a ride over to the gas station. A grim smile cracked his lips. A ride and some words of advice for Mommy.

He went inside, the bell on the door dancing and playing through the vast emptiness of the former print shop. Framed paintings covered the worn brick walls while sculpture pieces were scattered about on the ink-stained old floor. It might be a low budget operation, but there was a certain pleasant ambience about it.

"Mr. Van Horne."

Stephen turned and successfully fought an urge to sweep her into his arms. Joy's pleasant features were hung with a smile bright enough to shame the sun. There was no doubt that this family needed help but it certainly wouldn't come from him. He'd screwed up enough relationships to last a lifetime.

"What a surprise."

"Pleasant, I'm sure," Stephen replied dryly.

"Of course. What other kinds are there?"

Stephen tried glaring some sense into her but looking into the woman's face was like staring into the sun. He turned away, little spots of brightness dancing before his eyes.

"Anything in particular you're interested in?" she asked.

He let his eyes travel quickly across the room before letting them settle on her trim figure. "Actually I just came by to see how you and the kids were. I'm sure last night was pretty traumatic for them."

Joy laughed, a gang of elves tinkling their notes of happiness. "They're just fine. They look upon life as an adventure. We all do," she added.

Stephen frowned. A positive attitude was good, but this woman was too much. "How's the truck?"

"Fine. It just needed some minor repairs." She looked him straight in the eye, her features overflowing with good cheer and optimism.

He turned away to reclaim his soul and let his gaze settle on the paintings on the far wall. They were beautiful. Landscapes and old barns from the Michigan countryside. He walked over to look at them more closely. There was a starkness about them, but with enough fuzziness to give them a dreamlike quality.

"Nice," he said. "Local artist?"

"Those are some of mine."

"Oh." Maybe she wasn't as irresponsible as she seemed. Maybe she just lived in a world of her own and didn't see the harsh realities. Artists weren't known for practicality.

"I have all sorts of talents," she went on. "Besides painting, I can also tap dance, play minuets on the piano, and do a plié. Of course, the jury's still out on which of those skills are marketable."

"I didn't know anybody tap-danced anymore."

"I haven't since I was fourteen, but my tap shoes still fit."

"Better not tell Bruno. He might give you a whole new job classification."

She smiled, throwing Stephen's equilibrium out of whack. He cleared his throat and got back to the business at hand. "I just came by to give you a ride to Lou's station."

Joy frowned at him.

"To pick up your truck," Stephen reminded her.

"Oh." She laughed, ringing those thousand tiny bells again. "Lou just called a few minutes ago. Somebody or other had come in after all and they're going to bring it over."

Disappointment clouded Stephen's vision. She didn't need him to give her a ride. Lucky. But then life always rescued some people.

As Stephen searched for a way to warn her that life couldn't be counted on to always be that kind, Robbie clattered down the stairs in cleated shoes. Katie, barefoot and wearing her mother's broad smile, skipped along behind.

"Hi, Stevie," they chorused.

"His name is Mister Van Horne," Joy reminded them.

"I have a soccer game today," Robbie announced.

"They stay with you when you're here at the store?" Stephen asked.

"We live upstairs," Joy replied.

Stephen's eyes wandered to the street outside—a regular commercial street, heavy with traffic. It was well and good for her to live here, following her dreams, but not to subject her kids to such an environment. Not to mention hauling them around as she delivered pizzas.

"You want to come to my game?" Robbie asked.

Stephen had his mouth open, ready to issue warnings that he was sure Joy wouldn't heed, when Robbie's question penetrated. Stephen's lips snapped shut.

"It's fun," Katie assured him. "We holler at Robbie and tell him what to do."

The clean, bright faces shined up at him, their happiness overflowing. Stephen's eyes misted and he looked away. His eyes were caught by those misty paintings, pulling him into a dream world of dogs and kids and old tire swings. Going to soccer games in the spring, followed by baseball. Fishing in the summer and apple picking in the fall. These were all things a father did with his kids. Stephen's heart felt like stone.

"I'm sorry I can't," he replied. "I have a load of work waiting for me at the office." He turned abruptly and left, hurrying away from Joy's hazy dream world of happiness and contentment. Hurrying away before it smothered him.

"Hey, Robbie. You missed."

"Katie," Joy murmured.

Her daughter squirmed around in Joy's lap to face her. "But you said we were supposed to yell loud enough for Robbie to hear us."

"I meant nice things," Joy said. "Like, 'That's okay, Robbie, the next one will go in.'"

Katie's features were weighed down with serious misgivings. "But it won't, Mommy. Robbie misses a lot."

"They all miss a lot, honey. The important thing is they're having fun."

Robbie took another good shot that went wide of the goal to the other side. "Good try, Robbie," Joy shouted.

"I told you he misses a lot," Katie muttered.

Joy just hugged Katie close to her, kissing the top of her head as she breathed in the pleasant mixture of shampoo and fresh air. The ball had drifted back to the other side of the soccer field, away from Robbie and, although she kept looking at the field, Joy let her eyes mist over.

Robbie was a good athlete and he enjoyed having them come out and watch, but it was obvious that he was getting to the age where a man's approval was important. Otherwise, the poor kid wouldn't have asked that stuffed shirt to come to his game.

"Mommy, how come Stevie's always mad at us?"

Joy refused to wonder how Katie knew Joy was thinking about Stephen. "His name is Mr. Van Horne, honey."

"Stevie's easier."

Joy nuzzled her daughter's hair with her chin. "I don't think he's really mad at us. He's just—"

A burst of cheers pulled Joy back to the game. Robbie had scored a goal for his team.

"Way to go, Robbie," Joy shouted and clapped.

"Finally, he doesn't miss," Katie muttered.

Joy just laughed and let her vision cloud up again. No, Stephen wasn't mad at them; he wasn't the type to be mad for no reason. But then, how could she be so sure of that? She had no idea what type he was.

He was certainly handsome, in an aristocratic sort of way. And Beth said he was nice. No, that wasn't fair. He must be nice; he had come forward to help them out. Or was that just because he liked to run things?

Her head was starting to spin and she closed her eyes. It really didn't make any difference whether he liked them or not. He was a knight in shining armor and taboo. Better she should start thinking about important things, like how she was going to finish paying for the repairs on the truck.

"Hi, Stevie."

Katie's shout from just under Joy's chin caused her to jump. Stephen slipped right in next to them on the bleachers, his leg brushing hers, his arm just a breath away. Fortunately, he continued staring straight ahead at the playing field. She could let her startled heart relax into a mere frantic pace.

"I thought you were tied up this afternoon," she said.

"I hadn't realized until I checked my calendar that I was already scheduled to be out here this afternoon."

"I see," Joy said slowly.

"One of the organizations I'm active in is the Jaycees," Stephen said. "I'm on the board of directors."

"Oh?"

"And this soccer league is one of our youth programs."

Joy nodded slowly. "It's a good program."

"Jackie and Julie are here, Mom." Her daughter squirmed out of her lap and pointed toward twin girls getting out of a minivan. "Can I go play with them?"

"Okay, honey. But stay near the field."

Joy watched as Katie ran across the grassy strip. She felt rather vulnerable with the girl gone, but adults didn't hide behind children.

"So you're satisfied with the program?"

"Program?"

He was continuing to stare at the kids playing the game before them. From where she sat, his eyes seemed grim, his lips in an uncompromising straight line.

"The soccer program," he said. "Are you satisfied with the coaches, the referees? Is Robbie enjoying himself?"

"Oh, yes. Everything's fine."

Joy frowned and put her elbows on her knees and her head in her hands to better stare at the playing field. Damn. She was starting to sound like a talking doll. Push a button, pull her string and listen to the chatty doll talk.

Suddenly Robbie noticed Stephen and stopped in midplay. "Hi, Stevie," he hollered.

Adults seated around them chuckled while Robbie's coach yelled at him to pay attention to his game. Stephen's face remained stonelike. Oh, great, her kids were really getting under his skin.

"I'm sorry," she said. "I keep telling them to call you Mr. Van Horne."

He just shrugged. "Don't worry about it." Though his words were casual, his voice was stiff and cool.

Joy looked at him, trying to will his eyes to meet hers, but he continued to stare ahead of him. There was a wall there that he wasn't letting anybody past. He had a great body—trim and strong. His unruly blond locks invited touching and his eyes were the bluest this side of the universe. But No Trespassing signs were in everything he did.

Not that she was interested in trespassing. She had her hands full taking care of the three of them and getting her art store to fly.

Joy cleared her throat. "Do you coach any teams?"

"No." The answer was short and curt. "I'm involved in the financial and planning end of things. We try to keep the costs as reasonable as possible."

"Well, you've succeeded," Joy agreed. "The programs in the Chicago suburbs are much more expensive."

He nodded. "We also have an aid program."

"That's nice," she murmured. Robbie was about to take a shot but an opposing player took the ball away.

"Have you looked into that?" Stephen asked.

Robbie had recaptured the ball and had another shot on goal, but it sailed over the crossbars. "Looked into what?" she asked.

"The Jaycees financial-aid program," Stephen said. "We want to make sure that every child has a chance to participate."

Joy blinked in bewilderment. She and the conversation must have split up someplace along the way. "Robbie is participating."

"I'm aware of that," Stephen replied. "But maybe if you took advantage of the community resources available, there wouldn't be a need to deliver pizzas."

"What's wrong with delivering pizzas?"

Stephen didn't answer at all, seeming to concentrate even harder on the play of the children.

Joy felt herself getting closer to the boiling point. What was with him? "I mean, it's not against the law."

"Hauling your kids around with you at all hours of the night should be."

"I don't work all hours of the night." Her voice was rising but she didn't care. "I don't work beyond eight."

"It could be dangerous."

"What are you talking about? This is Holland, Michigan. Not some burned-out, drug-infested neighborhood in Chicago or Detroit."

Lines of tension formed around his mouth. "There are better things for your kids to be doing," he said.

"What's the big deal?" Joy said loudly, ignoring the people casting furtive glances their way. "Once a week or so, we ride around for a few hours, see different neighborhoods, meet people, stop to play in the park—" She paused to get control of her trembling. "We have fun. You should try it yourself sometime. Although first you'll have to pull that steel rod out of your neck."

He turned around and gave her the full frost treatment with those sky blue eyes. "Good day, Mrs. Chapin," he said with a curt nod.

"I'm sure it will be," Joy snapped. "Now that the dark clouds are rolling on."

He turned on his heel and stalked away without further words. Good, Joy thought. Stay out of my life. I don't need any extra depression at the moment.

Stephen rubbed the side of the old bureau he'd been refinishing for the past three months with the fine-grained sandpaper. The oak wood was taking on a golden sheen, looking even more beautiful than when it had been new. In another three weeks, he'd be done and ready to start refurbishing another battered antique out of his collection.

Except for his one misstep, Stephen had pretty much followed the path laid down by the men before him. After a stint in the big city, he'd come home to Holland where, as the eldest son, he continued a tradition of successful businessman and community leader.

He stood up and looked at the desk from another angle. Also, like his father and grandfather, Stephen used a manual hobby to rest his intellect and revive his soul. His grandfather chopped wood and his father raised roses. Stephen enjoyed refinishing furniture, putting life back into period pieces.

Shaking his head to clear the cobwebs, Stephen went back to his final finishing efforts. Given the events of the past twenty-four hours, it looked like he'd have to lengthen his running route and quickly find several more antiques. His tension quotient seemed to be shooting for the sky.

If he believed in that sort of thing, he would have sworn that Joy and her kids were some hex commissioned by one of his political opponents. The Chapins were getting under his skin.

A rough spot on the front of the bureau caught his eye and Stephen attacked with his emery paper. It wasn't that strange for Joy to be dancing in his mind. After all, she was a damn good-looking woman, carrying enough bounce and energy to fuel a medium-sized airline. There was enough woman wrapped around that petite frame to make a dead man sit up.

Suddenly he sensed something, an intrusion into his private preserve. Stephen turned and looked toward the door.

"I'm sorry," Joy said. "I didn't know you were busy. Beth said—"

He took a moment to settle his breathing. "No, that's all right," he said. "Come on in."

Joy moved a few steps into his workshop, sending the dark shadows scurrying for even further reaches.

"Trying to place another orphan pizza?" he asked.

She stuck her tongue out at him. Lord, but she was so beautiful. So full of life. Her name fit her personality like her skin fit the wonderful womanliness of her body.

"No, smartie," she replied. "Like yesterday, I delivered a pizza to your sister. One that she ordered."

He brushed absently at the desktop and shook his head. "It's a wonder she doesn't turn into a chunk of mozzarella."

"Or gain two hundred pounds," Joy added.

"She was always like that," Stephen said. "Eat a zillion calories and stay thin as a rail."

"I'm glad I didn't go to school with her," Joy said. "I was a little Miss Chubbs in junior high."

His eyes lingered on her T-shirted, jeans-clad body. Chubby? Stephen could think of many words to describe Joy. Full. Voluptuous. Sexy. But certainly not chubby.

The sudden warmth spread through his body and he quickly found another spot to sand. "Where are your kids?" he asked. "With a sitter?"

"No. Right now they're with Beth, listening to stories about your ancestor who invented pizza."

Stephen grinned. "According to my grandmother, our family is filled with such inventive geniuses."

"That's nice." She shifted her weight slightly and he felt her mood shift also.

"I can't always afford a sitter and getting the truck repaired makes things even tighter," she said. "But I only work a few hours in the early evening, and the kids enjoy riding around with me."

They actually were happy, healthy-looking kids. Maybe he should just mind his own business and butt out of the woman's life. One thing for sure, he owed her an apology.

"Sorry I blew up at you," she said.

Stephen stared at her.

"Today. At the park."

"No, no." He shook his head sharply. "I owe you the apology. I'm sorry."

Stephen paused a moment. His mother was always telling him that he shouldn't think so much, that he should just follow his heart. But the one time he did speak before thinking, he had put his foot in his mouth. Maybe mothers weren't always that wise.

"I put my mouth in gear before my brain was turned on," he said.

She stared at him a long moment before that mile-wide grin split her face. "Looks like we're even up now."

He nodded slowly, then returned to his studious sanding. His life was full and under control. There was no need to react to that bouncing energy, ricochetting off every one of his senses and turning him into one huge, vibrant nerve ending. She was right. They were even up now. Time to cut and run.

"Why don't you sit down and rest a spell?" Stephen said as he clenched his teeth momentarily. His mother should be happy now, seeing how brain-dead he was. "I'm sure Beth will let you know when the kids are ready to leave."

"I should be checking in. Saturdays are busy for Bruno."

For a moment, Stephen could see the battle of employee versus mother in Joy's face. Mother won quickly and Joy flashed another quick smile as she sat down. She picked a nearby bar stool, folding her legs into a lotus position and looking like some mythical fairy princess perched on a rose petal. He forced himself to breathe slowly and deeply while he sanded the desk's surface.

"My husband died in August. He had a heart attack."

The words leapt out at him, like a predator, giving no warning. A sudden mixture of emotions swirled in his stomach and Stephen quieted them with a dose of the practical.

"Did he have insurance?"

"Oh, sure."

He dared to sneak a look at her face. Joy's usual smile, now dimmed with sadness, was as beautiful as always.

"But it was used as collateral for business loans."

Anger came to sit on Stephen's heart. What the hell was with some men? They were surrounded with love and then didn't provide for this precious gift.

"Paul was a small real estate developer who wanted to be a big real estate developer. He was gambling that the sacrifices would pay off in the end."

Except that she and the kids were the ones who were paying. The anger still boiled within him so Stephen just kept on sanding.

"I grew up on the south side of Chicago," Joy went on a moment later. "We spent a lot of summer vacations over on this side of the lake. So when I found myself at the crossroads, I just came here and followed my dream."

"And what's that?" he asked, still not daring to look at Joy.

"Running my own art gallery. I put down a small down payment and I'm paying off the rest on a land contract."

His sanding grew even more vigorous. A land contract. Miss one payment and everything was down the tubes. And it was doubtful she had any kind of a financial plan. Hell, she couldn't even pay for routine maintenance on her truck. The silence yawned between them, begging to be filled, but Stephen didn't feel he could trust his voice.

"Beth said you'd been married."

"Yeah." He stepped back to eye his workmanship. "We met in grad school at Ann Arbor. Got jobs in Chicago and lived together. Then we thought we'd make it legal."

"Sorry it didn't work out."

"No big deal. Our careers were more important to each of us." Stephen shrugged. "And the big city grew on her, while I just grew tired of the dirt and congestion."

"So you came back home."

He found a speck that needed work. "Yeah, I guess." Came back home, back to these big old sand bluffs looking out over Lake Michigan, back to where his roots were sunk so deep that those huge bluffs looked like anthills.

"Probably best you had no children."

He saw his distorted reflection in the brass of the drawer handles and forced a reasonable facsimile of a laugh past his lips. "Beth is kid enough for me."

She didn't answer so Stephen hastened to explain. "Beth's the youngest of our brood and I guess she's just having trouble growing up. She's got the brains, but she can't do simple things like pick a major so she's no closer to graduating now than she was four years ago."

"As long as she's happy," Joy said quietly.

"Right." Stephen made a dour face. "In the meantime, she's my permanent, temporary boarder."

Joy didn't reply, choosing instead to come closer and inspect the bureau. "You do beautiful work," she said. "Chippendale one of your ancestors, too?"

"I'm sure he is." He let a smile lighten his face. "At least, according to my grandmother."

"That doesn't leave too many ancestors for the rest of us."

"Nobody good," he agreed. Though she must have had her share of good ancestors. She had to have gotten that strength from someplace, that determination, not to mention those beautiful cheekbones, those...

"Where do you sell it?"

"I beg your pardon?" He was lost.

"Your furniture. Where do you sell it?"

"I don't."

His voice was brusque and his mother's words stumbled into his conscience; something about gentle and turning the other cheek. But then he remembered trying that advice with Matt Holcomb, just before the bum broke Stephen's nose. He kept the brusqueness in his voice.

"I just keep them or impose donations on friends and family."

"I'd love to sell your pieces." Joy came closer to Stephen and the bureau. "It's so smooth, I'm afraid to touch it."

"We're . . . I mean it's sturdy stock—you won't hurt it." Her soft, flowery scent was surrounding him, creeping into his pores and befuddling his mind. "Here, run your hand over it."

He engulfed her small hand and found himself engulfed in turn by an electric-like charge that stunned him, making it hard for him to breathe. Her eyes sparkled, like her teeth between her full lips. He leaned forward.

"Mom," a voice called from the outside. "Where are you?"

"It's the kids." She was gone like a flash, leaving a void behind her that merged with the permanent emptiness he carried in the deepest, darkest corner of his soul.

"Stupid," he muttered to himself. He was a little old to pull such a stunt. That little experience in high school should have taught him not to play with his or anyone else's emotions. "Stupid, stupid, stupid."

Chapter Three

"They're real pretty, Mommy," Katie said, staring at the long line of little wooden shoes that Joy had painted.

"Thank you, honey." Joy gave the shoe in her hand a last check. "Have you finished your picture for nursery school?"

"Uh-uh." Katie climbed up on a chair and put her drawing on the counter.

Joy looked down at the scrawled, crayon picture and felt an ache in her heart.

"It's a mommy, a daddy, a big brother and a little girl. They're gonna go on a picnic."

It was a picnic scene all right. There was a tree and a big square box with a handle. Joy swallowed the lump in her throat. Daddy's hair was a big blotch of yellow. Paul's hair had been dark brown, just like Katie's.

The entry bells rang on the front door. Heaving a sigh of relief, Joy turned to welcome her neighbor from the residential street in back of her building. "Hi, Marlene."

"Hi, guys." Marlene was a computer software consultant but her loud voice, strapping frame and casual dress made her look more like she had just stepped off the farm she grew up on. "Amy and Lisa are already in the car, honey. Why don't you just run on out?"

"Okay." Katie grabbed her picture and slid off the chair. "Bye, Mom."

"Bye, honey."

Joy stared at the now-slammed door.

"You okay, kid?" Marlene asked.

"Yeah." Joy shook her head and brushed the hair back from her eyes. "I'm just tuckered out from painting these things, trying to get them ready for the Tulip Festival next weekend."

"Cute," Marlene said, picking up a shoe to examine it, then put it down to peer into a box on the counter. "Got another souvenir package from the folks?"

Joy grimaced. "This one's from Maine. Herbal tea for me, in case I'm not sleeping at night. Vitamins for the kids, in case I'm no longer feeding them and a dozen little jelly packets from the restaurants they've stopped at."

"Not bad. Maybe they're starting to have faith in you."

Joy just picked up another little wooden shoe. "They also sent along clippings about an art gallery that failed in Bar Harbor, three predicting the recession will deepen and that the sale of luxury items will be hurt and one article on raising guinea hens to eat the ticks in your yard so you won't get Lyme disease."

"Did they send you the chicks?"

"No."

"See? They trust you."

"Right." She painted the flowers on the back of the shoe. "You sure you don't mind taking care of the kids tonight?"

"No prob," Marlene called back over her shoulder as she stepped through the door. "Gives mine someone new to bicker with."

Long after Marlene left, Joy sat staring at the door but not seeing it. Her thoughts rolled and tumbled like clothes in a dryer. It wasn't enough that her parents were convinced of her incompetency; even on vacation, they had to send her stuff to keep going. She had a million more of these shoes to paint, and now her daughter's dreams were peopled by a tall, blond father. Were things never going to be easy?

Joy picked up a clean paint brush. A little Dutch boy stared back at her, blond-haired and blue-eyed with a dimpled smile. "Who says you guys have to be blond?" Joy muttered to herself.

The door chimes grabbed her attention before she had a chance to find the black paint. Her eyes went up to take in the tall blonde who had just entered her store and stood poised to storm her celibacy.

Joy turned away to glare at the little wooden shoe in her hand. Her feet itched to run. Not that she wanted to run away. She just needed to get outside, get some fresh air and quit breathing these damn paint fumes.

"Good morning," Stephen said with a curt nod.

"Good morning, Mr. Van Horne," Joy replied, taking a momentary and perverse pleasure in Stephen's frowny expression. Did Mr. Cool get up on the wrong side of the bed? "What can I do for you today?"

"I just came in to look around."

"This building's not for sale."

He ignored her and proceeded to check out the mostly empty rooms on the first floor. "You have a good amount of space here," he said.

"It's not for sale."

Stephen paused at the stairs and looked up.

"We live upstairs," Joy said. "And this building's not for sale."

The last sentence was almost shouted and Stephen turned to frown at her. "Do you have some kind of compulsion to control?" he asked. "I heard you the first time."

Compulsion to control? Joy's jaw dropped down as her blood pressure shot up. Look who was talking. She didn't butt in and try to run the world.

"Hey," Stephen said as he stopped in front of a painting. "Is this a real Brendan Sullivan?"

"No, it's fake. I put his name on the painting hoping to get arrested for fraud."

He frowned at her as if she was trampling on sacred ground. "As I was saying, you have a good amount of space here."

"I know," Joy snapped. "That's one of the reasons why I want to show your furniture. I have the space and you have the product." She smiled, proud of her businesslike attitude.

"I don't really have that much product," he said. "It's just a hobby with me. It takes me weeks, even months, to refinish just one piece. You could sell everything I give you and still starve to death."

Fine, so it wasn't a good idea. Did he have to pound it into the ground? Her father would have just told her point-blank it wouldn't work; Paul would have sounded interested, then let it die of inaction.

"So I checked around the area for some other folks," Stephen went on. "I found three others who do refinishing on a more extensive basis than I do."

"You what?" She was confused. He'd been turning her down.

"We all do antiques but slightly different stuff," Stephen was going on. "It'll make for a very marketable mix." Suddenly he strode off toward the back. "You have a patio or something back here?"

"Yes." She hurried after him.

Stephen peered out the door at the empty patio and postage stamp-sized yard. "Good." He turned back toward Joy. "I know a guy who makes patio furniture— wood, good quality. You can sell his stuff too."

All the time that Stephen had been striding about, Joy had been biting her tongue. He was into his Caesar act. Once he stopped and faced her, she forced a pleasant smile to her face.

"I'm glad you're discussing this with me before any decisions are made."

He blinked at her. "What decision? You have the space and location and I've found you the product."

"Just a cotton-picking minute, buster. We have some things to settle before a whole bunch of furniture comes piling in here."

"We most certainly do," he replied. "Since the product will be here on consignment—"

He wasn't listening to her at all. Should she just stand here and scream or throw something at him?

Stephen stopped and stared at her a moment. "You can't afford to buy the product outright, can you?"

His words pricked her balloon, releasing the hot anger into the atmosphere. All right, she admitted it—this was probably a great business opportunity. But couldn't he have suggested it instead of bringing it in as a *fait accompli?*

"Do you even know how well you're doing?" he asked.

Had some gentle slipped into Stephen's tone? Nah. It was just something she hoped for. And if there was one thing she'd learned in the past few months, it was that hoping wasn't enough.

"Are you making a profit?"

Joy looked up at Stephen then. "Sure," she said brightly. There still was money in the cash register. Of course, she hadn't looked at the bills for the past four days but details didn't belong in executive level conversations.

His eyes held hers for a long moment but she kept her smile in place. "I'm a CPA," Stephen said. "Why don't I look into your business, your procedures, that kind of thing? Set things up on an even keel."

Business procedures? Hers were based on grabbing the money from a customer and hurrying to the bank so she could pay the creditor that had been screaming the longest.

"I'm doing fine," she said. "I don't need any help."

"Maybe you don't need help," Stephen said. "But someday you might want a loan and a bank is going to want a little more than your sweet smile."

She knew that much. She wasn't just some empty-headed ditz, but neither was she ready to open up her business methods for his scrutiny. Once she had proof of her success in hand, she'd let somebody tell her she was doing things all wrong. "I'll think about it."

"I don't want to put my furniture and the others in here unless we know that you're on good footing," he said.

Joy felt her smile slipping again. "That sounds like blackmail to me. You got a shady side to your background, too?"

Suddenly his stiffness melted into the warmest smile this side of the equator. His eyes looked like a quiet inland lake. Someplace where you'd strip down naked and jump into—

She swallowed hard and looked away. Maybe a different tactic would work. "All right, all right already. Look into my books. But I need to warn you, they're quite extensive."

"Oh?"

"Yes, I have about three shelves full of romance novels and another of mysteries."

Stephen stared at her a long moment, then the smile returned, along with gentle laughter. "I guess I'd better plan on several days for the project."

"Several minutes should be more than enough time," she said.

He turned and picked up one of the shoes that she had been painting, turning it over in his large, gentle hands, looking at the windmills, little Dutch children and tulips painted on them.

"Getting ready for the tourists that will be swarming all over town this weekend?"

"I think it'll be fun."

He shrugged and put the shoe back with its mates.

"Don't you?"

He shrugged again. "I grew up here in Holland. I've sorted and packaged tulip bulbs as summer jobs. I've scrubbed Main Street and I've danced in my wooden shoes." He made a face. "I've done my share."

"Don't be such an old grumpy, fuddy-duddy," Joy said.

She turned her attention to the wooden shoes, carefully evening out the rows rather than watch him. She didn't want to hear about his past, to feel the bonds of friendship growing with someone who would be so easy to lean on.

"My kids and I are looking forward to the festival."

"You're going to work your fingers to the bone," Stephen said, his voice sounding almost angry.

"So what?" she snapped. She should have known he'd find something to criticize. "Some things are special and I'm not letting you spoil them."

Joy steeled herself for his response, one she was sure would be cold as well as angry, but none came. His silence hung heavy, like the air just before a storm. The door chimes gently bade Stephen farewell but Joy didn't breathe a sigh of relief. She sat staring at the endless rows of tiny wooden shoes.

It was late afternoon by the time Stephen made it back to Joy's with some of his furniture. The sun streaming in through the front windows had turned the polished wooden floors to molten gold and rainbows danced along the far wall from the sun-catchers hanging in the windows.

"Hi, Stevie," Katie called from her perch on a high stool where Joy was braiding her hair.

"Hi, yourself," Stephen answered. She was a cute little kid who would grow up into a beautiful woman like her mother. Twenty years from now, there'd be a whole new crop of befuddled and bedeviled men wandering around.

"Back again?" Joy asked.

Stephen frowned. "I said I was going to bring some of my stuff over later today."

"I know." Joy bent down and kissed the top of her daughter's head. "I was just teasing."

Her bright eyes danced and the glow of her smile filled the store to dull the sunshine. Love radiated about her. It was a good thing that she operated on her own power. If she'd pulled electricity from old Indiana and Michigan Electric there'd be a brownout in all of southwestern Michigan.

"Can I bring my stuff in?" Stephen asked.

"Sure, partner."

He chose not to address her cheerful words, instead going outside where two strapping young studs waited. "We'll put my stuff in the little room off to the right," he said.

The men nodded and Stephen went back into the store, carrying a maple swivel chair with him. Joy was still in the room at the foot of the stairs, putting out her own special glow, a combination of Katie's youthful innocence enhanced with Joy's own womanliness. He swallowed hard.

He had planned on taking them all out to dinner, but maybe that wasn't a good idea. His life was jam-packed as it was; he didn't need to complicate it any. Plus, Joy had a hard enough row to hoe. They didn't need a share of the gloom that he tended to carry with him at times.

Stephen forced himself to glance around the room, determined not to get caught by those sea green eyes, but his resolve wasn't enough. Her paintings called to a loneliness buried deep in his soul while the breeze, coming from the open window, wrapped her scent around him. Even the sunshine couldn't be trusted, as it stretched her shadow across the floor, teasing him with soft edges and flowing curves. Damn. Had he no will of his own?

Ah, what the hell. Her kids would be along. "Why don't you go upstairs and change," Stephen said. His eyes rested on her lithe frame, adorned with such smooth curves that he could navigate them with his eyes closed and not suffer a single bruise. "Nothing too fancy. We're going to The Spaghetti Works."

"What for?" The hardness in her voice brought his eyes up to hers. It was obvious that storms were gathering at sea. Now what?

"For dinner." Although it took considerable effort, Stephen was able to maintain a pleasant, easy tone in his voice. His mother would have been proud of him.

"You must have me mixed up with somebody else." Her smile flickered like a candle in a breeze. "First of all, I have to work tonight. Not to mention the fact that I don't remember you asking me."

Jeez! Stephen paused a moment to take a deep breath and unclench his jaw.

"I just thought we could celebrate our new partnership," he explained, proud that he was still able to maintain that calm and easy tone under these trying circumstances. Hell, it wasn't as if he was dragging her off someplace by the hair like some caveman. And her kids could use a break from riding around in an old pickup, delivering pizzas.

"My kids aren't going with me tonight," she said, as if reading his mind. "They're going to stay with a friend and her kids while I go out and deliver pizzas."

Fine. It was just as well they didn't go out. There was some kind of bad chemistry between Joy and himself, at least in social situations. It would be best if they restricted themselves to business hours only. Not that he needed the money from selling the furniture, but he wasn't one to back away from a commitment. His father didn't raise no quitters.

Stephen was about to attempt a graceful exit when Robbie stomped into the room, wearing about fifty pounds of grumpy on his thin features.

"What's the matter?" Stephen asked.

"Nothing," Joy replied for her son. "Are you all ready to go?"

"I gotta stay with a bunch of little girls," Robbie answered, ignoring Joy's glare.

Stephen turned back toward Joy. "Is he baby-sitting?"

"No, I told you a friend of mine was. Her two daughters go to preschool with Katie."

"And they're just as twerpy as she is," Robbie added.

"That's enough," Joy said.

At least the kids wouldn't be riding around in an old truck all night and that was all he cared about. He could hit the road with a clear conscience. Next time—assuming there was a next time—he'd know to make an appointment with the little princess. Maybe she could handle lunch. He began his goodbye, but the phone rang and interrupted him.

Joy snatched it up before either of the kids could. "Holland Arts. Oh, hi, Marlene." She paused for several long moments as concern spread across her forehead. "Oh, I'm sorry to hear that. No, don't worry. You just take care of your mother."

Stephen waited until Joy hung up.

"Marlene's mother fell," Joy said. "They're not sure yet, but she may have broken her hip."

"What about the kids?" Stephen asked.

She flashed him a glare that cast at least eighty evil spells over him. "They're going to have to come with me."

"All right," Robbie exclaimed, while Katie sat looking solemn.

Joy turned away from Stephen. "I'm going to be real busy tonight," Joy warned the two children. "I wasn't expecting that you guys would be with me, so Bruno assigned me a full delivery schedule. There won't be much time to stop at a park or anything like that."

"That's okay, Mom," Robbie said. "I mean, like what's there to do in a park anyway? Play on the swings?"

Stephen frowned at them, even though no one was paying him the slightest attention. "I'll watch them."

Three faces, all wearing masks of surprise, turned to stare at him. He glared back. Why did the simplest things always seem to surprise this crew?

"Are you really qualified?" Robbie asked.

Stephen turned up the intensity of his glare. "No, I'm really a pirate and I'm going to feed you to that alligator that chased Captain Hook around." He saw a flicker of uncertainty in Joy's eyes and softened his tone. "Taking care of little kids is like riding a bike. Once you learn, you never forget.''

The three suspicion-laden faces continued to stare at him. Not one of them exuded the smallest amount of excitement or even trust. He ought to leave. There were better ways to spend an evening. Like throwing rocks at streetlamps.

"Look, if Beth were around, I'd send her over," Stephen said. "But she's off someplace with friends."

What had he volunteered for? He'd enjoyed taking care of his siblings when they'd been growing up, but things had kind of changed after high school. It was harder to be around children, harder to let himself really enjoy their freshness and energy. He could handle them all right; but he'd just gotten out of the habit of being around them.

"Look, we'll be okay," he told Joy. "And if I really turn into a pirate, the kids can always call 9-1-1."

"I guess." She seemed to run through the alternatives in her mind then, obviously discovering there were none, forced a smile to her lips. It didn't exactly light up the room but it pushed some of the shadows back. "I want you both to get along now."

Her children nodded solemnly before she quickly closed up the shop. A few minutes later, she was changed and out the door. Both Katie and Robbie watched until the pickup disappeared down the road, then they turned and trudged upstairs. Stephen followed them.

"What are we gonna watch tonight, Robbie?" Katie asked.

"I dunno."

"We're not watching any TV," Stephen said. "We're going to have fun."

The kids exchanged glances full of suspicion.

* * *

Joy softly shut the car door, kicked off her sneakers and leaned back against the old truck. The light was on in her kitchen, although the kids were in bed by now.

At least, they'd better be in bed. It was past eleven.

She wiggled her toes on the coolness of the sidewalk and stretched. Three quarters of the population of Holland must have ordered pizzas from Bruno's tonight. And all of them wanted delivery. It was a good thing Stephen had stepped into the breach. Tonight would not have been a good one for hauling her little tykes around.

Her eyes drifted up to the light in her kitchen windows. It wasn't as if she didn't want to go up. She just needed a few minutes to relax, to let the cool sidewalk soothe her feet, to gather her wits about her.

She certainly wasn't afraid of him.

Joy almost laughed out loud at that stray thought. Who would be afraid of Stephen? Oh, he was stuffy and stiff. But it was the stiffness of a toy soldier. He was just a plain, ordinary nice guy accountant type.

A brief picture of his broad shoulders and blue eyes flickered before her mind's eye. Well, maybe he wasn't exactly plain.

The answering flicker of a spark deep within her spread through her body. All right, he wasn't ordinary either.

She shut her eyes tightly and remembered his "invitation" to dinner. He sure as shooting wasn't nice and definitely was stuffy.

Taking a deep breath, Joy bent down, picked up her sneakers and stomped up the back stairs. The house was silent, but not unwelcoming. The murmur of the television eased some invisible knot of tension from the air.

She padded silently into the living room where Stephen was watching a professional basketball game. "Hi," she said.

He started slightly, then turned toward her. "You should consider becoming a cat burglar. I didn't hear you come in at all."

Joy threw her shoes over by the sofa. "Unfortunately, that was one set of lessons I didn't get as a kid."

He stared at her shoes now lying lopsided on the floor. "Tired?" he asked.

She'd tried to throw out a flippant remark but couldn't quite make it. "A little."

Stephen slowly unfolded himself from the chair and came toward her. The closer he came, the more Joy regretted discarding her shoes. Sneakers didn't add that much to her height, but in her bare feet he seemed almost giantlike.

"Want a sandwich?" he asked.

Joy shook her head as she backpedaled into the kitchen. "I ate at work."

His eyes looked so soft but they really weren't. They couldn't be. Stuffed shirts didn't have eyes that were soft and dreamy. He just looked that way because the lights in the living room were so dim.

"Want some dessert? We made peanut butter cookies."

Now his voice was soft. And Joy knew that she couldn't blame that on the dim lights. A weak spot in her defenses suddenly crumbled as a picture of Stephen baking with her kids stole in.

"They make good bedtime snacks."

The warmth in her body inched toward a consuming flame. Damn. Joy clenched her teeth and hardened her resolve. What was with her? Stephen's baking with her children was nothing but a nice picture of his political file. Available when he ran for governor or something.

She busied herself flipping through the mail she'd left by the telephone. Not that the postcards from her parents were any more informative the second time around.

"I always liked milk with mine," Stephen said, walking over to the refrigerator. He took out a carton of milk and picked up two glasses from the cabinet. "Sit down."

That master sergeant tone had crept into his voice again but Joy ignored it. "That's okay. I'm not really hungry."

Stephen filled the glasses and brought them to the table. "You want me to tell your kids that you didn't like their cookies?"

Joy watched, her heart suddenly taking in the warmth and security of the scene before her. She and Paul had never had milk and cookies together late at night. There never was any time.

For just the smallest moment, Joy pondered running away, hiding some place where her heart wouldn't be under siege. But this was where her life was now. Any fleeing could only be brief, and when she came back, Stephen would be here waiting—with the milk. Sighing inwardly, she sat down while he took out a plate and heaped it full of cookies.

"Have one," he ordered her, taking one himself.

Joy remembered her mother's words about it being better to give than to receive. She considered giving Stephen a punch in the nose, but took a cookie instead. Maybe next time.

"They're good," she said.

Joy heard the words spill past her lips as another part of her mind wondered at her sanity. There would be no next time. She and Stephen were about as compatible as oil and water.

She concentrated on the cookie in her hand. Since there wasn't going to be any next time, maybe she should just go ahead and punch him in the nose now. "I hope my kids weren't too much of a problem."

He shrugged. "Prison officials know you have less trouble with inmates if you keep them busy. I think those theories were first developed with kids."

She sipped some milk to wash away the cookie crumbs, which weren't tasting all that good anymore. If he didn't like kids, he shouldn't have volunteered to sit with hers. They could have gone with her on the deliveries. It wouldn't have been the first time.

"We made airplanes," he said, indicating the ceiling.

Her eyes met his, then focused on the ceiling he was waving toward. Hanging above her were a squadron of paper airplanes, all shapes and sizes, most brightly colored with crayon. The room had been transformed into a sky show. It was marvelous. It must have been more fun than the kids had had in ages, yet how did that match up with the prison guard attitude?

A sharp stinging sensation invaded her eyes and Joy sighed. Was he a snob? Was he a gentleman? Did he like kids or didn't he? Damn. She wished that the real Mr. Stephen Van Horne would stand up.

The acid in her eyes turned into a wetness that her tired lids just couldn't blink away. Joy wiped at them with the back of her hand. Caesar, that's who Stephen was. Caesar, the emperor of the whole civilized world. Or at least the Holland, Michigan part of it.

"Joy?"

He had been across the table from her. Yet suddenly, so very suddenly, he was by her side. Strong arms pulled her up into the hard muscles of his chest and he kissed her.

A heaven came down to surround her and promise her a lifetime of gentle happiness. His arms tightened around her, almost as if they had vowed they would never let her go, even as his lips sung to her needs, to her hungers.

It had been so long since she'd been held, so long since she'd been cherished, that she'd forgotten how to react. Her knees trembled with the ecstasy of it; her heart quivered. Her lips had forgotten nothing though. They clung to Stephen's, taking nourishment from his soul and feeding her starving heart.

Ever so gently, he pulled himself away. "It's late." His voice was gruff. "You must be tired."

Tired? Her blood was pounding in her ears and her bare feet were ready to dance. Her fingers wanted to dash through Stephen's thick strand of blond locks. She felt sixteen and heady with the sensations of longing.

But she wasn't sixteen. She swallowed hard. "Oh, yeah. I'm really beat."

"See ya." Then with a quick nod he was gone, like one of those ancient Indian spirits of the forest.

Joy breathed a sigh of relief that for some reason hurt. She picked up the empty glasses and put them in the dishwasher. After turning off the lights, she walked down the hall to her room, but the house seemed filled with unexperienced memories. Sleep was as far away as solvency.

Chapter Four

Four weeks of school left and Robbie had finally concluded that homework was a waste of time. Joy dug her hand shovel into the earth with a vengeance, uprooting the dandelion plant. Robbie just wants attention, his teacher had told her. It's hard on a boy losing a father, the principal had said. Was his father into airplanes? the school counselor had asked. His father hadn't been into fathering, Joy had wanted to tell them all. Robbie couldn't miss a companionship he never had. He could very well be missing the supposed security of their former life, but she feared it something a lot more straightforward than that.

"Hi," a voice said from behind her.

Joy practically jumped out of her skin, scattering dirt, pulled weeds and her hand-gardening tools. "Why are you sneaking up on me?" she demanded of Stephen.

"Boy, you're sure a bundle of charm."

That was one thing she hadn't been with him, a bundle of charm. She tossed the dandelion into the bucket near her. Maybe you couldn't worry about bills and your kids' well-being and still be charming.

Not that she wanted to be. After all, what would charming get her? A softening of her spine as she slipped back into those treacherous leaning habits as she had the other night. A return to habits of dependency that had been built over a lifetime, starting with her father and going on to Paul.

"What do you want?" she grumbled as she bent to pick up her tools.

"What do you want?" His mimic of her sour tone was gentle. "Crisp and short, yet filled with nuances of care and concern. You should consider going into public relations."

"You'll find people in a more receptive state of mind if you don't sneak up on them," she pointed out.

"What's with this 'sneak up' bit? These aren't exactly my sneak-up shoes," he said, pointing down at his sturdy wing tips. "You should have heard me clicking on your flag-stones all the way from the street."

Maybe. If she had the leisure to enjoy the sunshine while she did her gardening, instead of using the time to stew over problems.

"I have a lot on my mind." And now that Stephen was here, she had a lot more. "What do you want?"

"Glad to see we're back to warmth and charm."

Joy brushed her hands on the front of her jeans. "I really am busy. Did you come on business or just to harass me?"

His forehead crinkled a moment in thought before he replied. "Business. What other reason would I have to come here and get abused?"

An icy stillness came over her. Her question had been stupid. Why else would a handsome, successful, dynamic man-about-town like Stephen Van Horne come to visit someone like her?

"I brought over the garden furniture that I was telling you about." He nodded toward a large truck pulling in behind his own beautiful car that her kids still talked about. "Remember? We talked about putting a display out on your patio."

Did she remember? She remembered a lot of things—his deep voice, his soft eyes, his—

His damn overbearing attitude. "Things are moving a little fast," she said. "Faster than I like."

Stephen frowned at her. "You have the space," he said. "And, as your business adviser, I recommend that you strike while the opportunity is hot. Besides, you're not investing any of your money."

Joy could feel her shoulders slump. Or was it just her heart? Logically it was the right move; it was just that she felt that any move that brought her closer to him was the wrong move.

"And I'm not using the space anyway," she murmured.

"Right. Now you got it." His tone turned brusque and bustling again. "I'll go down and tell the guys where the stuff is going. Why don't you go in back and make sure the merchandise is arranged properly? I'm sure you have a better sense of layout than any of us."

She didn't let herself read that as praise of her artistic sense, but just watched him walk over to the truck. She was tired of being manipulated like some Barbie Doll, viewed as an incompetent who could be trusted with only the simplest of tasks.

"Nuts," she muttered under her breath and walked through the store toward her patio in back.

Stephen wasn't really manipulating her. He was just a knight in shining armor. A guy who moved in and exuded leadership, when he felt there was a damsel in distress. If she didn't want him taking charge of her life, then she'd just have to demonstrate that there was no need for his services. She'd just have to make sure that she didn't leave a vacuum. It was all in her hands.

And in her hands is where she kept it for the next half hour, directing the guys in laying out the furniture so that it was shown off to its best advantage. The lounge chair here and the love seat over there, the end table under the window where it could hold a low vase of flowers, and the picnic table off to one side. If only life was as easy to arrange as furniture.

The young movers left and Stephen put his suit coat back on. "Well, that was fun," he said.

Joy took one last look at the furniture, then walked back toward the front of the shop. "Thanks for getting the merchandise to me."

"Just servicing my client."

Servicing? Joy felt her cheeks burn as if they were on fire. That was an interesting choice of words. She'd been in this rural-dominated community long enough to know that service was what a bull did for cows.

Stephen was looking at her, his blue eyes sparkling like the lake on a quiet summer's day while, within the taut confines of his lips, teeth flashed like whitecaps in a westerly wind.

Peace and turmoil. That was Stephen Van Horne. And Joy knew that she didn't need either. What she needed was businesslike competence.

"I think I'll put some baskets and such around the furniture. Show how livable the stuff is."

"Good idea." Stephen looked quickly at his watch. "I have some time this afternoon. Why don't we take a look at your bookkeeping system?"

Joy stopped breathing for a long moment. She'd meant to get some business books from the library after he'd first mentioned looking at records; she really had. But with the Tulip Festival coming up and everything, she just hadn't gotten around to it.

If she let him check out her bookkeeping now though, he'd become a full-fledged member of the *Take Care of Little Joy Club,* instead of the associate member he presently was. For some reason, it was important that he think her competent. And she thought it still possible, in spite of all the help he'd already given her.

"I need a raincheck on your accounting help," she told him and opened a box of miniature wildlife castings. "I have a lot to do today."

"We shouldn't put it off too long," Stephen said.

Just until she started making some money so that her system was unique, not crazy. "I'd like to organize my records first. Some of my methods are rather unusual."

"No problem," he said with a shrug. "Most small businesses are like that."

She unwrapped two geese about to take flight and put it on the display case. "Well, I'd just feel a little more comfortable if I had them ordered a little better."

Maybe she could hire a different CPA to organize things first. Then she could show her books to Stephen and he'd be so impressed he'd be speechless. Trouble was, she didn't have money to hire even a high school student with a semester of accounting.

She unwrapped another set of geese and carried them over to the lighted case where she would show them before turning back to Stephen. "I really have a lot to do," she said.

And she really did. She had to unpack this box and then arrange some craft items on the furniture. A task that couldn't be done just any old way. It required thought, analysis and time. Lots of time. Three lifetimes even.

Maybe four. Surely by that time, she'd have found a way to win his respect.

The bell on the front door announced visitors and Joy looked up to see Marlene and her two daughters walk in. Katie started jumping up and down, waving both hands.

"Just a minute, please," Joy said around the pins in her mouth. "Two more pins and I'm done."

"We got a whole bunch of new stuff out back," Katie said, standing as still as a statue. "Can I show Lisa and Amy, Mom?"

The last pins in, Joy pulled the dress off over Katie's head. "Just remember it's not really ours," Joy warned.

The three little girls ran out to the patio as Joy folded up the dress, putting it on her desk where it would no doubt leak pins all over her precious records. She wondered how many of Stephen's other clients had straight pins buried among their bills and receipts. She came out of her office to find Marlene looking at a desk of Stephen's.

"Quite a few changes around here," Marlene said.

"I took on some new merchandise, furniture." Joy took a long moment to look around the store's rooms. "I have the space, so why not try something new?"

"Right." There was a twinkle in Marlene's eyes that Joy couldn't quite define. "And I noticed you've taken on a new partner. Stephen Van Horne's been around quite a bit lately."

Just twice. Well, maybe three times. But that wasn't all that much. "He's going to do my books for me." Once she got them cleaned up enough to show him.

Marlene nodded sagely, raising Joy's level of aggravation. "I hear he's good. I mean, as an accountant."

She really didn't like Marlene's smile. It looked like a good time to change the subject. "How is your mother?" Joy asked.

"Lucky," Marlene replied. "She's just badly bruised. Nothing's broken."

"Then she'll be home soon."

"A week or so," Marlene said. "I'm sorry to have left you in a lurch. Did you find somebody else to sit with the kids?"

"Yes," Joy said, but didn't volunteer any names. It wasn't something Marlene would be interested in anyway. "Want something to drink? We can test out the new patio furniture."

"Good idea," Marlene agreed. "Besides we should be out there anyway before my little monsters really break it in."

Joy went into the kitchen to get a pitcher of lemonade while Marlene went out onto the patio to supervise the kids. By the time Joy returned with the drinks the girls were crawling around under the tables pretending they were caves.

"This stuff is really nice," Marlene said as she took the glass Joy offered. "It should sell well once people see it. How'd you ever hook up with the maker?"

"It was somebody Stephen knows," Joy said, then took a long drink of lemonade. "I really love having the patio. Back in Illinois, we lived too close to the airport to sit outside much. Not that it was quieter inside when a 747 was passing right overhead."

They'd talked about moving, but it was always a plan for next year or the year after that. When the next big sale came through. Paul had never realized how important it was to have time to sit together in the evening, to have a quiet little Eden to call your own. She thought of Stephen's workshop and the patio behind the house, surrounded by bushes so that you would feel like you were the only person on earth. Or the only two.

"You have to watch him," Marlene said, flinging words out of the blue.

Pulled from her reverie, Joy could only blink. "Who?"

"Stephen," Marlene said. "He's sort of a quiet type. But before you know it he's running everything his way."

Nothing wrong with that, Joy thought as she watched the ice cubes swim in her glass. The world needed order. Just as long as those he was ordering about wanted him to.

"Are you listening?" Marlene demanded.

"Of course, I am," Joy said.

"All right, what was I talking about?"

"This isn't grade school and you're not my teacher," Joy said.

Marlene's facial muscles struggled for a moment before letting the laughter roll out.

"What's so funny?" Joy asked.

"Life."

They sipped at their drinks, clinked the ice cubes and watched their kids. Maybe she should let the kids sit around on the furniture on weekends. Just like putting the craft pieces out, the kids would show off the items better, but she doubted if the kids could sit still long enough. Of course, all their jumping around would show the customers how sturdy the pieces were.

"He was a class president, captain of the football team, leader of the debate team."

Joy slowly returned to Marlene and her conversation. "The Big Man On Campus."

"There and everywhere," Marlene agreed. "He was a scout leader, captain of his little league teams, that kind of stuff."

Her glass was empty, but it didn't mean she had to look up at Marlene. She stared down at the ice cubes. They weren't swimming anymore but she could watch them melt.

"Some people are like that," Joy murmured.

Stephen was her business partner, her adviser in a few matters and only if they related to her business. She wasn't interested in any part of his personal life or his past. But it really wouldn't be polite to ignore Marlene's words.

"You went to school with him?" Joy asked.

"He was two grades ahead of me."

A silence fell over them, looming like a vulture until Joy leapt in to fill the space. "He baby-sat for my kids. I couldn't get anyone else." She said it like it was a guilty secret she'd been hiding. "I didn't try all that hard. He sort of volunteered."

Marlene nodded. "He'd be good at that kind of thing."

"My kids like him."

"He was the oldest child. And very responsible."

"They like him a whole lot."

"Everyone does. He's a little stiff but a heck of a nice guy."

Some of the ice had melted and Joy raised her glass to drain the water. Popular man. It didn't sound like he needed any more friends, which was fine with her. She wasn't looking to add any friends to her roster right now anyway.

"Stephen did throw us all for a loop in high school though," Marlene went on. "He had this girlfriend, Laura, and they went together for years. Everybody expected they'd get married and raise a passel of kids. He'd be their little league coach, she'd be den mother and chief neighborhood cookie maker. We all thought they were the most perfect couple around."

Laura didn't sound like the CPA he'd married. "That's not the way he described his wife."

"That was someone else. He never married Laura." Marlene shook her head. "Laura moved away during their senior year. We all thought Stephen should have followed her and carried her off, but he didn't. Just stayed here and graduated, then went on to the University of Michigan."

"Fairy tales don't really happen," Joy said. Though she had spent twelve years married to Paul, waiting for hers to come true.

"No, but when you're fifteen, you still think they can." Marlene drained her glass. "I can still see them holding hands as they walked through the halls, oblivious to everyone but each other. I sometimes wonder if he still loves her and that's why his marriage didn't last."

Joy stared off into the backyard, at a blue jay hopping around on the lawn and searching her little spot of green for lunch. Was there such a thing as a perfect love that happened only once in a lifetime? She didn't think so, but was that because she'd never experienced it? She'd loved Paul, but not with that all-consuming fire that would never burn out. She felt too tired, too much betrayed by his shortsightedness, to feel that he could never be replaced in her life.

Yet Stephen was so self-possessed. He was always in control. She could see him loving so completely that no other love would ever come close.

"Well, I told Mom I'd come by and see her. I'd better get going," Marlene said, popping up. "Come on, kids."

Katie bounced on out with her friends while Joy stared unseeing at the patio around her. Sometimes a person just couldn't manage things to come out the way they wanted. Not even a man like Stephen Van Horne. She felt a touch of sorrow for him, locked in a prison of his emotions and knowing that there was no escape.

Stephen gathered up the small pile of knobs and screws and tossed them all into a shoebox. A couple of washers bounced out and, muttering darkly, Stephen retrieved them. This time making his pitch much more gentle. Then he set the box high on a shelf and went to the door to stare down his driveway.

The daylilies lining both sides of the blacktop were growing nicely. It had been an early and warm spring. Wouldn't be surprising if a few of them started blooming before the end of the month. By June, they'd be a riot of color.

"Hell," he muttered to himself and walked to the patio where he sat down on the lounge chair. He felt a blue funk coming on and it looked like it was going to be a humdinger. He'd had his regular three-mile run, a shower and a light dinner but none of it had done any good.

He rubbed his eyes and sighed. He was so damn moody he wished Beth was around to talk to, but she was gone off someplace. Actually he'd much rather sit down and have a pleasant chat with someone else. Female, like Beth, but short and curved rather than long and lean.

Slipping easily into a frown, he shook his head sharply. He didn't need to talk to anyone. What he needed instead was activity.

He stood up and started down the driveway toward the street. A walk would be nice, a pleasant stroll through the neighborhood. Enough to get his heartbeat up but not so much that he couldn't pause for a chat about the weather or whatever. Putting a lightness in his heart, Stephen stepped briskly down the street.

Almost an hour later, he found himself in Prospect Park, nurturing the reemergence of a good grump. He hadn't found a single person walking. A lot of people waved from their yards and even more honked at him from their passing cars but that was it. He was still alone with his gloom.

He sat down under a big maple in the center of the park. Off to his right, a soccer game was going on, kids of about eight or ten. He tried concentrating on it—the cheers, the coaches shouting instructions, the small single-engine plane flying overhead—but it was no use. The whole pleasant picture retreated as dark clouds rolled in from Stephen's past.

It had been a boy. Laura's father had told his mother that much. He and Laura had made a boy child. A son whom he'd never seen, not even for an instant.

They were supposed to get married. It was going to be hard, both of them knew it, but each had some money saved up. They would finish high school, then Stephen would go to college. After he graduated, Laura would go.

But when Stephen had driven up to Laura's house that Saturday morning, he and Willie Van Eck—who was going to be his best man—the house was empty. No one was there, not even Buster, Laura's dog. There was just a note sticking out from between the doorframe and the screen door.

With shaking hands, Stephen read the note, his heart hearing the message even before his eyes took in the printed words.

Laura was going away. She said she wasn't ready to be a wife and mother, she still had a lot of growing up to do. She would put the baby up for adoption.

The rest of that day danced in a haze. Willie drove him home and explained everything to Stephen's parents, as Stephen seemed unable to talk to anyone. Eventually the haze cleared, though, and life went on. Laura never did come back to Holland. Her Dad took a job out West someplace and the whole family was gone.

Stephen had known that Laura had corresponded with some girlfriends, for a while at least, but after his attempts to get in touch were rejected, his mother convinced him to let her go. They'd given each other more than enough pain, enough to last a lifetime.

So he let her go, but the pain they'd shared stayed with him. The weekend of the Tulip Festival their senior year, he learned he had a son, a tiny scrap of life that might carry his eyes, his fondness for chocolate, but never his name. Somehow Stephen had always connected the fields and fields of tulips dancing in the spring breezes with unbearable loss.

Cheers from the soccer field tugged and pulled at him. Stephen focused his eyes to see the red-shirted group of kids jumping up and down. Somebody had scored a goal.

His son would be eighteen this weekend and probably was graduating from high school. Would he be going to college? Did he like sports? One thing was for sure, Stephen wouldn't ever know him. He'd missed all the joys and pains of seeing him grow up, and now he'd miss the friendship that a parent and an adult child could have.

Stephen started walking down toward the soccer game. He needed something to get the monkey of gloom off his shoulders. Watching a bunch of kids having fun might be just the thing.

Then he stopped. This was Robbie's team. There was Joy over at the sidelines and Katie was farther off, frolicking with some girlfriends.

Suddenly, he wanted nothing more than to go to Joy's side, to let her laughter blow all the dark clouds from his mind, but his feet refused to move. She had enough of a load to carry without him adding to it. It would be better for both of them if he kept the relationship a strictly business one. He'd tried for love once and that had been enough.

He turned and began walking toward home. Best to find some dark corner, hunker down, and let the blue funk run its course. It always did.

Chapter Five

"Now what?" Joy asked. Her nerves were stretched to near breaking. She'd stayed up half the night trying to organize her business records according to the methods recommended in those library books, but Stephen did not seem impressed. He just sat there, shaking his head and making little *tsk, tsk* sounds as he pored over her books.

"I would have expected a certified public accountant to be more dignified," she said.

This time a soft smile flickered on his lips, distant yet definite. She tried to concentrate on business matters.

"Do you have any comments?" Joy asked. "Verbal ones, that I might be able to understand."

"Like you said, your record-keeping is rather unique."

He didn't look up when he spoke and Joy was just as happy that he didn't. She had discovered that there were many dangers in having Stephen as her CPA, not the least of which were his baby blue eyes. This business relationship was going to be a challenge, maybe too much of a one.

"You know," she said. "I'm really very small potatoes."

"That's no excuse for sloppy business practices."

She clenched her jaw as she thought of the long hours she'd put in trying to clean them up, then tried again. "I'm not sure that I need a high-powered CPA to take care of my books."

He brought his gaze up and Joy held her breath. Fortunately, those baby blues were cool and still, like the lake on a calm winter's day.

"At the moment, you need all the help you can get," he said. "You're skirting the edge of being a real business, one that makes a profit."

Warmth seeped into her cheeks, and Joy eagerly seized the emotion. Anger she could handle.

"What I'm trying to say, and it should be very obvious to you, is that I can't afford a high-priced accountant like yourself."

"I don't have to be high-priced," he said.

His voice was almost a murmur, soft and gentle. Any relationship with him would carry too high a price tag, and it wasn't her checkbook she was worried about. Not that that was something she was about to admit to him.

"I don't need charity," she said.

"I'm not talking charity." His eyes turned colder. "Charity is for people who can't help themselves. Help—business help—is for people who have some problems at the moment."

Her points shot down, Joy's argument died like a campfire doused with a bucket of water. She wished her childhood had included a course in arguing. Miss Anita's Tap, Ballet and Arguing School. That would have been a useful skill to acquire.

"I want to make it on my own," she said.

"You will," Stephen agreed. "But your odds will go up if you're smart about it."

He reached over and put his hand on hers. His touch was light, but safe, hopefully. Touching should be okay, she just didn't want him to hold her. That would be too much like protecting.

"All smart people hire expertise they don't have," he told her.

But who ever accused her of being smart? If she was so smart, she wouldn't have him as a business partner. She wouldn't be listening to his advice. She wouldn't be sitting here, letting him start taking over.

Her heart trembled ever so slightly. Maybe she wasn't as strong or as competent as she tried to pretend. Maybe she had leaned on someone so long that she couldn't stand on her own. Maybe her parents had been right; there was no reason for her to move out here except stubborn pride that she should have outgrown.

"Hi, Mommy," Katie shouted over the door chimes as she came bounding into the room.

Ah, the cavalry had arrived. Joy pulled her hand away as she got to her feet. Katie flew into her arms. "How was school, honey?"

"Okay." Katie wiggled from Joy's embrace and climbed up on a chair to pull over the cookie jar Joy kept on her desk. "We don't got no more cookies," the little girl said accusingly.

"Why don't we have lunch instead?" Joy said. "Stephen, would you like to have—" She'd turned to him and the words died on her lips. A distant bleakness had come to his eyes, like winter at sea.

"I should be going," he replied, standing up. "I have a number of people to see today and I'm running late."

"Look at my picture," Katie said, thrusting a crayon drawing at Stephen. "It's how I'm going to look in the Tulip Parade tomorrow."

He barely glanced at it. "Very nice."

The words were short and curt, the smile was stiff and forced. The man changed moods more than the lakeside weather.

"I'll go over those payables later," he said with a short nod, then he was gone. The door chimes called out a plaintive goodbye to his ramrod-stiff back and Joy felt strangely abandoned.

"Hey, kid." Stephen knew he was growling, but didn't much care. The Tulip Festival had more tulips than anything else, but kids came a close second. "You get any ice cream on my shorts and you're going to be wearing that cone on your ear."

The young boy, who looked slightly younger than Robbie, had been bouncing all around them the whole time they'd been watching the parade. He'd been waving his cone like a weapon, but Stephen's tone sent him scurrying to the other side of his mother.

"You certainly have a way with children," Joy said.

Stephen shrugged. "It's a gift."

"From some loving ancestor, no doubt." Joy watched the boy, still hovering quietly by his mother's side. "I think you scared the little tyke half to death."

"That's the only way to deal with them."

He should have known that his blue funk would come around; he should have stayed home, by himself. Today was his son's eighteenth birthday.

"Sweet," Joy replied, as she scanned the parade before them. "Robbie should be coming by soon with his Cub Scout troop."

Joy's presence pushed itself in, wrestling with his dark clouds of gloom for space in his soul.

She looked so beautiful. Her clothes were ordinary, but her face radiated such love and happiness. She knew her kids were the most precious thing she had, and in having them she was wealthy beyond all measure. It hurt him to watch her. Yet he couldn't keep his eyes away. There must have been a masochist somewhere amid his ancestors. According to Grandma Van Horne, they had everything else. He forced his eyes to watch the high school band passing by.

"All kids are a pain," he groused once the pain had subsided. "But tourists' kids are the worst. They should just stay home and send their money."

Joy shook her head. "You're in a great mood today. Somebody beat you up with a tulip when you were a kid? There must be a reason why you love the Tulip Festival so."

"Hey, my plan would work out great," he insisted. "Our merchants would make their profit and the tourists would save themselves the hassle."

"It wouldn't work," Joy said.

"We could mail them trinkets to leave around the house. That way everyone would think they'd gone away on vacation."

"Right," she said.

"Okay. Along with the trinkets we send them a picture book—*Places to See and Things to Do in Holland, Michigan*. That way they could make up lies about what they'd seen and done during their fake vacation."

"People have enough fake in their lives today," Joy said. "That's why they come to places like this. Places full of tradition, old-fashioned values and friendly people. The whole nine yards."

He knew all that. Hadn't he moved back here for the very same reasons? But in the last few weeks, his life had felt empty. The tradition and old-fashioned values didn't seem to have the zip they used to have.

"That's why I came here," Joy said. "I wanted a place where my kids could walk to school, bike to the park and know everybody in town. My business is my dream for me but I also have dreams for them."

Suddenly, Robbie's Cub Scout troop came into view and Joy darted away to snap pictures. Some of Robbie as he approached, others as he was across from them and shots of him as he had passed by. She probably had albums full of photos at home. Every occasion would be there on paper to remember and cherish. Even after the boy was a man, she'd be able to relive his childhood. The memories would warm her through long winters. She'd never really be lonely.

"You sure you have enough pictures?" He tried not to sound like a grump, but he didn't quite make it.

Joy seemed not to notice. "Paul would have enjoyed seeing the kids in all this."

Stephen didn't reply at all, concentrating instead on the Brownie troop that was now passing before them. Any father would love to see his kid in a parade, in a ball game or just doing the silly stuff kids do.

"But then I don't ever remember him taking a Saturday off during our entire marriage," Joy said, as she forced a laugh. "So even if he were alive, he wouldn't have been here to see the kids."

What a fool the man must have been. His treasures were left with him, yet he wouldn't take the time to savor their beauty.

Stephen kept his attention on the parade, afraid to speak, afraid to even look her way. Afraid Joy would see the anger and pain boiling in his eyes.

"And I would have been hauling Robbie to one event and then running across two suburbs to haul Katie to something else.'' Joy craned her neck to look around the crowd, for Katie's float probably. ''So, like I said, I came here to follow my own dreams as well as to give the kids a richer and lower-key life.''

''Took a lot of guts to come to a totally new place and start life all over.''

She just shrugged. ''I guess, though some people might say lack of sense. Oh, look, there's Katie.''

He just watched as she took more pictures of the little Dutch-girl float Katie was on, wondering if the three of them knew how lucky they were.

''Philistines.'' Stephen slammed the door after a small group of tourists and stomped back to where Joy stood near the cash register.

She gave a short laugh that hid the confusion in her heart. He was certainly in a rare mood today. If he hadn't wanted to spend the day with her, why had he come over?

She leaned forward on the counter and put chin in hand. ''It's a good thing you didn't go into sales.''

''All those fools want to buy is junk.'' He glared toward the door, his eyes dark with storm clouds.

''Junk is profitable. I've just about sold out my wooden shoes.''

''Yeah, but you'll need to sell about a million of them to generate a decent income.''

She shrugged. ''It's better than nothing.''

''You've got to get a mix of sales. Big ticket and small ticket.'' Stephen straightened a perfectly straight painting on the wall. ''I can't believe they don't want to buy some of these. They're really good.''

''Maybe you're pushing too hard.''

''I'm not pushing.'' He looked hurt, like such a little boy. ''I'm just pointing out the obvious. Damn tourists. They must be brain-damaged.''

Swallowing her laughter, Joy looked out her window. This grumpy Stephen ought to be easier to deal with. She ought to feel safer with him when he wasn't sweet-talking his way into her heart. But the truth was, she didn't feel safe anywhere around him. Her knees went all mushy at just the sight of him and her mind watched for signs that he respected her, not as a woman, but as a businessperson. Grumpy or not, he was starting to affect her all too much.

His pull was easier to fight when the kids were around. She glanced at her watch. "What time did Beth say the play would be over?"

Stephen was exchanging the vase of flowers beneath one painting for a statue of two puppies frolicking, then stood back to admire the effect. "She said four o'clock, but then she was taking the kids for ice cream and souvenirs."

"They should be home about five, five-thirty then."

Satisfied with his rearrangement, he came back to the cash register and stood glaring at the door. He was too close for her peace of mind. She could smell the faint scent of his after-shave. It tickled her senses and suggested dreams for her heart to follow. She concentrated on his dark and fierce frown.

"I could offer you a penny for your thoughts," Joy said. "But I don't think I'm brave enough to handle all that mean."

"I'm going to sell one of your damn paintings this afternoon or else."

"Or else? Or else what? Are you going to beat some sweet old lady half to death if she doesn't buy?"

"Whatever it takes," he muttered darkly.

She came around the counter to perch on her high stool, pulling the tray of little wooden shoes over to straighten. "Aren't you taking this sales thing a little too seriously?"

"Your business needs the income that the big ticket items can generate."

And he was the one who had to pull it off, of course. "I'm doing fine."

Stephen didn't answer her, but just kept staring at the door as if he could will in the proper customers.

Did he give all his clients this same level of intensity? One part of her liked believing she was special, yet another part said that was being weak.

"I really am doing fine," she repeated a little louder. To herself or to Stephen?

He turned toward her, his eyes boring into hers, stripping them of their veil, leaving her feelings exposed for all the world to see. Her hopes, her longings, her dreams and her fears were now an open book.

"All right, all right." She pulled some strength from a hidden pocket and turned away. "So my figures are a little disordered at the moment. I know I'm going to make it. Besides, when things get tight, I can always fall back on my pizza delivery profession."

There was no mistaking the tenor of his grunt. It had no neutral tone in it whatsoever.

"Look." The heat was coming back into her own voice and Joy welcomed it. "Paul gave me safety and security but I wasn't happy with it and I don't see where it made him happy. I'm doing what I want and I'm not destitute. So I'm happy."

Fortunately the door chimes rang, signaling a time-out between the two of them and announcing the arrival of possible customers. Stephen fixed a smile of welcome on his face and stepped out to greet the tourists, like a shark greeting a school of fish.

Joy finished straightening the tray of wooden shoes, then decided to start closing out her day's receipts. Stephen didn't need her help, and her equilibrium didn't need to stay out here listening to the murmur of his voice as he walked through the rooms with the customers, or watching the way he moved his hands as he spoke. She'd spent enough time thinking of those hands and the wonder they would bring. It was time to be assertive with her whimpering soul and ignore Stephen Van Horne.

She was almost done counting the cash on hand when the conversation between Stephen and the tourists grew a little louder and more animated. Should she listen in and check out his sales technique? Nah. He wouldn't really fight with a customer. He was all blustery talk. He showed her some action a few times, a little shadow reminded her. He'd hardly sweep a customer off her feet. Joy took the receipts into her office in back.

The murmur of the voices still drifted back but they were distant and not disturbing. She balanced her tapes and began filing some invoices. Stephen would be proud of her when he saw how she was straightening things up. The door chimes signaled the departure of the tourists just as Joy filed the last invoice.

"Ta-da." Stephen stepped into her office, arms spread wide in a triumphant gesture.

"You sold a picture?"

"I sold two."

Joy felt as if her eyeballs would pop out of her head. "You sold two?"

"And for list price. I didn't discount them one penny." He stood there for a moment, grinning in triumph. "You may congratulate me," he announced.

Now it was Joy's turn to feel shaky. Two pictures at list! She'd marked all of them at five hundred or more just to look respectable. Never in her whole life had she really expected to get that for a picture, much less for two.

Joy stepped slowly around her desk, her knees all atremble. How did one congratulate one's star salesman? Buy him a new car? Take him out to dinner? Kiss him until he cried out for mercy? She stuck her hand out.

Stephen stared a moment at her outstretched hand, then shook his head with a laugh. "That's not what I had in mind."

With a wicked twinkle in his eye, he stepped over to grab her into the heaven of his arms. She could only stare up at him as he swept her outside the little office and into the display room, where he twirled her around until she was dizzy.

"Stephen, I can't breathe," she said with a laugh. But it was a token protest, made only to satisfy the warning lights that were flashing in her mind. She shouldn't be in his arms, shouldn't find such peace and delight there.

But his only answer was a laugh. His hold tightened as his eyes locked with hers. She felt a jolt, a sparking charge, race along her spine that seemed to numb her to everything but the feel of his arms and the soft whisper of his breath.

Slowly, he stopped his twirling, but Joy's dizziness only grew worse. She needed his embrace to hold her up, but it was that very embrace that stole all her breath, all her willpower. She could think of nothing but the wonder of him.

"You are so beautiful."

The whisper was carried on the air, so soft, so gentle that Joy wondered if he'd actually said the words. Then all time for thinking was past as his lips came down on hers.

It was all the heaven that their last kiss had been and then more. His touch was magic, lighting fires that raced along, demolishing any coherency she possessed. She wanted to rest forever in the shelter of his embrace and know the power of his strength.

His hands slid over her back until she was burning up, yet even as they pulled her closer and closer into his arms, she felt too far away. She couldn't share in his strength. She tasted it, she felt it quiver as her own hands roamed over his solid muscle. But she was still too far from him.

She would regret this later, her mind warned her. Giving him power over her for the moment would only increase the way he took charge in the future. Stand up to him, that little voice screamed. But being in his arms was just too much heaven to leave.

"Whatcha guys doing?"

Her daughter's voice stung like the tip of a bullwhip, and Joy jumped from Stephen's arms. There in the doorway stood Katie, Robbie and Beth.

"Nothing," Joy said. Her voice sounded strained and tight even to her and she stuck her hands into her pockets as if that would fortify her.

"Looked like some serious huggy-huggy to me," Robbie said, gazing sternly at her.

"We were celebrating," Stephen said.

Joy guessed that was what they'd been doing, although the sale hadn't remained first and foremost in her mind for very long.

"What's celebrating?" Katie asked.

"Looked like hugging to me," Robbie grumbled.

"Robbie," Joy said, flicking a stern glance the boy's way, but Stephen was concentrating on Katie.

"Celebrating is when people show how happy they are because something good's happened to them," he said.

A smile worked its way onto Katie's sweet little face. "What kinda good thing happened?" she asked.

"He got to first base with Mom."

"That's enough, Robbie," Joy snapped. She was quite conscious, without him telling her, that she'd acted stupidly. She dusted her hands off on her skirt as if dusting off her weakness where Stephen was concerned. "Mr. Van Horne sold two of my paintings this afternoon."

"For a thousand dollars," Stephen added for good measure.

"Wow!" Beth's eyes widened in amazement. "Congratulations."

"Yeah," Robbie added. He found a smile also, though it looked a bit grudging. He was probably wondering what selling some paintings had to do with her melting in Stephen's arms, as she herself was wondering.

"I say we all celebrate," Stephen said.

Robbie's face quickly reverted back to his normal frown. "I ain't hugging nobody."

Joy put her arm around the boy's shoulder. Maybe she could absorb some of his common sense by osmosis. "That's not what he meant, honey."

Stephen looked annoyed, but was it because she was trying to gain common sense or at Robbie's surly attitude? "I meant we should all go out to dinner," he said.

Luckily, she had a perfect excuse. "I'm afraid we can't." With a final pat of Robbie's shoulder, she went over to one front window and closed the blinds, then moved on to the others. "I have to work and Robbie has a sleep over."

Stephen frowned at her. "Work?" he said. "After selling two paintings, you should tell Bruno to jump off a bridge with his stupid delivery job."

That was her financial adviser speaking? More likely, that know-it-all side of him that had to boss everybody around.

"Mom, I gotta get ready to go," Robbie said.

"Go on, sweetheart." She watched as he ran up the stairs, then turned to Stephen. "Two paintings are not going to support us for the rest of the year. I can't give up a steady income, even if it is small."

"You could miss a night," he said.

"I can go celebrate," Katie said.

"Me, too," Beth chimed in.

A sense of relief washed over Joy and she just grinned at them, before turning toward Stephen. "Well, there you are, celebration companions."

He glowered at her.

"I'll wash my face and hands," Katie said, then looked down at her sandaled feet. "And my feet."

Beth looked down at her own feet. "I'll wash my hands and face but I'll skip the feet," she said. "They'll just get dirty again."

He ignored Beth and Katie. His frown deepened as he glared at Joy. "Why don't I go to work with you?" he suggested.

Her relief vanished like stones in a pond. "What in the world for?"

"Can we come too?" Katie asked.

"No, you can't," Joy said. She took a deep breath. That wasn't fear clutching at her heart. It couldn't be. "Nobody's coming with me."

But Stephen had stooped down to Kate's level. "Why don't you and Beth go out to dinner?" he suggested.

"I want to go with Mommy," she said.

Beth joined him at Kate's eye level. "How about if we get some money from Stevie? Then the two of us can go out to dinner."

"It's fun riding around with Mommy," Katie said.

"This really isn't necessary," Joy pointed out. "I have a neighbor lined up to—"

"We can get a movie and watch it at my house on our big TV," Beth said. "Then you can sleep overnight with me."

"Can we see Mickey Mouse?" Katie asked.

"Sure."

"Marlene's little girls are looking forward to having Katie over," Joy said, but knew no one was listening to her. Drat the man! Why did everything have to be done his way?

Stephen gave Beth some money. "Have fun."

"Let's get your pj's," Beth said, taking Katie by the hand. The two hurried up the stairs, leaving Joy and Stephen alone.

"Well," Stephen said. "When do we leave?"

She would not be pushed around. "*We* don't," she said. "You let your kids help you."

She didn't want him along, wrecking her good intentions and distracting her from her goals. But even now, here alone with him with the memories of his touch still singing in the air, she felt her strength ebbing. "They're a lot less trouble than you'd be." She turned off the display lights in the small sculpture case.

"I won't be any trouble at all."

"Right." She moved on to the lights above the paintings.

"Look," he said. "I promise not to whine and I won't ask to play on the swings."

Robbie came running down the stairs, sleeping bag in one hand, duffel bag in the other. "Mr. Maloney's here." He paused to receive a quick peck from Joy before flying out the front door.

By the time Joy finished turning off the other display lights, Beth and Katie were down. Beth had Katie's Mickey Mouse overnight bag under her arm. Joy felt everyone was abandoning her.

"See you tomorrow, Mommy," Katie said, planting a wet kiss on Joy's cheek, then she, too, was gone.

"Bye, hon," Joy called to the closing door. Was she or was she not in control of her own life?

"So are we going now, too?" Stephen asked.

Joy went over to lock the front door. "I really don't need help," she said.

"Who said you did?" He beat her to the light switch and the showroom was bathed in shadow. "I think you owe your top salesman a drink at least, and I want to collect. We get your pizzas delivered, then you can pay your debt.''

It sounded so reasonable, so sane, but she wasn't reasonable or sane around him for long. ''It'll be hours before I'm done,'' she pointed out.

''So that gives us hours to plan where to go.''

''My truck isn't very comfortable.''

''I'm pretty tough.''

So somehow he came along. Where'd she go wrong? she asked herself as she drove to Bruno's. She hadn't wanted him to go to the parade with her this morning, hadn't needed his help in the afternoon and sure didn't need his companionship this evening.

Then why had she let him drive them all to the parade? Why had she let him talk to the customers in the store? Why was he here in the pickup with her?

She was relieved to pull into Bruno's lot and get down to business. The busier she was, the less time there'd be for stupid questions and distracting presences. Joy hurried inside to get her pizzas. She wasn't weak; she wasn't in need of support. She wasn't in need of Mr. Stephen Van Horne.

''So where to?'' he asked as Joy climbed back into the truck.

''Elberdine, then Graafschap.''

She pulled back into the street, conscious of his arm resting on the insulated carrier on the seat between them. If he moved it just an inch or two...

Stop it! she scolded herself and took a right turn a bit more sharply than she meant to.

''There's a great little club on the east side,'' he said. ''We can have a late dinner and a little dancing.''

Dancing? Spending more time in his arms? Letting him lead her around even more until she couldn't think for herself? She cut sharply into the left lane as she overtook a dark blue sedan.

"What are you doing?" he asked.

She glanced his way to see him grabbing the door handle. She wondered what he'd say if she told him the truth. *I'm fighting off my attraction for you.* She played it safe with a puzzled look. "What are you talking about?"

"You're driving like a maniac all of a sudden."

She just shrugged. "I just don't want to get stuck behind some slowpoke."

She was a maniac. A certifiable maniac to have let him come along with her.

"Neither of those cars you passed seemed to be going all that slow."

She paused at a stop sign, her hands beating a tattoo on the steering wheel. He shifted slightly, turning toward her so that the inside of the truck suddenly felt even smaller and more confining. She floored the gas pedal and roared away across the intersection.

"Get 'em while they're hot," she said. "That's Bruno's motto."

"A fine motto to die for."

"You promised you weren't going to whine."

"I didn't know that you were going to drive like some kind of nut case."

She screeched to a stop in front of a white frame house, sending Stephen pitching forward.

"Thank God for seat belts," he muttered as she climbed out of the truck.

Thank God for deliveries that got her out of the truck and away from him. Unfortunately, there was someone waiting at the door, money in hand, and she barely had enough time to catch her breath.

She lost it again as she got into the truck. His eyes were frowning, but about such mirrors of his soul she hardly cared. His lips seemed a magnet for her gaze, as her heart relived the surge of delight at their touch.

Damn.

She climbed back into the cab and pulled away, tires squealing. Maybe she could leave her weakness back at the house on Elberdine and escape from it.

"Will you stop driving like a nut?" he cried.

"Oh, don't be such a wimp."

"I'm not a wimp," he snapped. "I just have a sane and rational concern about my safety."

"I don't need this hassle." She didn't need anything from him.

"Fine, then let me drive."

"I'm not going to church," she snapped. "I'm delivering pizzas."

"You keep on driving like this and you'll be riding to church real soon, in a hearse."

If she kept on seeing him, she'd die of a broken heart, of broken promises she'd made to herself. She took a sharp right turn, then a left and barreled out on the straightaway.

"Hey, where we going?" he asked.

A sensible question since they were on his street. They squealed to a stop in front of his house. An answer to his sensible question.

"Out," Joy ordered.

"What's with you?"

"You," she said. "I can't concentrate on my driving. You're going to make me have an accident."

"I'm going to make you have an accident? I'm not the one driving like a nut."

"You promised not to whine." She latched onto the technicality like a lifeline. "You broke your promise, so out."

"Are you serious?"

"Damn right, I am. Out, out. This other pizza is getting cold."

"This is unreal."

"Out," she screamed.

He stared at her in disbelief, then got out.

"Don't worry," he said before he closed the door. "I'll take care of your kids. I'll tell them how you died in the line of duty, making sure a Bruno's pizza was never delivered cold."

He barely had time to slam the door before she fled.

Chapter Six

Joy growled through her clenched teeth as she shoved with all her might, but it didn't help. The desk that Stephen had refinished stayed in place, stubbornly, just like its owner.

Stop it, Joy silently berated herself as she leaned on the desk. An inanimate object was not affected by the personality of the man who'd worked on it. Joy heaved a deep sigh. That's not to say that Stephen wasn't stubborn. She wasn't going to back down from that opinion. No, it wasn't an opinion, it was a fact.

The jingle of the door chimes was a welcome excuse to derail her thoughts. She hurried into the front room and found Marlene had come in.

"Just the person I needed to see," Joy said.

Marlene just eyed her suspiciously. "Why does that worry me?" She stopped and looked around the room. "My, you certainly have been a busy little beaver."

"I just changed a few things around."

"A few things? You either had an earthquake or an army swoop in here. Your Mother's Day must have been a bit more exciting than mine."

Her Mother's Day was quiet, spent with her kids and her paints. It was just coming down here this morning and seeing Stephen's desk that brought the demons back.

"I just wanted to make some changes," Joy protested. "Come on into the back room, I need some help."

Carrying her silence lightly, Marlene followed Joy into the room where Stephen's furniture was displayed.

"I want to move that desk over to the far wall," Joy said.

The smile disappeared, replaced by a deep frown. "You want it moved all the way over there? What do I look like, a horse?"

"I don't want you to do it by yourself. I just want you to help me."

"Where's your boyfriend?" Marlene asked. "He's the one with the beautiful muscles."

"I don't have a boyfriend."

"He could move it by himself."

"I don't have a boyfriend." Joy said the words more distinctly this time, so there'd be no misunderstanding them.

"All right, so where is Stephen?" Marlene asked, sitting down in a dark maple swivel chair. "I haven't seen him around for a few days."

Joy remained standing. She guessed this was progress. At least the relationship was more defined. "I really wouldn't know. I presume he's out taking care of his other clients. He has his life and I have mine."

She stared at the desk, her arms folded across her chest, as if she could move the thing by the force of her will. It looked like he'd finally taken the hint the other night when she'd thrown him out of the truck. She was glad.

Of course, Stephen could certainly move this desk with what Marlene called his beautiful muscles. Unfortunately, that wasn't the only thing that was beautiful about the man. There were his baby blues, there was his smile, there was his everything.

But most beautiful of all was Stephen as a person. He was strong but gentle, serious but with a sense of humor, caring but—but so damn pushy. Always telling her what to do. Like suggesting he drive instead of her! There was nothing wrong with her driving that getting him out of the car didn't fix.

Joy let a frown build across her face, one that was good and fierce. That's all Stephen Van Horne was, a big, bossy bully.

"Well," she said to Marlene. "Are you going to help me move this thing or do I use dynamite?"

"Mommy, I'm itchy."

Joy turned to find Katie at the doorway, scratching at her arm. "What's the matter, sweetie? You got a bug bite?"

But the red spot Joy expected to find turned out to be a bunch of them, spread out all over Katie's arms and neck.

"Oh great," Joy said on a sigh. "Chicken pox."

"That probably means my kids will be next," Marlene said. "Looks like we're going to be busy for the next week."

Dare she hope to be too busy to think of one blond, bossy, bully?

"How come Robbie gets to stay so long at Teddy's house, Mommy?" Katie asked.

Joy was tired, bone dead tired. They'd started out with Mommy full of sympathy, but then as the days and nights filled with whining, crying, and sleeplessness, Joy found herself fighting growing irritation. That passed and now she and Katie were twin zombies, too tired to even whine.

"Robbie'll be home in a few days, honey. Just as soon as you're over the chicken pox."

"How come Robbie ain't sick? He eats chicken stuff, too."

Joy hugged her daughter to her bosom. "It doesn't have anything to do with eating chicken, baby. He had it when he was about your age."

"Was he sick like me?"

"Yes, honey."

"Was he grumpy?"

"Real grumpy." She kissed the top of Katie's head, noticing that she wasn't feverish any more. That meant she was leaving the sick stage but still afflicted with a terrible case of the itchies. Another few days. Another few days and a good night's sleep, and things would be normal again. It was downhill now but sleep still seemed a distant pleasure.

Katie's hand went down toward her leg and Joy gently took it. "Don't scratch, honey."

"But it's itchy, Mommy," Katie whined.

For just the shortest moment, Joy closed her eyes and sighed. *But it's itchy, Mommy.* Those words were going to be forever engraved in her mind.

"How about a baking soda bath, honey?" Joy said. "That'll make you feel better."

"All right."

The words were agreeable but the tone was doubtful. Poor baby. Joy carried Katie to her bedroom. Her little girl was almost too heavy to carry. Where were those big beautiful muscles when you needed them?

"I'll start the water running, honey," Joy told her daughter. "Pick out some clean jammies and come in for your bath."

Once Joy was in the bathroom, out of Katie's sight, she let the weariness overflow. What in the world was she thinking of? Here she was with a sick little girl who needed her help and she was letting her mind drift to some good-looking hunk.

She sprinkled the baking soda into the tepid water. I don't need his help, she reminded herself. It was one thing to hire the man for his business expertise, but it was another to seek his help in her personal and family life.

He probably wouldn't be that much help anyway. He'd just order her about and point out how inefficiently she was doing things. She certainly didn't need that, what she needed was a nanny. Someone who'd give Katie her bath, put Joy to bed and clean the house.

"I don't want no jammies. I want my Pooh Bear shirt."

"Oh." Joy almost jumped out of her skin.

"Did I scare you, Mommy?" Katie's solemn eyes looked up at her.

"No, honey. I was just daydreaming."

"You do that a lot."

Joy helped her daughter into the bathtub. "Mommy has a lot on her mind." Or a lot to keep off her mind.

Soon the baking soda was working its magic and Katie was happily playing with her family of duckies. Joy sponged water onto Katie's back and various ducky parts as Katie instructed. It was exacting work, requiring her total concentration.

The bath made Katie feel better so she was able to fall asleep, giving Joy the promise of a few hours of uninterrupted peace. Should she zonk out herself, clean up or eat? Trouble was, she felt too tired to do anything but sleep and almost too tired to even do that.

The doorbell rang as she stood in the hallway, drowning in indecision. "Damn," Joy exclaimed. All she needed was for Katie to be woken up. Joy ran to the door and jerked it open.

"Hi."

Great. Just who she needed to see when her resistance was down to zero. "Hail, Caesar," she muttered. Stephen's baby blues seemed filled with concern.

"Somebody else delivered Beth's pizza tonight," he said. "Is something wrong?"

Nuts. They were filled with concern. Joy shook her head more to shake out the guilt than to emphasize her words.

"I'm fine. Katie has the chicken pox so I sent Robbie to stay with a friend." Why did he have to come now, when she looked like something no self-respecting cat would drag in? She was tired, she hadn't showered at all today, and her hair was an absolute, low-down, frizzy mess. "I'd invite you in, but it wouldn't be wise."

He squeezed his way past her into the kitchen anyway. "I had chicken pox when I was a kid, and both sisters and younger brother had it. I should have more than enough immunity by now."

She didn't want him here. Just because idle thoughts of him had possessed her mind over the last few days, it didn't mean that she really had wanted him here. She didn't. She was strong and competent and...beyond protest of any kind.

"Why don't you close the door?" Stephen said. "Come in and sit down."

She heard the bossiness even before the words and, if she hadn't been so tired, she'd have thrown him out on his butt. She shut the door, but stayed where she was. A token protest.

"Where's Katie?" he asked. "Sleeping?"

She nodded.

"Not your usual chatty self, are you?"

"I'm tired." Joy knew that a wail had crept into her voice, but she was beyond caring. She was just so tired.

For a moment, she thought he was going to take her into his arms, but then that idea passed. "Hey, no need to apologize," he said. "I find the change rather pleasant."

A little flame of anger sparked into life and was enough to burn off the edge of her weariness, like the morning sun burned the mist off a dew-laden field. "What do you want?"

"The pleasure of your company," he replied. "People have been polite to me all week and I'm starting to feel uncomfortable. I'm basically a humble man and I don't handle adulation well."

"Go home," she said.

Stephen looked at her, his face crinkling around the corners of those baby blues. She really wanted to pick him up bodily and throw him out, but was afraid of what she'd do if she laid a hand on him. She'd enjoy it, whatever it would be, but probably wouldn't think well of herself in the morning.

"Just go away."

This time he didn't even bother to acknowledge her order; he was too busy looking around the kitchen. It, too, was done in disaster-area decor.

"I just want to take a nice bath and then collapse."

His eyes came back to her. "Better make that a shower," he advised her. "Less danger of drowning if you fall asleep."

"Thank you. I'll take your advice under consideration. Now why don't you just leave?"

But Stephen was already piling up dirty dishes on the counter. "Go take your shower. I'll see what I can do about putting this place back together."

"I don't need your help," she protested. He wasn't the nanny she wished for. He was too tall, too blond, too male.

"Beat it," he said. "I'm going to clean up and make us some dinner."

Even on her best days, Joy doubted that she could physically throw Stephen out on his ear. And she would feel better after a shower and some food. Then she could try throwing him out.

Stephen had the kitchen cleaned in a matter of minutes. It felt good to have something to do after his initial surge of worry when that stranger had come with the pizza.

He'd tried to tell himself that she had quit Bruno's, or that it was just her day off, but the worry hadn't subsided a bit. He tried pointing out to his stubborn nature that she had no use for him—their lovely delivery drive together last Saturday was proof of that—and that he really preferred organized, pleasant women. *Childless*, organized, pleasant women.

So why then, when that stranger had appeared in a Bruno's cap, had he hightailed it over here to see a disorganized, grumpy woman with two kids, figuratively if not literally, hanging on her apron strings?

His ex-wife Donna had always said he had a compulsion to manage and organize, but he didn't agree. It was just that he had no willpower when he saw someone who needed his help. Maybe Florence Nightingale was an ancestor. He'd have to remember to ask his grandmother. Frowning, Stephen took himself over to the refrigerator.

Joy could use a solid meal. Most likely she'd spent the past few days grabbing a bite on the run. And maybe, just maybe, a little food in his own stomach might help quiet his other hungers.

His frown deepened as Stephen scanned the inside of the refrigerator. Things were getting a little sparse in there. Damn. Why hadn't she called him? Either he or Beth could have helped out.

Stephen shook his head as he took out a carton of eggs. She was always talking about the joys of a small town, yet she didn't know how to use the facilities. You didn't have to beg, either. Just drop a little hint on your neighbors and the troops would be out in the blink of an eyelash. The house would be cleaned and a sick child cared for while the parent grabbed some necessary sleep.

Besides twenty-seven packets of orange marmalade, she had a little ham, some cheese and even half of a green pepper. Plenty enough to make a nice omelet for the two of them.

By the time Joy was out of the shower, Stephen was ready to flip the omelet. Her hair was wrapped in a towel and she had a knee-length terrycloth robe wrapped around her body.

Stephen noticed that her feet were bare and briefly wondered if the rest of her under the robe was also bare. That was not an easy thought to handle at the same time he was flipping the omelet. Squinting his eyes, Stephen concentrated on the pan and spatula in his hand.

When the food was safely turned, Stephen let out a sigh. "Why don't you put down the toast?" he told Joy in a tone befitting the financial adviser he was.

"Yes, Caesar."

He sent a glare her way but her back was turned to him as she slipped bread into the toaster. What was with the Caesar bit? He just happened to have a strong manner in dealing with life. If she wanted a wimp to do her accounting, then that's who she should have hired.

Stephen took the pan off the stove and walked to the table. She was getting to be as much of a wiseacre as his younger brothers and sisters.

"Which do you want to do?" he asked as he held the frying pan over the plates. "Cut or pick?"

"Whatever you want is fine with me," Joy replied.

Stephen frowned, but she was pouring their milk and didn't look up. Boy. First she berated him for taking charge and now, when he gave her a chance to make a decision, she backed away. There was no understanding her. He took great care to cut the omelet exactly down the middle.

The toaster popped up and Joy buttered their toast before she brought everything to the table. Stephen put the empty frying pan in the sink and turned just in time to see Joy staring at both portions on the plates.

"I cut them in equal parts," he pointed out. "But pick whichever one you want. Make your own decision."

"You certainly have a tender little psyche," Joy said, laughing.

She sat down at the table and her robe parted slightly, exposing her milk-white cleavage. Oh, Lordy. He might have a tender psyche but he was willing to bet that Joy had more tender things than he had.

Swallowing hard, Stephen went to the freezer and took out an ice cube for his milk.

"The milk is cool," Joy said. "I just took it out."

"I like things cold," he snapped. "Do you mind?"

"Not in the least." Her voice turned cool enough to freeze his milk. "Have a few more ice cubes if you like. Have several. They're on the house."

Angry words milled around on his tongue, pushing and shoving, eager to get out, but Stephen bowed his head and gave his full attention to the omelet in front of him.

Damn, she was an argumentative little thing. The folks in the baby factory must have had a good batch of ornery left over from when they were making some Ninja warriors and they had given it all to Joy.

And another thing, who the heck gave her a name like Joy? The only time she was happy seemed really when she was berating him or pounding him down.

"There's jelly in the fridge if you want some," Joy said.

"I noticed. What'd you do? Hold up a pancake house?"

"My parents sent them. They're on this vacation they've planned all their lives, to see the whole country in one long trip, and they send me little souvenir packages from each place they stop. They're in Florida now."

He should have guessed. "Orange marmalade."

"So we won't starve. Mickey Mouse bandages for when the kids are playing unsupervised and fall down, a Donald Duck indoor-outdoor thermometer so I won't send them outside in shorts when it's freezing, and five newspaper articles prophesying doom, gloom and the spread of killer bees."

Her parents must be worried about her. "The jelly probably comes in handy," was all he said though.

"And will until the year 2200." Joy finished her meal. "That was very good. Mary Poppins one of your ancestors?"

"I'd rather claim Nana," he said. "I was always more impressed with her ability to spot the inherent danger of Peter Pan than Mary Poppins's ability to fly with her umbrella." He drained the last of his milk. "Do you have any fruit?"

"I'm sure I have some canned peaches," Joy replied. "Would you like some?"

"No, I meant for you."

"I'm full, thank you." The sweetness in her voice seemed just a trifle strained.

"You need a balanced meal. It's obvious that you've been under a lot of strain the past few days."

"I don't want anything else."

"You can have the peaches with ice cream."

"I'm not a little kid." There was definitely more strain than sweetness now.

Stephen sighed. "I'm not saying you're a little kid. I just want to make sure you're eating properly."

Joy's frown lines deepened and her face took on a little more red to add to its pink. Apparently patience and understanding had a negative effect on her.

"Would you like anything else?" she asked. "If not, then I'll clean up."

"I'll clean up," Stephen said brusquely.

"You can help," Joy said.

In strained silence, they cleaned up the dishes, then Joy suggested they sit out back for a while. He knew she was dead tired and needed sleep, but her invitation sounded sincere, so he stayed. Leaving the door ajar, they went out onto the open second-floor balcony and sat on a swing.

The night was bright and clear, under a canopy of a million stars, and propelled by a gentle spring breeze. The sensual erotic breath of Mother Earth gently caressed his body.

Stephen straightened his leg sharply and sent the old swing off at a faster pace. A warning should be posted in all high school literature classes—poetry can severely stress one's peace of mind.

"Hey," Joy protested. "Why didn't you tell me that we were going to encounter some turbulence? I would have fastened my seat belt."

"Sorry." Stephen slowed the old swing.

"I didn't say you had to stop," Joy said. "I just didn't want to go off into orbit."

He increased the pace a bit while Joy pulled her feet under herself and tilted closer toward him. There was something potent about the night and the stillness. He reached out and put his arm around her shoulders. She didn't resist.

"I'll try and control things," he said. "But I'll also hold on to you. Just in case we hit any more turbulence."

Joy laughed softly. "That's very kind of you."

"I'm very protective of my clients."

"Hmm."

It was just a little sound but it seemed full to overflowing with skepticism. "I am," he insisted.

"I'm not disagreeing in the least," she said.

Maybe it was time to leave well enough alone. He let the silence flutter in the breeze and they viewed the stars, marveling as lovers had from the beginning of time, at what wonders must lie beyond them.

Lovers? From what subconscious dream had that come? He wasn't even sure they were always friends.

But even as the thought stirred in his mind, he and Joy turned into each other and their lips met. Softly, tentatively at first, it was as if each expected the other to protest. But as the moment for pulling back disappeared, so did the tentative feel. Their desires grew, eagerly devouring any shadows in their way.

She was all woman beneath his touch. Soft, warm and made to fit just right against him. Holding her in his arms, he felt he could do anything just to keep her safe. He felt strong. He felt powerful. He felt consumed by the need to bury himself in her warmth.

Suddenly they broke apart as if the bond holding them together was too weak to hold up under his thoughts. He could feel each beat of his heart echoing in the veins in his temples.

Whoa! His normal rigid control called out to his feelings. Pull it back. Did he really want to get in that deep? He took a shaky breath. More importantly, was it fair to Joy to take such advantage of her? After all, she'd already spent several days nursing a sick child. What she needed was sleep, not passion.

He got up and walked to the porch railing, leaning his hands on it and looking out at the night. Maybe what she needed was the sound night's sleep that came after being loved quite thoroughly.

"Beth said you guys all grew up here in Holland, Michigan," Joy said.

Her voice was a little hoarse, a little strained. Or was it just his imagination? His heart was still beating fast and he didn't dare look her way.

"Yes, we did," he replied, still staring out into the darkness. "You always live in Chicago?"

"Somewhere in it or around it," she said. "I grew up mostly in Beverly, a quiet, middle-class neighborhood in Chicago. Both my parents were the first generation born in America. Until I was about four, we lived above the grocery store my dad's folks ran in Bridgeport, an older, ethnic area in Chicago. I can remember sitting behind the counter as a little kid, being fascinated by all the different languages being spoken there. They seemed like pieces of different colored glass glittering in the sun.

"I was starting to pick up little bits of everything—could say hello in German and Polish, count out change in Spanish and swear in Lebanese. Suddenly, we were moving out to Beverly. Had a split-level house with a patio and a two-car garage and I took every kind of lesson anybody in the neighborhood took except for languages."

"To get 'American,'" Stephen said. He came back over to the swing, but sat on the edge, resting his arms on his knees and keeping his hands clasped in front of him, where they'd stay out of trouble.

"To live the American dream to the hilt," she agreed. "Except my parents were still living the fifties version of it and hadn't noticed that no one else was." She paused. "No, that's not true. Civil rights, Vietnam, burning bras and draft cards. They noticed all that. It just scared the hell out of them and they tried doubly hard to preserve the world they had just reached."

"They weren't the only ones."

"No, but it seemed that way at the time. I loved them so much, but I hated being the coddled little princess. I used to watch the war protests on the news at night and envy the protesters their strength to defy authority."

He was catching glimpses of the girl she had been and could see why she was so determined to make it on her own. He could also see why her father had protected her so, not just because of his dreams and fears, but because there was something about her that brought that out in a man. She was like a delicate rose, maybe strong enough to weather the storm, but too precious to take the risk.

"You must have rebelled," he said. "Everybody does in some fashion."

"In stupid, little ways. I dropped my tap and ballet lessons, and wore jeans occasionally, though my mother would iron them so I didn't quite look the hippie."

He smiled into the darkness, seeing her at fifteen with that same ornery look of determination, but too gentle to hurt anyone in the process. "A real rebel," he teased.

"About the same time Saigon fell and ended the war protests by ending the war, Dad had a heart attack. He recovered and went back to work, but I had gotten a glimpse of life's fragility and lost my taste for rebelling if it would distance me from Mom and Dad. I finished up high school and started at Xavier College on the south side."

"You meet Paul there?" The peek into her life only made him hungry for more. He suddenly wanted to know all about her.

"No, actually I met him through Mom. She was a secretary in a realtor's office and he was the rising star."

"So you met, fell in love and married."

"Yep. And I let him make all the decisions just as I let my father make them before because I was too afraid of hurting either of them by demanding more of a say. In the long run, I was the one who was hurt. It's hard to hit the ground running, when you've barely had practice walking.''

"What did your parents think of the move here?"

She laughed and it was like a rainbow crinkling up into a million pieces to shower over them. "My dad had a fit. Years ago, he'd gotten me out of Bridgeport and into the good life, and here I was, moving the kids and myself back into an apartment above the store."

"What goes around, comes around."

"The one thing I've learned is that you can't please everybody. There comes a time when you have to follow your own dreams."

Stephen looked down at his hands, but saw the past. "Life is a series of choices," he agreed. He saw his choices back in that beautiful fall night in his senior year, and Laura's when she left to have their baby. "And you can't have it all."

"But people should follow their dreams."

"If they can," Stephen said. Dreams sometimes collided and whose took precedence?

"What were your dreams?" Joy asked.

"Pretty much what I'm doing now."

"Aw, come on." Her tone was nowhere near gentle. "You wanted to be an accountant all your life? Even as a little kid?"

He had to smile at her intensity. It was so little-girl-like. As if things were always simple and straightforward. "I guess I wasn't very imaginative."

"You're patronizing me again."

"I am not," he protested. "For the most part I've always wanted to stay around here and be a part of things. This is home."

"I told you my dreams," she grumbled. "There's no reason for you to keep yours such a big secret."

They were dancing on the edges of an argument again. To her, dreams were intense and immense. She wasn't going to believe that he avoided all of that. Keep the dreams within reach and keep your heart intact. It was time for him to hit the road.

"Katie's been quiet for some time now," he said. "Maybe you should catch a few zzz's yourself."

She stretched her legs out and put her feet up on the balcony rail, wiggling her toes. The moonlight was bright, so bright that he couldn't miss a single curve on those beautiful legs.

Stephen stood up. It was definitely time to go. "Good night."

Joy stood up also and put her hands into the pockets of her robe. It was too dark to see the green of her eyes but their sparkle was evident.

"Good night," she said after the longest moment, then she went inside.

He stayed out on the porch until he heard the lock turn in her door and saw the kitchen go dark, then he slowly made his way down the back steps. Joy was always beautiful, no matter what time of the day or night, but she was especially warm tonight. So warm and so womanly.

Should he have tried to stay? He'd be willing to bet the farm that she would have let him.

But then, why would she have let him? Because she was so tired and her defenses were down? What kind of man would impose himself on a helpless woman? Or was it her true longings that came through when her defenses were down?

He expelled the air from his lungs and started the car, wondering if he had any ancestors who had been monks. If so, he'd wished he'd get some help from them.

Chapter Seven

A couple nights of uninterrupted sleep worked wonders for both Joy and Katie, so when Stephen came over Monday evening, Joy felt able to face him.

"Hello, ladies," he said when Joy let him in.

Katie ran across the room with a squeal and grabbed his leg in a giant hug. "You're my hero," she exclaimed.

"What?" Stephen's face reflected such a mixture of horror, surprise and embarrassment that Joy had to laugh out loud.

"You saved my Mommy's life," Katie explained. "Just like a knight on a big horse who rescues the princess from the scary old castle."

"Katie," Joy cried out, the horror in her heart echoing in her voice. "I never said anything like that."

"Did too."

"I said Stephen was a lifesaver." She'd never spoken aloud about Stephen being her knight in shining armor.

Now it was Katie's turn to look bewildered. "That's a little candy with a hole in the middle."

"That's me," Stephen said. "Only I'm a lot sweeter."

Katie's bewilderment grew by leaps and bounds and her face scrunched up. "You guys are making fun of me. You tell Robbie it's not nice. Well, it ain't nice for you neither."

Joy felt her horror subside as she tried hard not to laugh. "I know, baby. I'm sorry."

She caught Stephen's eye and felt his smile, even if he was forcing it back. Something passed between them, a sharing of a gentle moment. It caught her off guard and off balance.

Stephen turned back to Katie. "I brought some cartoons," he said, holding up some VCR tapes.

"What kind?" Her tone indicated that Katie was interested, but not quite ready to forgive them.

Stephen glanced at the titles. "*Lady and the Tramp* and *Sleeping Beauty.*"

Katie took a moment to look serious, even though she loved both films. "Okay," she finally said. "But I get to sit in your lap."

Now it was Stephen's turn to make faces, but instead of bewilderment, his seemed to carry a touch of fear.

"Okay," he replied after a long pause.

Joy followed them to the doorway, watching as they set up the VCR. Once that was done, Stephen allowed Katie to choose the spot on the floor where they'd sit, bring a pillow for his back, then plop herself into his lap. Both leaned back once the movie started.

In a matter of seconds, Stephen's expression seemed to change. The wariness gave way to a kind of awkwardness, as if Katie was made of china and might break if he moved the wrong way. Then that changed to surprise and warmth. He was such a strange mixture with the kids, standoffish and then tender. With her, too, come to think of it. She never knew when he was going to be gentle and understanding or when he was going to be the heavy-handed bully.

For the moment, such a mixture of emotions danced across his face, that she almost felt like she was intruding. What had happened to make him so reluctant to express his gentle side? She told him a lot about herself the other night, but he'd said very little. Was he just more reserved or was there something he couldn't talk about?

Robbie came in the back door and she joined him in the kitchen. She wasn't certain she was ready to look at the vulnerable side of Stephen Van Horne; afraid that would make her all the more vulnerable to his knight-in-shining-armor-qualities.

"So how was practice?" she asked Robbie as he dropped his cleats by the door.

"Good," he replied.

"Hungry?" Joy asked.

"Starving." Hearing sounds from the living room, Robbie walked to the doorway. "Hi, guys."

"Hi," Katie and Stephen greeted him in return, although his sister did not bother to look up at him.

"Whatcha watching?" Robbie asked.

"Sounds like *Lady and the Tramp* to me," Joy answered.

"Oh." Robbie turned back to the kitchen. "What's to eat?"

"Sloppy joes."

"Super."

While Robbie poured himself a glass of milk, Joy filled a bun with the meat, then sat down with her son. She wasn't really avoiding the living room and Stephen. She just had to digest this new side of him, if she was going to continue being strong.

"Learn anything new in practice?" she asked.

"Nah."

Joy tried to think of another question. "But you said you had fun."

"Yeah."

"What makes practice fun?"

"We do stuff," he replied, gobbling the sandwich and chips.

"Stuff?"

"Yeah, soccer stuff." He finished his milk and took his dishes to the dishwasher. "I'm gonna watch the movie."

Joy sat alone in her kitchen, watching the evening shadows creep in with the night. All her conversations with Robbie were like this. Short and cryptic.

What her son needed was a man to talk to. Laughter floated in from the living room and nudged at her ear. No, there was a limit to what she could ask of her CPA.

Besides, Stephen seemed closer to Katie. It wasn't that he and Robbie disliked each other. They just hadn't developed a rapport. Maybe Robbie was jealous of Stephen.

Joy got herself up and out of her chair. That was stupid. There was no reason for Robbie to be jealous and he knew that. Maybe they'd like some popcorn. She threw herself enthusiastically into the popcorn manufacturing.

She and the popcorn were welcomed with enthusiasm and they watched the movies with the warmth and familiarity that belonged to a family. Then, after the kids went off to bed, Joy and Stephen settled down on the floor to watch *Key Largo*.

Her eyes stayed on the TV screen but she could feel Stephen beside her. His arm was so close that she'd barely have to move to touch him. She could be in his embrace in the blink of an eye.

"Katie seems a lot better," Stephen said.

"Yeah. As full of energy as ever."

He moved a little closer to her, his breath tickling the hairs on the back of her neck. "And how's her mom?"

"She's better, too."

She turned as she spoke and found his lips so close to hers. So close that she didn't have to think, didn't have to make a choice. She just followed her instincts and pressed her lips against his.

They'd shared so much over the last few days, from chicken pox to popcorn. Sharing their bodies seemed right and inevitable. She sighed with pleasure as his tongue slid between her parted lips, and she lay closer into his arms.

There was a darkness in her soul, a lacking that the sunshine couldn't reach, but here in Stephen's arms, the shadows seemed to grow dimmer. Life and happiness—real, rich happiness seemed not only possible, but inevitable.

His hands moved across her back, spreading the fire of his touch as his mouth lit an answering flame in her soul. Her heart began to race, pounding a rhythm of urgency that echoed across the universe. The time had come to forget, to feel the rhythm of life once more, to dance amid the magic again.

His mouth left hers to taste the softness of her neck, and shivers of delight raced down her spine. She liked being touched, being slowly brought alive again. She felt like Sleeping Beauty, but was she really in the market for a Prince Charming?

The idea was jolting enough to create a sudden stillness in her heart that Stephen must have sensed. He pulled back and they discovered that the movie was over and the credits were running.

"Guess we weren't paying very good attention," Stephen said with a shaky laugh as he hit the rewind button. "Want an instant replay?"

Of the movie or the kiss? "I don't think so." She got to her feet, finding her knees were willing to try to support her, and picked up the empty popcorn bowl. "It's pretty late and I'm afraid I don't bounce back as quickly as Katie."

"I guess I'd better take off then."

Take off what? But she didn't say the words, choosing another meaning to latch onto. "Yeah, I guess you'd better."

In a matter of seconds, he was out the back door and she was alone in the sleeping stillness of the house. She turned off the lights and walked slowly down to her bedroom.

She came alive under Stephen's touch in ways that she never remembered feeling with Paul. Maybe now she treasured the sense of fire that a caress brought, or maybe she and Stephen matched in ways she and Paul never did.

Either way, she had wanted him to stay. She had wanted him to stay very much. And that realization scared the hell out of her.

"Come on, Uncle Stephen. Let's go outside and play catch."

"Not right now, Jill," Stephen told his niece, barely glancing away from his baseball game.

"How about we play some soccer?"

Stephen looked up then, giving his nephew Joey, Jill's twin, a frown. "How about you guys don't bug me?"

"Watch it, kids. It looks like Uncle Stephen got up on the wrong side of the bed. Like usual."

Stephen gave his sister Jane a full-blown glare. She was the second in line, just two years younger than himself, and had always been the mouth of the family.

"Don't give me that look, big brother," Jane said as she sat on the sofa across from him. "You've been a regular Jekyll and Hyde since we got here."

"Who are those guys?" Jack asked.

"They're monsters that Uncle Stephen keeps in his closet upstairs," Jane replied.

Two pairs of young eyes, framed in a mixture of concern and doubt, glanced up at the ceiling.

"Jane," Beth scolded as she helped Jennifer, Jane's youngest, put a dress on a doll. "You're scaring the kids."

"It's good for them," Jane replied with a smile. "Keeps them on their toes."

"What kind of a mother are you?" Beth asked.

"Normal."

"You've never been normal since Mom caught you eating your paste in third grade," Stephen grumbled.

"None of that explains your mood swings, brother dear."

Beth snickered as she gave Jennifer the doll. Stephen tried glaring his younger sister into silence, but Jane already had a mean smile on her lips.

"What's her name, Stephen?"

"Whose name?" He'd learned long ago that Jane didn't bluff easily but that didn't mean that he couldn't try.

Jane turned toward Beth. "Okay, kid. Give me the low-down skivvy. Sherlock Holmes is in my blood."

"Well." Beth drawled out the word. "Stephen's developed a taste for pizza."

"I thought he was getting a little thick around the middle."

"I am not," Stephen protested.

Jane ignored him. "Where does he get this . . . pizza?"

"There's a lady that delivers," Beth replied.

His sister's smile turned even meaner. "Oh," she crooned. "How convenient."

Jane had been terrible when they were kids. Always goading him, always trying to one-up him. They hadn't been able to treat each other as decent strangers until both had graduated from college. He was saddened to see her reverting back to her nasty juvenile self.

"This woman just delivers pizza part-time," Stephen explained. "She also owns a shop downtown where she sells art, home furnishings, that kind of thing."

Jane nodded wisely. "I see," she said.

Stephen considered hitting her. Unfortunately, he was no longer into sibling violence. "I'm her financial adviser," he said. "I do her taxes and advise her on procedures."

"Hmm," Jane said.

"She also sells some of the furniture I refinish." His voice had risen and he could feel his cheeks growing warm.

"That's nice," Jane said.

"Now, if you don't mind, I'd like to watch my game," he said. Maybe he should rethink his position on sibling violence. It certainly wasn't admirable, but there were times when it was a necessity.

Jill plopped herself on the sofa next to her mother. "I wish we had something to do," she moaned.

"Yeah," Joey agreed. "I mean, like, this is really boring, Mom."

"Why don't you watch your uncle's stupid baseball game?" she suggested.

Stephen sighed as Jane's twins chorused an "Aw, Mom." This sure was going to be a fun weekend. Bickering with his sister who'd dropped in unannounced from Chicago and listening to her kids whine. He could think of a lot of other things he'd rather do. Hell, he'd even be willing to go on a pizza delivery run.

His stomach tightened and he felt about ten times more alive. Maybe he should go out with the kamikaze pizza lady. Live life out on the edge.

Actually he didn't want to deliver pizza any more than he wanted to review her payables, but he sure wouldn't mind getting a movie and cuddling with her on the living room floor as they had last night.

"I don't want to watch this game," Joey grumbled. "It's just the Cubs."

Not that Stephen really wanted to get involved. He had a nice, easy kind of life, except when his sister visited with her kids, and there was no reason to upset the old apple cart.

"I hate watching baseball," Jill moaned.

Stephen gritted his teeth. On the other hand, it isn't as if he'd taken a vow that denied him a drink and a few laughs.

"Mommy, I gots nothing to do."

His lips twisted in pain. There was nothing like the whine of a preschooler to rip your nerves raw. He ought to take them all for a ride on some back country road and lose them. Get rid of—

A bright light lit up his brain. "How would you guys like some of the best pizza in town?" he asked. "And two extra kids to play with."

Beth's smile turned into a definite smirk.

"Robbie can play with you twins and Katie can play dolls with Jennifer."

"Awright," Jill exclaimed as she and Joey exchanged high fives.

Stephen hurried off to the phone before his sisters could come up with any comments. Joy answered on the first ring.

"Hello," she said.

It was a common enough greeting but her voice gave it such an uncommon feel.

"Hello," she repeated. Her voice was louder and sharper.

"Hi," he said quickly. "This is Stephen. I was wondering if you could do me a favor. My sister Jane is over with her three kids. Jane and Beth want to gossip and the kids want to play. Do you think Katie and Robbie would like to come over? I'll spring for pizzas and they can sleep over."

"I'm sure they'd love to," Joy replied.

"Good." He paused and swallowed the memories of last night. "Are you delivering pizzas tonight?"

"Yup." Her voice had tightened. "But I can bring the kids over beforehand."

He wasn't looking to start a fight. "Can you bring over about three pizzas at the same time?"

"Okay, see you around six."

"Ah, Joy? Want to go to dinner after you're done?" he asked. After all, providing the kids with entertainment didn't mean he had to be there to share it.

Unfortunately, she didn't reply. Damn. He'd thought she'd been having some second thoughts last night. Was she going to keep him at arm's length now?

"You know, to a nice place with tablecloths." His words trailed off lamely.

"Sounds good to me."

"Great." He hung up, feeling his lips stretch into a broad grin. Hot dog!

Stephen reined in his emotions and drew his lips into a tight line. No use going off the deep end. Given a choice between a date with a charming lady, and Jane and her kids, only a fool would choose to stay home.

And his father didn't raise no fools. At least not of the eldest son variety.

"Whoo whee," Marlene exclaimed when Joy slipped into low heels. "Bruno's sales are going to go through the roof after tonight."

"Oh, God." Joy felt the pit of her stomach fall about seven stories. "Do you think this is a bit much?"

"For delivering pizzas, yes, just a tad. It's perfect for a date though."

Joy chewed on her lower lip as she looked in the mirror. She was a mess of confusion. She wanted to have dinner with Stephen, but her stomach was churning. Maybe she should call and cancel. She smoothed down the front of her cream blouse with the full sleeves and brushed at some lint on the sides of her best pair of dress slacks, a snug-fitting pair of peg-leg navy blues. Maybe she should change into something less date-like and pretend that it's a chance for them to discuss her sloppy business practices.

"I haven't been on a real date for a long time. I don't know if I'm too dressed up or not enough."

Marlene chuckled and came over to hug her. "You're going to do fine, kid. Just relax and let it all flow naturally."

"I don't remember what's natural anymore."

"Don't worry," Marlene assured her. "It's just like riding a bicycle."

"Right. You never forget." Joy brushed at her unruly locks. She wished she believed that old bromide. Right now, she just knew that she was going to screw up worse than a junior-high kid.

"I better get going," Joy said, looking at her watch. "I'm late already." She rushed out into the kitchen, Marlene following close behind, where Katie and Robbie waited. "Let's go, guys."

"Did you order the pizzas?" Robbie asked.

"Yes," Joy replied. She ushered everybody out and slammed the door shut. "We're going to pick them up, then go straight to Stephen's house."

"And extra hats?" Katie asked.

"Yes, yes, yes." Joy hurried down the steps well ahead of her own kids. She had the old truck's motor fully revved up and growling as Katie and Robbie were still scrambling in.

"Have fun," Marlene called out after her.

Joy just waved over the roar of the motor as she spun into the street. She wasn't sure she was ready to start dating again. But she was ready to snuggle on the living room floor while watching movies? a little voice asked. Maybe she wasn't ready for either. Or maybe she was just afraid to feel again. If she lived through tonight it would be a miracle.

Fortunately, they got to Bruno's before her doubts made her turn back. The pizzas were ready and waiting for her, along with a pile of Bruno's hats. Robbie carried the pizzas and Katie the hats. The traffic was light and they were at Stephen's in a few minutes.

He answered the door, his smile so warm and welcoming that she wanted to fly into his arms on the spot.

"Hi," he said.

"Hi yourself." She stuck her hands into her pockets so that she'd keep them out of trouble, but couldn't keep herself from returning his smile in force. Maybe she was ready to date again.

"Mom," Robbie said. "The pizzas are going to get cold."

"Oh, right." She followed the kids inside with an apologetic smile at Robbie that he grimaced at. They were met in the living room by Beth and another woman.

"For heaven's sakes, Stephen," the other woman scolded. "What are you doing out here all this time? Well, hello."

Stephen made a face at the change in the woman's tone. "Joy, this is my older sister Jane. Jane, this is Joy."

"Cute, Stephen." The woman stepped forward and took Joy's hand in both of hers. "Stephen is older than me. I just happen to be the oldest girl."

"That makes you my older sister," he said.

Joy just watched the byplay with interest. Stephen appeared to have come from a strong-minded family. One that could easily swallow her up, if she didn't clutch her independence fiercely.

"I'd better check on the kids," she said and edged toward the kitchen.

Jane came along with her. "That's a lovely outfit. I can see why my brother is so smitten with you."

"Oh, but he's not," Joy insisted. Or if he was, it should be a silent smitten, not one his family knew about.

"Stephen, you old devil," Jane said, laughingly over her shoulder. "Still playing that old keep-'em-guessing game."

Joy breathed a sigh of relief once they entered the kitchen. Everything seemed quite in order. A box of pizza was open and the kids were in place, each with a slice in hand, Bruno's hats on their heads and broad smiles on their faces.

"You guys behave yourselves," Joy warned.

"They will," Beth assured her.

Stephen took her by the arm and led her out of the kitchen. "The sooner you get done, the sooner we can get together," he murmured.

Joy was beginning to feel like she was a dim-witted pendulum, needing to be led back and forth. "Don't worry," Joy said. "I'm going to burn rubber all up and down this old town tonight."

Stephen's face turned into such a mask of horror that Joy found herself laughing. "Don't be such an old worrywart," she said. "I'll drive carefully. I've never had an accident in my life."

"That's because you've been lucky so far," he grumbled as they stood out on his porch. "Everyone gets out of your way."

"Boy, what a fuddy-duddy you are."

He took her into his arms and kissed her lightly. "I'll show you fuddy-duddy," he said. "Just you wait and see."

A delicious excitement rippled through Joy's body and demolished any worries meeting his sister had awoken, but she kept her voice tough. "Is that a threat or a promise?"

Stephen smiled. "I don't make threats and I always keep my promises."

This was too much. Her heart was racing out of control and her tongue was paralyzed. She couldn't believe that she was out here, word-playing like some coed on a first date. She backed away and waggled her finger at Stephen, not daring to trust her voice.

"Be careful," he said. "And I mean that."

After saluting sharply, Joy dashed for her truck. Be careful? Absolutely. No problem. She was just going to lay out a string of pizzas on this town in about thirty seconds flat.

Unfortunately, things went a bit beyond thirty seconds. It was more like three hours but she delivered a volume that would normally have taken her four hours. Good thing Stephen wasn't with her. She would never have heard the end about tonight's driving. One more delivery and she was done, free for the evening.

"Come on, come on," Joy muttered to herself as she leaned on the doorbell. No one came, though the house appeared open. She rang the bell again, then called out, "Hello?"

Still no answer so Joy wandered off the porch. She followed the driveway to the back of the house and found two kids playing on the patio out back.

"Pizza," Joy said.

"All right!" they cried. "We're starving."

One ran to the picnic table and sat down as if ready to dig in, while the other one ran to the screen door. "Mom," he called into the interior. "Pizza's here."

Joy had tried calling into the same darkness inside and had gotten no response, but maybe the kid knew the magic password. Joy pushed the gate open and stepped into the yard, seeing the other kid mouthing some words, but the sound was drowned out by the roar of the huge dog suddenly charging at her. Fear only paralyzed her for a split second, then she held the boxes in front of her like a shield, letting them catch the full brunt of the dog's weight.

They smashed as he hit them—gooey warmth oozing out all over Joy's chest. The dog seemed torn between licking Joy's face and licking the pizza. Damn.

A woman materialized from somewhere. "What the hell are you in the yard for?" she cried as she pulled the dog away. It finally sat down, wagging its tail in frantic excitement.

"I was trying to deliver your pizzas. No one answered the front door," Joy said. Her blouse was a disaster and her slacks just shy of one. Just when she had wanted to look special.

"That's no reason to barge in like that."

What was she supposed to have done? Sent them a telegram to expect her? People usually expect the pizzas to be delivered once they've ordered them.

"Are those our pizzas?" one of the kids asked.

"Not on your life," the woman snapped. "I'm not paying for that mess."

"No one said you had to."

Joy stomped out of the yard and threw the pizzas into a nearby garbage can. Now what? Did she go home and change, which would delay the evening, or go over to Stephen's and tell him what happened? It was almost nine-thirty already, so, reeking of pizza, she drove to his house. Luckily, he answered the door and he quickly stepped out onto the porch with her.

"What happened?" he asked, his eyes just a bit too sympathetic.

"Oh, I just ran into a pizza-loving dog," she said, trying for a laugh. This was supposed to be such a special night and now it was all ruined. "Sorry, I'm late, but I think we should just skip this whole thing."

"We can go to your house and you can change," he said. "It's not that late."

Late? It was far too late. She had her chance at happily-ever-after with Paul. She wasn't going to get a chance for even a pleasant morning-after with Stephen. She was stupid to think that she could balance her job, her gallery, the kids and a relationship. She was just as incompetent as Paul feared she was, as her father knew she was.

"I can't just go home and change," she said, her voice echoing the trembling of her heart. "This is my one good summer outfit. Tonight's off, tomorrow's off, the whole rest of eternity is off. I'm never going to try to date again in my whole life." Then the dam burst and tears ran down her cheeks to mingle with the tomato, cheese and sausage.

Somehow Stephen got her into the truck and he drove them to her house.

"It's not really so bad," he assured her about the ten millionth time. But then he hadn't prepared for his first date in eons by coating himself in pizza. She was just so humiliated.

He kept up his soothing talk until he had her in the bathroom, had turned on the shower and handed her a stack of clean towels. "Want me to stay and help?" he offered.

But she found the strength to shake her head and he left. Once the door closed behind him, she stripped off her yucky clothes and scrubbed a zillion times until every smidgen of tomato paste and oregano were gone. Then she put on a pair of shorts and a T-shirt and stomped into the kitchen.

"Hi," Stephen said, all too cheerfully.

"Hello," Joy mumbled.

"Care for a little pizza?"

If looks could kill, Joy would have dropped Stephen in less than a second, but he just laughed. "Just a little humor," he said. "I didn't think you'd want to look a pizza in the face for a while."

"For the rest of my life would be too soon."

"So I went out and got us some hot dogs, some potato salad, some sherbet and a nice bottle of wine." He held out a glass of a blush wine toward her. "Skoal."

The wine was sweet and cool and went down all too easily. It seemed to wash away all her tensions, all of her silly worries about the evening. She and Stephen were friends. There had been no reason for her to get all tense. She didn't need to look perfect. Lord, he had seen her when Katie had the chicken pox. If he was going to duck out of her life, it would have been then.

She looked up and found him watching her, his eyes promising her that the delight and sweetness of the wine could go on. She felt a sudden tingle, a tightness deep in her core and took another sip of her wine. The tingle grew and along with it, a reckless desire to feel alive. She finished her glass of wine.

"I must have looked hysterical, trying to fight off that dog with a box of pizza," she said, looking away. Did she need more time or was their loving inevitable, the haven their meetings had been leading them to all along? "I thought he was going to eat me, but all he wanted was the pizza."

"Ah, but was there a difference between you and the pizza?" Stephen asked.

His voice was velvet, patching up the tattered parts of her heart. It was the mist, covering the craggy cliffs that she dwelt on. It was the steel that could give her strength.

"Not once he greeted me. The pizza and I became as one."

The very notion of becoming one tempted and tantalized, her throat growing dry with the effort of decisions.

She held her glass out for a refill on the wine, but once she got it, she didn't drink it. She stared into it.

The softly pink color was the dawn. The promise of a new life after the darkness was dispelled. She sipped at it, feeling an easiness slide down into her heart. The dawn would come if she would let it.

She looked up at Stephen, feeling the night and all its secrets surround her. What would it be like to know his touch, to rest in the safety of his arms?

"I'm not really very hungry," she said softly. "What do you say we watch some TV and relax?"

"Fine by me."

They settled onto the sofa, the television offering them the choice of news or reruns. Stephen's arm slipped around her and she lay against him, letting her eyes droop closed. She was strong, she was independent, but could she stay that way if she followed her hungers for the night?

She sat forward, using the remote control to change the channel. The next one up was the weather channel.

"How about this?" she asked.

Stephen cleared his throat. "Exciting," he said. "But you won't see Holland on that weather map."

"Why not?"

"Because to forecast the weather in Holland, you need an expert."

"And that guy isn't?"

"An expert needs to be on the scene. Now, take tonight, for example. There was a severe threat of storms earlier."

"There was?" She didn't remember any clouds in the sky while she'd been rushing around. Then once she'd met up with the dog . . .

His meaning suddenly dawned on her. "Oh, there was."

"Now, though." His fingers traced along the side of her cheek, drawing a soft little line toward her lips. "Now, we still have a chance of turbulence, but there's also a chance that the clouds will pass."

"Leaving high temperatures and sunny skies behind."

His finger had reached her mouth, but left to be replaced by his lips. His touch was gentle, and yet demanding, drawing everything from her. She felt the walls of her foundation slide into oblivion, her worries and fears melted away, pulled out of her by the magic of his lips.

"You know," he whispered on the breath of the night as his hands slid under the loose fitting T-shirt. "I like this outfit just as much as the other one. Maybe better."

His hands felt cool, yet left her skin blazing hot. "Oh, Stephen," she sighed.

His hand cupped her breast as his lips came to hers for another assault. His kiss was deeper, hungrier, but left an answering hunger in her. Fire spread out from his fingers; her heart trembled with need, with a tightening heat deep inside her. She arched against him, wanting the iron of his muscles against her.

He pushed her T-shirt up so that his lips could take the place of his hands. His mouth sucked at her breast, his arms encircling her to draw her closer to his heart. She held him, running her fingers through his hair and feeling his hot trembling beneath her touch.

His lips came back to hers, pressing hard into them, even as he lay her back into the sofa. His hands took up their exploring again, but this time roamed lower, sliding beneath the waist of her shorts. Her body ached for his completeness. She tugged at his shirt, pulling it free of his shorts so that she could touch him, feel the fire beneath the rock-hard surface of him.

After a moment, she gently pushed back. "I think those high temperatures are here," she said, and sitting up slightly, pulled his T-shirt over his head.

He did the same for her, sighing as he beheld her nakedness before him. But then, as if her body was a magnet, he pulled her into his embrace. His cool chest met her blazing one; his muscled iron met her softness and their arms entwined to hold them as one.

She took his weight on her, reveling in the pulsating need of him. Her hands felt the dampness of his skin as they slid over his back. Then she pushed at his shorts, willing them away so that she could feel all of him against her.

He sat up, leaving her cold and bereft. "I feel like a high schooler necking on the sofa," he said, but his hands came back to tease her, warming her breasts and her heart. "One false move and I fall on the floor."

She reached up, unable to deny herself the pleasure of touching him, of feeling him come alive beneath her caress. "There are alternatives, you know." She ran her fingers lightly through the soft hair on his chest.

"The balcony?"

"The neighbors would enjoy that. I was thinking of the bedroom."

He stood up, leaning back down to pick her up in his arms. She felt dizzy. She felt like she could reach the stars and beyond.

"Point the way, milady."

He carried her through the darkened hall and laid her on her bed. The softness swallowed them up, the shadowy night bespoke of urgency and all time of play was over. The heavens awaited. The stars sang of love and need and hunger.

She slid out of her shorts, feeling him do the same, then they lay intertwined. Their hearts beat as one as the passion consumed them. She opened herself to him, taking him inside her heart as well as her body. The world spun out of control. Nothing was real, but only them, only the fever that devoured them.

The night was magic, not misery. Memories lay waiting to be made, not waiting to haunt and mock. She felt a shiver of wonder course through her. This was real, this was now. All that mattered, all that ever really mattered—being truly one with another, even if it just lasted for a few moments.

The earth shook and was left behind. Then, slowly, the night came back to claim them. But it soothed and left a heady peace in its wake. She felt Stephen's arms wrap around her as she fell asleep.

Chapter Eight

Joy stirred and pulled the blanket tighter around herself. Blanket? Just a plain simple old blanket? Where were the strong arms that had held her so securely?

She sat up and looked around. She was still in her own bedroom, covered up for warmth, but alone. Where was Stephen? Had he snuck out?

Her shorts were off to the side near a pair of men's shorts. Stephen had to be around someplace. It was hard to imagine a CPA skulking about Holland, half-naked in the night.

Snatching up her robe, Joy went looking and found him out on the back porch. She paused a moment until her heartbeat returned to near normal, then stepped outside. The cool wood surface felt good on her bare feet.

"Hi," she said.

He looked over at her. "Hi."

"Couldn't you sleep?" she asked. "Or do you always get up around four in the morning?"

He stared a long moment out toward the alley and the string of houses behind her. "I've never been much of a sleeper."

So quiet, so subdued. She hadn't expected cartwheels on the lawn, but not this pensiveness, either. She walked up behind him and began to massage the muscles across his shoulders. His skin was smooth, like soft leather covering steel, and touching him brought back memories of the passion of last night, actually of a few short hours ago.

She couldn't tell if her touch awoke like memories in him though. He sat quietly throughout her ministrations, staring out on the star-draped darkness covering her backyard. There was so much tension beneath her fingertips. He was wound tight like a steel cable. An uneasiness crept up to envelop her, like a damp fog rising from a Louisiana bayou.

"A penny for your thoughts," she said.

"Save your money," he said. "Don't waste it on something so worthless."

Her hands stayed on his shoulders but they grew more tentative. She'd like to think that nothing would change between them because of last night, but what she had feared was an increase in his protectiveness, not this sudden distancing.

"Would you like something to drink?" she asked. "A glass of wine?"

"No, thanks."

He was back to short, cryptic answers. Was it a lack of enthusiasm for their lovemaking, for her? She grew even more fearful. Maybe it hadn't meant a thing to him.

"Mind if I sit down?" she asked.

"No, go ahead."

His answer was hesitant and slow, her steps followed in the same path. She pulled a chair over next to his and sat down.

For a moment he said and did nothing. Then he reached over and took her hand, holding it with surprising need—a blind man's only link to the world. "I'm sorry I'm such a grump."

As she tried to enclose his one large hand in both of her small ones, she felt a little piece of him relax.

"Is something wrong?" Joy asked.

"Not with you, that's for sure."

The dimness of the night's half-light created shadows on Stephen's features but not enough to hide his pain. She lifted his hand to her lips, brushing it gently.

"Stephen?" she whispered.

His hold had been tight enough to suggest he'd never let go, but then suddenly he did, casting her adrift.

"I haven't been honest with you," he said. "But I don't know quite how to tell you the truth."

His words caused panic to set into her heart, but she kept her voice soft and calm. "However you like and whenever you like."

He sat back with his silence and she gazed out over the yard. A faint light was edging up over the eastern horizon and a few early birds began to tentatively welcome the new day.

Which did she want, the new day or the old? The passion that they'd shared or the dawn, suddenly filled with an unknown.

"I have a son."

The words came spilling out, bursting forth without any warning, without even a hint of what message they would deliver.

Joy said nothing, concentrating instead on breathing. Her mouth had forgotten how to speak and her heart ached with a dull weariness. He had hidden his child from her. Not just hidden, but lied about having one. During all these weeks, while she'd been opening her soul to him, he'd been keeping her at a distance.

"Does he live with your ex-wife?"

Stephen sighed and stared away at the hinting dawn for a long, long moment. "Donna and I never had any children, by our choice. I fathered my son when I was in high school."

The ache eased a fraction, though Joy was not sure why. Maybe it was the hint of anguish in his voice. Maybe it was the knowledge he'd been just a kid himself when he'd become a father.

"Who does he live with?" she asked.

"I don't know." This time there was no hint. There was definite anguish. An anguish that seemed to rip Stephen apart, opening up his heart so that she could see his agony within.

Joy waited a moment, scarcely breathing, as she felt him struggle within himself for control. More birds stirred and truck traffic rumbled on a far distant expressway, indicating that the new day was serious about stepping forth.

"Laura gave him up for adoption," he went on after a while. "I know nothing about him except his birthday and that they were going to name him Michael."

His voice was bleak, lifeless even. The eastern light crept higher and the birds' chorus increased in volume. The new day would not be denied.

"I loved Laura. At least I thought I did. We dreamt of a life together the way only the young can dream, reaching for a kind of happiness only the young can reach. But then she changed her mind and decided to give the child up for adoption. I didn't know what to do."

Stephen closed his eyes and shook his head.

"My parents were supportive. They didn't harass me in any way but they were honest with me. They pointed out that I might have legal rights to the child, but morally, ethically, I shouldn't make it any harder on Laura than it already was. Their advice was to pray for God's blessing on the child and get on with my own life."

He looked off to the east and gazed for a long moment at the light, now stronger, but still hiding behind the horizon. Joy couldn't tell whether he was pleading with the dawn to hurry up or wishing he could send the new day running and keep the protective darkness of the night's cloak about him. What Joy knew for sure was that his soul was full of misery.

"Most of the time I'm okay and I do go on with my life. But then there are other times. When I wake up in these early hours before dawn and there's nothing to distract my thoughts, or when I see some boys playing baseball. Then the blue funk comes to sit on my head."

"Have you ever looked for him?" Joy asked.

"No." His voice was sharp and invited no comment. "I mean, why? What could I offer him except misery, pain, confusion and everything else negative?"

"How about yourself?"

Stephen made a disgusted sound that said he didn't think that was much to offer. "I'm his biological father, that's all. I wasn't there when he was growing up, I wasn't there during any of his crises. I'm not now and never have been a part of his life."

"How do you know his crises are all over? He should be getting out of high school about now. Maybe he needs money for college."

His lips turned up but more like a grimace of pain than a smile.

"Money can't buy love."

She touched his cheek gently, a soft caress meant to soothe and bring peace. "Stephen, why are you torturing yourself like this? So you made a mistake. You weren't the first kid to have done so and you won't be the last. Forgive yourself. Let go of the guilt."

"I'm not the letting-go type. Every kid I see awakens the pain all over again."

It was as if she had gotten a peek into his soul, saw a slice of who he was at a very basic level. She wished there was a way to ease his pain, but she had no idea how.

Joy just let the silence cover them and watched the sun pull itself up over the horizon, triumphant in its struggle to bring forth a new day. She'd always looked forward to that new day, more than happy to welcome the hope it brought with it, but her heart felt inordinately heavy this morning.

Stephen paused halfway up the steps to Joy's back porch. The sounds of laughter drifted from the window above him, forming part of the background hum of a small town Sunday afternoon. He stood there, savoring the sounds of hearth and home, like a hobo savored the smell of a cherry pie cooling on a windowsill. Green eyes danced over a wide smile, he could feel arms gripping him, sheltering him in their strength, caressing him with their softness. Joy. They'd shared a night of love and he was her prisoner, forced to lay the reality of his soul at her feet.

A lot had changed last night and early this morning. He had confessed things to Joy that he'd never told Donna, and he'd been married to her for four years. But that had been back in his tough-guy days, when he didn't allow things to touch him.

He blew out a lungful of air and rubbed his eyes. So why did he spill his guts to Joy? Was he getting weak in his old age? Stephen sighed. Hell, he wasn't old. He wished he could be as emphatic about his strength.

His feet stayed rooted to the steps and his eyes wandered the backyard scene before him. Sure, thoughts of his son had been lying and festering in his soul for a long time now, but he'd always been able to control it. Periodically, he'd fall into a blue funk but he'd always rode it out and came out as good as new. But not this time.

He looked around the backyard. Joy wasn't here now. He could just turn and run. Run away from Joy's soft strength that pulled him into a world of total openness and honesty, a world he didn't want to wander in.

Then he took a deep breath and straightened his shoulders. His daddy didn't raise no quitters. Stephen Van Horne had never run away from anything in his life. He'd made the one mistake but that was it. He'd just put the genie back in the bottle.

One thing would certainly help—he needed to concentrate more on the business assistance he was supposed to be providing her and less on her green eyes. He pushed his hovering blue funk out into the bright sunshine, hoping it would wither in the heat, and continued up the stairs, walking hard to announce his arrival.

"It's Uncle Stevie," Katie cried out.

"Hey, Stevie," Robbie shouted.

He needed to concentrate on joking with the kids, include them in more activities. That way he would see Joy, but they would have little space for serious discussion.

"His name is Mr. Van Horne," Joy admonished them.

By the time he walked through the door, Stephen had a natural smile on his face. "That's okay."

"No, it's not," Joy protested as her eyes searched his, obviously trying to read his mood. "I'm trying to teach them to be respectful of their elders."

"Are you an old man?" Katie asked.

"Absolutely not," Stephen replied. He smiled back at Joy, a controlled smile that said he was fine, that she needn't worry about him.

Katie tugged at his sleeve. "We're making cookies," she told him.

"Super," Stephen replied, keeping his smile firmly in place.

He looked down at the rows of cookies sitting in front of Robbie, now leaning on one hand, his baseball cap askew, placing a chocolate kiss in the center of each piece. The boy looked about as grumpy as Stephen had wanted to feel.

"Aren't you enjoying your work?" Stephen asked him.

Robbie shrugged. "It's okay."

"You prefer eating them."

"Yeah."

"Robbie's grumpy," Katie announced.

"Katie," Joy said.

"But he is, Mommy. You said he was."

"I may have said that," Joy pointed out. "But we don't have to tell the world all about it. I don't think Mr. Van Horne wants to get involved in our moods."

"Then what's he come around for?" the girl asked.

"Katie."

"I came to do some accounting for your mother," Stephen said.

Two pairs of young, innocent eyes just stared at him.

"It's business stuff. Something she needs done for her store."

Apparently satisfied with his explanation, Joy's little helpers went back to their cookie chores. She just frowned at him.

"You don't have to do that kind of thing on a Sunday."

"I'm not too much of a hammock cowboy," Stephen said with a shrug. "And we really need to put a system in place for you before your busy season starts in a few weeks." Not to mention that he needed something to keep him from thinking.

Joy made a face. "I suppose."

"Hey, I want to make it easier for you."

"Want a cookie?"

Joy popped the morsel into his mouth before he could reply. He chewed, savoring for a moment the delicious combination of peanut butter and chocolate. Was it the cookie or the infectious gleam in Joy's eye that started the ice in his heart melting? He slammed a lid on those thoughts. He didn't come here for any soul dancing.

"Don't try and divert me," Stephen said. "It's my sworn duty to make sure that your accounting systems are efficiently supporting your needs."

"Boy," Joy snickered. "You're really a fun kind of guy."

"You want fun, I'll take care of that later."

Joy smiled, her eyes seemed overflowing with warmth and acceptance. "Whoo, another one of your promises, sir?"

The kids' eyes had been going back and forth between them as if watching a tennis match and were now focused on Stephen. It was obviously time for him to get to work.

"Later," he murmured before hurrying down the stairs.

"Oh, boy," Joy exclaimed, an exaggerated enthusiasm carrying her words. "That's two promises. My cup overfloweth."

Joy's words followed him down through the main store, and into her office, but then the silence washed over him, wiping away his smile as easily as a sand castle built too close to the shore.

She was right in telling him to let his son go. But that was easier said than done. Michael was locked into his heart, but Stephen was the one being held prisoner. Gritting his teeth, he forced himself to turn on the office light and get started. Michael was somebody to bring out in the dark, wee hours of the morning when he was all alone.

In barely two hours, Stephen had a new ledger system in place, as well as a new filing system and a controlled system of aging the store's invoices. He leaned back and pondered the results of his efforts. It would all work better with a computer system but he doubted that Joy could afford one at the moment.

Although she could almost not afford to have one. He wondered if he could get her a secondhand system. He would look into it.

Suddenly, he jumped, startled almost out of his chair. Robbie was standing at the door, staring at him.

"Have you been there long?" Stephen asked.

"Nope."

"Watching me work?"

"Yeah."

"Do you want to be an accountant when you grow up?"

"Nope."

"Not interesting enough, huh?"

"Nope."

Stephen took a slow, deep breath. This wasn't an exciting conversation, but then he and Robbie weren't exactly buddy-buddy pals.

"What do you want to be when you grow up?" Stephen asked.

"A baseball player."

Stephen smiled softly. The typical all-American dream of a ten-year-old boy. "You're a good soccer player."

"Baseball players make more money."

"Just in the United States," Stephen said. "Professional soccer players in Europe make just as much or more."

"Yeah?" But the flicker of interest Robbie showed quickly dimmed. "I can't go that far. I need to stay close and help Mom."

The blue funk that had wanted to sit on Stephen's shoulders all day buzzed closer. Responsibility. Taking care of those who belonged to you. That was what growing up was all about.

"I was going to be a professional basketball player when I was your age," Stephen said.

"Why aren't you?"

Stephen laughed. "Too slow and I could never get my jump shot to hit."

The boy nodded solemnly. "I don't think I'll be tall enough for basketball. My Dad was sort of tall but Mom is really short. So it's got to be baseball. That's the only way I can make a lot of money and help her out."

The boy's adult-like solemnity would have been humorous had it not been so painful. He seemed to be carrying so many burdens. Stephen wished he could help him.

"So, how is your baseball career progressing?"

The solemnity stayed in Robbie's face. Not a good question, Stephen thought as Robbie shrugged.

"I can catch good but I'm having trouble hitting."

Stephen nodded. Not an uncommon problem, especially at Robbie's age. The eye/hand coordination necessary to hit a baseball came slowly to most.

"If my Dad was here, he could help me. He used to be a good baseball player."

According to Joy, Paul had spent all his time working, but Stephen just nodded. Some myths needed to be kept intact.

"My grandfather used to be real good, too," Robbie went on. "But he doesn't do anything anymore. He says his shoulders hurt too much to throw a ball."

"That happens," he said, his eyes drifting to a hazy netherworld of impossible dreams, where Stephen's own parents played catch and baked cookies with his son Michael. It hadn't been just his loss, but theirs as well. Michael was their first grandchild and Stephen had seen the pain in their eyes even as he had struggled to bury his own. There certainly was no need to drag Joy into that world.

He looked up at Robbie, the boy's face clouded with the certainty that he was alone in his struggle. "I can pitch for you sometimes when you want to practice," Stephen offered.

Robbie's eyes flickered over to Stephen, then back to a point on the far wall. Was the boy interested?

"Okay," Robbie replied with a shrug. "Sometime when I'm practicing batting."

"Right, you let me know."

"Okay," Robbie replied.

"Sounds good to me."

Robbie nodded and wandered off, while Stephen took up the job of staring at the far wall. The boy had learned fast not to trust that others will help you reach your dreams. He was lucky and smarter than Stephen had been. But the realization only made it easier for his blue funk to settle on his shoulders.

"Sure you don't want the rest of this?" Joy asked. A few spoonfuls of the chili remained in the bottom of the pot, the magic spoonfuls her mother had always believed it was a sin to leave.

But Stephen's eyes just took on a look of horror as he pushed his plate away. "I'm going to burst as it is."

Joy was relieved that he seemed closer to his old teasing self so she was willing to let the magic spoonfuls go to waste. He had given her such pleasure and splendor last night, she couldn't bear to see him hurting. She walked around behind him and mussed his hair. "Don't burst," she said. "It would be too much of a mess to clean up."

He got to his feet then—to avoid her touch? She couldn't help but wonder.

"Maybe some exercise would help," he said, starting to clear the table.

"You don't have to do that," she protested.

"Sure I do. My mother raised me to be a helper person."

Joy forced a laugh, but her eyes looked beyond his teasing manner. She didn't really think he was avoiding her touch, most likely he was avoiding all touching. The pain was still there. That had to be it.

She longed to help him, but had no idea how the healing would begin. Joy began loading the dishwasher.

"Speaking of family, want to spend Memorial Day with mine at our annual picnic?" Stephen asked. "My folks have a cottage in Grand Haven and we all descend on them for a day of volleyball and fried chicken debauchery."

"Sounds great. We'd love to."

Katie's happy shriek came through the open windows along with the patter of her little feet on the stairs outside. "Mommy," Katie hollered as she burst through the door. "Robbie's throwing water at me."

Joy looked at her daughter. Katie's eyes were bright, her cheeks rosy. Joy was suddenly overwhelmed with the wonder of love for her children. She couldn't imagine a life without them, and felt for the first time the real cloud of emptiness that Stephen lived under. To know you had a child, but that you'd never see the light of laughter in his eyes or be there to wipe his tears away.

Joy caught Katie in her arms. "Maybe we need to go to the park," she said. "Think Robbie could behave there?"

"Nope, he don't behave no place." Katie squirmed free and raced toward the door. She stopped to look back at Joy. "Is Stevie coming with us?"

"If he wants to."

The sheer force of Katie's gaze made Stephen stop wiping the table and look at her. "Wouldn't miss it, kid," he said.

His voice wasn't too enthusiastic, but the weight dragging it down seemed more weariness than cynicism. Did being with her kids help or add to his pain?

Katie wasn't worried about such fine points. She abandoned the door and climbed up on the chair next to Stephen, pulling over the salt/pepper/sugar turntable so that he could wipe where it had been. "We gots swings at the park," she told him.

"Wow," Stephen replied, his voice seemed tight as he finished wiping the table.

"And slides."

"Double wow." A bit looser?

"And things to climb."

"Triple zillion quadruple wow." He'd almost reached pretend excitement.

But Katie was frowning. "Is that good, Mom?"

"Sounds good to me," Joy said. "Go tell Robbie we're going and he should come in and wash his hands."

Katie bounced back outside, and once the echo of the screen door slamming faded away, Joy found the courage to speak.

"You don't have to come if you don't want to," she said.

"I know that," Stephen assured her. "Where do the crackers go?"

She pointed out the cabinet to him and let the silence fill the room again. The kids came rushing through as they raced to the bathroom to clean up, causing the house to ring with their alternate bickering and laughter. The normality of the sounds brought a strange mixture of feelings to Joy's heart, gratitude for her own good fortune and an ache for Stephen's hurt.

"What was Paul like?" Stephen asked suddenly.

Joy started, and dragged her thoughts back into the past. "Sometimes I wonder myself," she admitted. "When I look at our life together, it seems like I was a different person and then I wonder what he was really like."

She pondered a moment, watching a bird flick by her window. "I think he was almost afraid of love, of closeness. He embraced his work so eagerly. I'm sure it was because he felt more comfortable there."

She stopped to rinse out the sink.

"A lot of men feel that way," Stephen said.

"He said he was doing it all for us, and I know he believed that. But I would have been happier with more of him than with the promise of riches for tomorrow."

"That never came."

She shrugged. "Even if they had, I don't think it would have been worth the price."

He was silent for a while, the sounds of the kids' laughter echoing through the halls, and she grew suddenly worried. "I'm sorry," she said. "When I said I would have rather had more of him, I didn't mean to remind—"

He stopped her words with a shake of his head. "Hey, I didn't tell you about Michael so that you'd watch everything you said from now on."

"Why did you tell me?" she asked. The question had been nagging at her all day.

Stephen looked at her and then away. From the movement of his throat, Joy could tell that he was swallowing. She waited for his words to come.

"It just came out I guess." He tried fitting a smile to his face. "I'm rather vulnerable at four in the morning."

The kids raced in and Joy let the subject drop, eagerly embracing the distraction of herding them all out, down the stairs and on out to the park.

Joy and Stephen walked slowly along as the children skipped, hopped and bounced ahead of them. They walked hand in hand but silent, each carrying their own thoughts.

So, Mr. Stephen Van Horne was vulnerable, but only at four in the morning. Poor man. There were only a few moments that he felt he could let his guard down and they were when he was alone; the rest of the time he wore an enormous mask of control.

When they reached the edge of the park, the kids made a mad dash for the swings. Stephen dropped down onto the grass nearby and lay back.

Joy sat down next to him, picking at the grass for a moment. "Don't you want to go on the swings?"

"Nope," Stephen replied.

"Poor baby." Joy brushed his blond locks back off his forehead. "Did the walk wear you out?"

"No, but watching those two sure did."

Joy forced a chuckle and watched the kids for a few minutes. When she glanced back at Stephen, his eyes were closed. She saw the little lines of tension around the corners of his eyes.

Had they always been there and she just hadn't seen them? Certainly the pain had always been there.

"To be honest about it," Stephen said quietly. "It did take me a good while to get over everything."

Joy lay back down across his chest, though she kept a watchful eye on her children while she listened to Stephen. They had found some kids from the neighborhood so she relaxed.

"I guess mostly I felt betrayed." Stephen shook his head. "It's not like I was into some kind of male power thing. You know, like I made the baby and she was going to do as

I told her. But we'd talked about everything. Getting married, our education, where we were going to live, everything. And then, without a word, she went off on her own and made some earthshaking decisions.''

"Maybe on her own was the only way she felt she could make those decisions.''

Stephen frowned as he looked at her.

"Well, you can be a little overpowering at times.''

"This was back in high school,'' he protested.

"Were you a shy little fella back then?''

Stephen grimaced and looked away.

"It couldn't have been easy on her,'' Joy said. "But I'm sure she did what she thought was best for everybody concerned.'' She kissed him lightly on his lips. "Especially the baby.''

Stephen continued to look away.

"She wasn't ready and she knew it. She was scared, Stephen.''

"Yeah, I guess.'' His words were reluctant, but there might have been a hint of understanding in his tone.

"Can I ask you a question?'' She sat up, brought her knees up to her chest and wrapped her arms around them. "Are you still in love with Laura?''

"Laura?'' He looked dumbfounded at the question, then recovered to shake his head. "No. Whatever I felt for her died when she gave our son away.''

"Stephen.''

He sat up himself, leaning back on his elbows as he looked at the kids playing. "Sorry,'' he murmured.

"She may be regretting her decision as much as you.''

Stephen stood up and brushed off the back of his shorts. "She's probably got a family and a big house in New York or someplace like that.''

"You have a big house here in Holland.'' She got to her feet, too. "And I can't imagine that even if you had a million kids, you would forget the one you no longer had. You shouldn't make presumptions about her anymore than she should about you. You don't know what life's handed her or what turmoil she's gone through. Have you ever tried to look Laura up?''

The kids must have seen them get to their feet because they came charging over before Stephen chose to answer.

''Do we have to go now?'' Katie whined. ''It's not very dark yet.''

No, but the evening shadows were creeping up on them and darkness would be in full force by the time they got home. '''Fraid so,'' Joy said. ''There'll be lots more evenings in the park for you two.''

''Aw, Mom.''

But amid their grumping and groaning, they began trudging home. Before a full block had passed though, they were laughing and telling jokes. The three of them were, anyway. Stephen was silent, smiling occasionally at the kids' jokes, but the smile never found his eyes and Joy knew his thoughts were elsewhere.

She had expected him to leave once they got back home, but he didn't. He played a card game with Robbie while Joy bathed Katie, then offered to read the girl a story. Robbie sped through his own bath so that he could hear it, too. It was a silly story about rabbits that was about as far from a classic as Saturday morning cartoons, but Robbie hung on Stephen's every word as if the wisdom of the ages could be found in the doings of grocery store-owning rabbits.

Joy watched from the doorway, wondering if Stephen knew how the kids were treasuring these times with him, wondering if he could find solace for his own loss in their needs. Probably not until he'd been truly healed.

The story over, she tucked the kids into bed and kissed them good-night. When she went back into the living room,

Stephen was watching TV. He looked up as she entered, then patted the sofa next to him.

"How are you?" she asked, letting her fingers play with the hair on the back of his head.

"Okay."

His voice was brusque and deep but pain still lurked in the corners of his eyes. She wrapped her arms around his neck and gave him a deep, long kiss that sent shivers through the universe.

"I guess it's time I forgave Laura," he said with a sigh.

"It's time you forgave yourself," she replied.

"Maybe."

There was no maybe about it. Not if she had anything to do with it. Joy leaned toward him and took his lips. She felt him come alive beneath her as she lowered herself on top of him. At that moment of contact she knew a power in her heart that she'd never felt before. She could bring delight. She could bring ecstasy. She could bring healing.

"Do you have to get home?" she asked.

"Not unless the spiders in my basement miss me."

"They don't," she told him. "Spiders are very self-sufficient." She took his hand in hers, weaving their fingers together as if she could weave their hearts.

"I find that rather sad," he said. "The very creatures I share my life with aren't going to miss me."

His voice was light and teasing, but she found it sad also. That the only thing he was willing to share his life with were the accidental co-occupants of his house.

She leaned over and took his lips with hers, speaking promises to his heart, telling him of peace and magic, of love. Her hands slid under his shirt and added to the tale.

Stephen's hands found her, but his touch held a kind of despair, as if in holding her, he could find a moment's solace. She felt her body come alive with desire, a wanting to belong, to bring delight to his heart, but her mind threw cold water over her.

She pulled back slightly. "I'm not sure the kids are asleep yet," she said, her voice sounding breathy and weak.

"Want me to go?"

"No." That wasn't at all what she meant. "Maybe we'd better just slow down."

She got a blanket from a hall closet and wrapped it over their shoulders, creating a little cave that was safe from any prying eyes. Stephen put his arm around her and she lay against him. They watched a ball game and then the late news as the silent stillness of the late night descended on the world.

"Maybe I should go home," Stephen said suddenly.

She felt his gloom covering him, and knew only she was strong enough to keep it away. "You aren't going anywhere, except to the bedroom."

On silent tiptoe, she led him into her room and shut the door. She had found wonder and delight in his arms here last night; tonight he would begin healing.

Chapter Nine

"Where's Mom?" Robbie's tone was demanding, his expression no-nonsense, as his eyes searched the kitchen.

"She's sleeping," Stephen replied. After the peace she'd given him last night, the least he could do was give her some in return.

"Is she sick, Uncle Stevie?" Katie followed close behind her brother.

"No, she's not sick. She just wants to sleep a little longer today."

"I think I should see how she is," Robbie said.

"No," Stephen said. "You'll just wake her."

Robbie hesitated. "But she could be really sick."

"I already checked." The boy stared at him but Stephen couldn't read his face. "Trust me."

Robbie walked to the cabinet and pulled out bowls for himself and Katie.

"Want me to make something for breakfast?" Stephen asked. "Pancakes? Waffles? French toast?"

Robbie just shook his head and kept right on pouring cereal. Stephen tried not to mind. Cereal was probably their traditional school day breakfast and no kid in the world took to change easily.

"Where did you sleep?" Robbie asked around a mouthful of sugared cardboard bits.

Stephen blinked, struggling to bring his thoughts to bear on the boy's question. Robbie's expression was emotionless and closed.

"On the sofa?" Robbie continued his question. He must have seen the blanket on the living room floor.

"Yes," Stephen replied.

Apparently satisfied, Robbie turned his attention to finishing his breakfast as the clock in the living room sounded the quarter hour. Stephen knew that the kids went to school, but he wasn't sure when or how either of them went.

"What's the drill today, guys?" Stephen asked. His question was greeted by a pair of frowns. "I mean, like who goes to school, how and when?"

"I walk to school," Robbie replied. "I leave as soon as I rinse my dish."

"I goes to school, too," Katie said.

"How about lunch?" Stephen asked, directing his question to Robbie.

"Pizza day." Robbie rubbed his stomach and spread a wide grin across his face. He stuck his rinsed bowl into the dishwasher. "I get to buy lunch today."

"I has lunch with Mommy," Katie said.

Robbie picked up a backpack from the counter. "Katie goes to nursery school with Mrs. Jansen's kids. Mom drives today."

"We got to wake Mommy up," Katie said.

"I'll drive you," Stephen said. His offer was greeted with great suspicion, but Stephen ignored it. "Where do the Jansens live?" he asked Robbie.

"The green house in back," Robbie replied, pointing as he dashed out the door.

The door slammed after him, then all was silent. Stephen cocked an ear toward Joy's bedroom as he and Katie exchanged stares. There were no sounds of stirring so apparently Joy had slept through the noise.

"What time do you have to be at school, kid?"

"Nine o'clock." Katie thoughtfully chewed the inside of her cheek for a moment. The same habit Joy had when she was pensive. "And we can't be late."

"We won't be," Stephen assured her.

"We gots to wake Mommy up."

"I'll take you."

"Mommy knows where everything is."

"I've lived here longer than your Mommy," Stephen said. "So I know about a lot more stuff in this town than she does."

Katie's expression remained skeptical but his confident demeanor kept the child in her chair and out of Joy's bedroom. The two of them shared almost a half hour of long silence while Stephen puttered around the kitchen, sort of cleaning up but mostly keeping Katie in the room.

"Okay, kid," Stephen said as the clock approached eight-thirty. "Time to go."

"I never been late," Katie reminded him.

"If you're late today, you can throw rocks at me."

"Big ones?" Katie asked, dragging her feet in the shambling manner of a lifer in prison.

"Giant ones."

"Giant ones are too heavy," Katie replied. "I can't lift them. You gots to get things way up high to throw good."

"How about a big stick?"

"Okay," she replied, perking up a bit.

Stephen sighed as they finally reached the car and he buckled Katie in. The kid was the spitting image of her mother, small and ornery.

The Jansen kids and a woman were waiting by the curb as Stephen pulled up. She was probably their mother and she looked vaguely familiar.

"Hello, Mr. Van Horne," the woman said as her daughters stared inside the car. "I'm Marlene Jansen. I used to be Marlene Koenig."

"Oh, yeah," Stephen replied. "You were a couple of grades behind me."

"Stevie stayed with us all night," Katie announced. "And Mommy's all tired out and she's still in bed."

"Oh," Marlene said, her face turning the same kind of bland pleasantness that his sisters used to achieve when he got into trouble.

Damn. He felt his own face grow warm and the smile that he'd worked up for this meeting was now downright painful.

"Stevie wouldn't let us wake Mommy up," Katie continued.

"That's very nice of him," Marlene said.

"Stevie don't know where we go to school," Katie said, her face curling up into a nasty kind of grin. "And if we're late, I gets to hit him with a big stick."

Marlene blinked a moment at Katie before looking up at Stephen. "It's at the First Christian Church. You take them in the side door."

"Better luck next time," Stephen murmured.

The Jansen girls had crawled into the back seat and Marlene buckled them in while Katie slumped down in her seat, disgust and disappointment flooding every corner of her being. Once the door was closed, Stephen quickly pulled out into traffic.

"Don't you like me?" Stephen asked Katie. "I thought we were friends."

"I like you," Katie answered.

"Then why do you want to hit me with a big stick?"

Katie smiled and shrugged her shoulders. Realizing that line of questioning would go nowhere, Stephen concentrated on his driving and got everyone to the school on time.

Stephen drove back to Joy's in a pensive mood. He didn't have any appointments until early afternoon and Joy's store wasn't scheduled to open until eleven, so he had thought they could have a leisurely breakfast, but he hadn't counted on the four-year-old public service announcer.

He didn't know how Joy would take being a gossip-column item in Holland, but he didn't like it at all. Knowledge was power and he didn't like losing even the tiniest bit of control to anyone.

He walked tentatively into the house and peeked into the bedroom. Joy was still asleep. He'd make some breakfast for her and then they'd have a little chat.

His hands busy preparing the bacon and eggs, his mind took its own little trip. He hadn't liked Katie spilling the beans, but in reality he'd done the exact same thing in telling Joy about Michael. He'd blurted out something that was nobody else's business and in doing so lost some control over the situation.

There had been no need for any of it. The kid had never been and would never be a part of his life. And Lord knew what Joy would do with the information. She was the type of woman always trying to make things right.

Stephen placed Joy's breakfast on a tray and walked toward her bedroom. It would be hard, but he'd have to take back control of the situation. Concentrate on other more enjoyable aspects of their acquaintanceship.

"Wake up, sleepyhead," he said and opened the drapes to let in the sunshine.

Joy purred sleepily and rolled over onto her back, stretching her body like a cat. The curved landscape that the thin blanket covered sent a surge of desire coursing through his veins. There definitely were other parts of the relationship to concentrate on. She smiled up at him as if she was thinking the very same thing. But first he'd better tell her about Katie.

"That's enough of that," he scolded. "You keep that up and you'll never get a chance to eat."

"Promises, promises."

"Come on," he ordered. "Sit up and eat."

Joy lay there and smiled impishly at him.

"Up," he said, raising his voice. "I have scrambled eggs and bacon, toast, coffee and orange juice." He frowned at her. She was rapidly making him forget everything he wanted to tell her. "Sit up."

"You'll never make it as a butler," she grumbled and pushed herself to a sitting position. "You're too damn bossy."

"Come on, you need a good breakfast."

"I need a lot of things," she replied. "Breakfast isn't on the list."

"Eat," he said, setting the tray on her lap. "Or I'll stuff this in your ear."

Joy sipped at her orange juice. "You're a real bundle of charm."

"I work at it."

She started to pick at some of her scrambled eggs and bacon. He sat down on the edge of the bed, gingerly, as if she shattered easily.

"I got the kids off to school."

"Oh, no," she said with a sudden gasp. "Today is my turn to drive in our nursery school car pool."

"I took care of that." Stephen looked out the window. A cardinal sat on a branch, preening its feathers. "I met Mrs. Jansen and Katie happened to mention—" He cleared his throat. "That I stayed overnight."

The bird outside looked at him and snickered, it seemed, then flew away. Damn coward.

He turned back to Joy, who looked remarkably unperturbed as she bit into the toast. "Didn't you tell me once that there were no secrets in a small town?"

"Probably," he replied.

"Well." She shrugged with a half grin. "There you go."

He felt something in him sag with relief that she had taken it so well. Now the only thing left was to get her to forget his stupid confession. Kicking his shoes off, he scooted over closer to her.

"Did you have any breakfast?" she asked.

"I had some cereal with your kids. I offered to make them pancakes but they turned me down."

"They think stuff like that is special, something for the weekend." Joy shrugged. "Probably my fault. Weekends are about the only time I make a regular breakfast."

Stephen shrugged in turn. "I don't think it matters. We always had cereal when I was a kid."

"I'm getting close to full." She held a forkful of eggs out to him. "Let's share."

They both picked at the breakfast until the tray was just about empty. With each bite he took, he grew more certain that he could pull this off, that Joy would just forget—

"You know," Joy said, putting the tray off on the end table. "I've been thinking—"

Uh-oh. "That's a bad idea," Stephen said, rolling over and pinning Joy down with his body.

"Why?" A frown filled her face. "Don't you think women can think?"

"Never said that." He rained light, little kisses on her neck that sent massive shock waves through his body. "It's not a good idea for anybody right after breakfast."

"Oh?"

"It screws up your digestion." He took her lips and kissed her hard. "Didn't you ever hear about not thinking for an hour after you eat?"

"I thought that was swimming. Don't go in the water for an hour after you eat."

"Same thing."

"I see. And you wouldn't happen to know of something that might help my digestion, would you?"

"I might." He kissed her again. Longer, harder. This was what they should be doing. Taking care of the present and not worrying about the past.

"Hi, strangers," Beth said, drawing Stephen's front door open as wide as her smile.

"We're not strangers," Katie said.

"She's just joking, honey," Joy said, herding her two children before her as she stepped into Stephen's house.

"But we can't be strangers, Mommy," Katie said, continuing her protest. "We're here all the time."

Joy felt her cheeks grow warm under the increased radiance of Beth's smile. They weren't here all the time. True, they'd stopped by a number of times this week after work, but Stephen had invited them. Well, he did tell them to drop by anytime.

"What kinda ice cream you got?" Robbie asked.

"Robbie," Joy exclaimed.

"Why don't you go in the kitchen and check?"

Stephen came slowly down the stairs, wearing a soft and easy smile. His deep voice drowned out everything for Joy, that is everything except her embarrassment. She wanted to say more to her kids but they were already running off, laughing and talking to Beth.

"I can see I'm going to have to have a little talk with them," Joy said.

"That's nice." He came down the rest of the way into the foyer and took her into his arms as if it was the only way to welcome her. Maybe it was. "Mothers should have a lot of chats with their children."

When he let her go, she found her voice again, though it seemed to lack a certain determination. "It's going to be more than a chat. It's going to be a strongly worded lecture on good manners."

"They're fine. Don't be too hard on them."

He put his arm around her shoulders and led her out onto the front porch. His short blond hair lay flat and wet on his head, and he smelled of soap. He'd obviously just taken a shower and the idea of his body all wet and glistening made it hard for her to concentrate on lectures and scoldings.

They sat down on his porch swing, jointly setting it to swaying. A breeze was coming in off the lake, chasing away the heat of an unseasonably warm and muggy day, like a shepherd dog chasing away a wolf. Gentle street noises of children playing and voices from television and living rooms floated up to them. A man walked his small dog, taking the time to let the animal carefully sniff for the messages left behind. It felt so much like home that it should be scary, except that Joy had forgotten how to be scared. Not when Stephen still had such pain buried deep in his soul. She just didn't know how to address it.

"My kids are going to have to stop seeing Beth," Joy said. "I think they've put on fifty pounds since we've met."

"Beth thinks ice cream is the elixir that cures all." Stephen chuckled. "But you can relax for the rest of the summer."

"Why? Is she leaving?"

"Yeah, she's taken a job as counselor for some kids' camp in the Upper Peninsula."

"I'm going to miss her."

"Yeah, me, too." Stephen paused a moment. "We'll have to find a new baby-sitter."

Joy poked him in the ribs. "That's not why I'm going to miss her. My kids like her and so do I."

"Hey, I like her, too," Stephen said. "Sometimes."

Joy considered poking him again, but he quickly brought his right arm across his body for protection. "No violence."

She relaxed, knowing that she could get him later. "Has Beth always been that thin?"

"Yep," Stephen replied, nodding. "All the other female relatives hated her. She'd eat all kinds of junk and still stay thin as a reed."

"I never had to worry about that."

Stephen moved closer and tucked her under his left arm. "What you have is not a problem. It's a gift."

"A gift for all mankind?" Joy asked with a laugh.

"I certainly hope not for all mankind." He bent down and kissed her. "I had in mind a gift for one man."

Joy snuggled into Stephen's arms, awash in contentment. Maybe he found strength in her arms, just as she found such peace in his. She had to find the way to help him heal.

"Have you ever tried to find Michael?" she asked.

His muscles tensed up, like rods of steel, and for a moment Joy thought she'd angered him. Then he sighed and she felt his tension flow away.

"No."

Short and curt. Now it was Joy's turn to sigh. "You seem to have a great need to know him."

The tension came back again, but only for a moment. "For a while, I was angry. Mad would be a better word. I didn't even want to think about Laura or anything connected with . . . with what we had.''

Joy waited, silently listening to him breathe.

"That anger carried through college and into graduate school. Then after I married, I started wondering about him. Donna and I had agreed not to have children, and that was okay, but . . .''

Stephen was silent a moment before shrugging and going on. "I thought about him, but he would have been living with his adoptive parents for some time. Hell, he might not even have known he was adopted. His life was all settled and I would have just been barging in on it, bringing nothing of value.''

He was silent a long moment, but Joy wasn't fooled. It was obvious that whatever decision he may have reached years back, his son was still on his mind. And also obvious, this was a wound that would not heal on its own.

"And now?" she asked.

"Now?" He let out a short laugh, totally absent of mirth. "Now he's near to grown-up and he doesn't need anything I could give. And even if he did, he'd probably spit in my face.''

Joy didn't have the words to wash away the pain and didn't even try. That bitterness in his voice was only an echo of the real agony in his soul and that would take more than a few simple words from her to ease. She snuggled up closer to him, listening to his heartbeat. Poor Stephen. Such a tough guy on the outside and yet so afraid of rejection on the inside.

She had to help him resolve his feelings of guilt. The quick fix would be easy—just take him into her arms and love him. No, he needed to be healed permanently. And she was going to find a way to do it.

Chapter Ten

"Would you stop picking on yourself?" Stephen exclaimed.

"I'm dressed like a bum," Joy said.

"I told you six zillion times, that's the way everyone will be dressed. It's just a picnic on the beach at my parents' house."

Joy glared at him as he turned his attention back to the road. He wasn't dressed like a bum. His white knit shirt clung like second skin, his red shorts looked like they'd been ironed, and he had brown docksiders on his feet. She was wearing cutoff jeans, a halter and canvas slip-ons.

"Didn't you come here on vacation when you were a little kid?" Robbie asked Joy from the back seat.

"No," Joy replied. "We're going to Grand Haven. My parents rented a cottage in South Haven."

"Some kind of haven. Same thing."

Joy stared out the window as she fought to keep from laughing hysterically. South Haven was south of Holland while Grand Haven was north. South Haven was little beach cottages. Grand Haven was old Victorian homes on the bluffs above Lake Michigan. Grand Haven was ladies in big white hats sitting on the veranda drinking iced tea. Grand Haven wasn't going to be any kind of a haven and she should never have agreed to come. "I should have brought some other clothes."

"Geez, are you a fussbudget," Stephen said. "If you don't stop that, I'm going to leave you on the side of the road."

"No." Katie reached over the top of the back seat to grab Joy around the neck. "Don't do that. She'll be good."

"Are you sure?" Stephen asked sternly.

"Yes." Then Katie put her mouth next to Joy's ear and whispered loudly, "You got to be good, Mommy. You hear me?"

"They can hear you in that car way up ahead of us," Joy replied. "And how good can I be if you choke me to death?"

Katie loosened her hold on Joy's neck.

"Now sit back and put your seat belt back on. You could be hurt if Stephen has to stop suddenly."

"I won't throw your mother out," Stephen assured her. "I was just joking."

"Okay."

They turned north off the main highway, onto a narrow county road and Joy knew that they would be there soon. She put both her hands over by the door, shielding them with her body so that Stephen wouldn't see her twisting her fingers. She forced herself to breathe deep and slow. She'd met Jane and Beth before and liked them both. Everything was going to work out just fine.

And what difference did it make if it didn't? she asked herself. It wasn't like she was going up here for his family's approval. She was Stephen's client and friend; she doubted he needed permission from his family to carry on such relationships.

Thick, dense woods crowded down to the roadside but Joy could smell the water and knew they were close to Lake Michigan. As if by instinct, Stephen turned into a gravel lane and within moments, they popped out of the trees into a clearing. Cars were parked in a disorderly sprawl off the driveway.

Joy looked up at the house and stopped breathing. Oh, no. Her worst nightmare had come true.

The "cottage" was a huge, old two-and-a-half story Victorian with blue siding and white trim. A porch encircled the house, a circular tower was off to the lakeside and intricately carved woodwork was along the top of the porch.

"Wow," Robbie marveled from the back seat.

"It looks like a castle," Katie said.

No one came forward to greet them and Joy wasn't surprised. The ladies would be sitting on the front veranda drinking tea; the men playing croquet on the broad lakefront lawn. Everyone would be dressed in formal whites. They would know instinctively that she was dressed grubbily and that they needn't bother greeting her. She got out of the car, wishing the earth would just swallow her up. She helped the kids out.

"Hey, guys. Come on in."

Joy turned to find Beth had come out onto the porch.

"Bethie." Katie ran forward to be scooped up into Beth's arms.

Good old Beth. Joy's heart did a backflip when she saw her. Beth was wearing an old Chicago Bears T-shirt with the arms torn out, paint-spotted jeans and no shoes. The white-gloved ladies could have their tea and crumpets. She and Beth would have their own party of pretzels and beer.

"We're so glad you could come." Beth came forward, carrying Katie on one hip, to give Joy a hug and a kiss. "Come on in. Everyone's looking forward to meeting you."

Beth put an arm around Robbie's shoulder as she turned. "Hey, big guy, how are ya?"

"Okay." He looked relieved that Beth had stuck with just a hug and skipped the kiss.

"Come on." Stephen was by Joy's side and had taken her arm.

They walked through the house to get to the lakeside porch. The rooms were big and airy, furnished with a mixture of Stephen's refinished antiques, rustic camp furniture and Salvation Army rejects. Some small children were bouncing on a couch, and bedrooms, filled with unmade beds and clothes-strewn floors, were visible off to the side. Joy started to breathe again.

As she stepped out onto the porch, Joy's worries slipped completely away, shed like an old winter coat. There was a white-haired man in shorts and sports shirt with tails hanging out, bouncing a gurgling baby on his lap. And off to the side, an older woman in an oversized T-shirt and clamdiggers was successfully coaxing smiles from a tear-stained little face. Children dashed about, squealing, and adults relaxed in various stages of dress.

"Mom, Dad," Stephen announced. "This is Joy. Joy, Trudy and Dave Van Horne."

His mother hurried over and hugged her. "It's a pleasure meeting you, dear."

Stephen's father rose to his feet, holding a baby with one hand while he shook hers with the other. "Joy," he said. "Looks like the name fits."

"Thank you," Joy murmured.

Stephen took her around, introducing her to everyone. She remembered Jane, and got to meet her husband Jeff and Stephen's brother Robert and his wife Susie. Then there were dozens of cousins, nieces and nephews and assorted friends. By the time they'd made the complete circle, a little old lady had taken up residence on the porch.

"Joan of Arc," she said as Joy and Stephen came up the steps.

Joy glanced over at Stephen. "Another ancestor?"

"Yours, I think." Stephen walked over to the little old lady and bent to kiss her cheek. "Hi, Gram. I want you to meet a friend of mine, Joy Chapin."

"Hello," Joy said as the old woman squinted at her.

"Joan of Arc," she said again. "She's an ancestor of yours. You look just like her."

"I do?" Joy just looked at Stephen for guidance, but he was biting back a smile.

"It's a good match," the old woman said. "Saint Michael is one of Stephen's ancestors." She patted Stephen's hand. "Now, you listen to him."

Stephen didn't say much until they were halfway across the lawn a few minutes later. "Did you follow that?"

"Follow is not to obey," she said and waved to Robbie who was playing a game on the bluff with some boys near his own age.

"Want to enlighten the dense?"

"Saint Michael was one of the voices Joan heard."

"One she listened to and obeyed?" Stephen said with a new note of interest in his voice.

"And look where it got her, burned at the stake."

"But she's a saint now."

"What price glory? I think I'll take my chances on my own. Besides, I'll need proof that an archangel was your ancestor."

"Don't I make you soar?" he whispered wickedly into her ear.

"Hey, you two," Jane called over. "We need some more bodies for volleyball. Boys against the girls."

Joy jumped at the distraction to cover her reddening cheeks. "I haven't played volleyball for years."

"No negative thinking allowed," Jane scolded. "We're going to stomp their butts."

"Nice talk," Stephen muttered as they all started down the steepest, ricketiest wooden stairs Joy had ever seen.

Actually, they seemed fairly steady, but they curved and twisted to follow the line of the bluff. Joy didn't see how stairs that high could possibly not collapse.

"You aren't afraid of heights, are you?" Jane asked.

"No." Not heights in general, but falling down them, perhaps.

"You should have seen these stairs before they got fixed last year," Stephen said.

"They were worse?"

Jane just shrugged. "They looked worse. I don't think they were dangerous. The elements just make everything look worn-out faster here."

Once down on the beach, Joy looked back up. The house appeared to be in the sky. The bluff had to be at least two stories high.

"Want to go back up and skip the game?" Stephen asked her.

"Afraid of losing?" Beth sang out and grinned at Joy. "He's always been like that. If he can't win, he won't play."

"Who says us guys can't stomp you girls?" he said.

"We do," Joy said and was immediately slapped on the back by his sisters as they dragged her over to their side of the net. Robert's wife Susie was there, along with a couple of cousins.

"Don't believe anything they say," Stephen called across the net.

"Too late, Stephen. She's ours now and you don't stand a chance," Jane scolded.

"Were you guys always this competitive?" Joy asked.

"Hey, this is really friendly. We're actually talking now," Jane said.

The game began with both sides looking pretty rusty. Joy didn't feel too bad when her serve hit the net, because just about everyone else's did, too. Unfortunately, her net ball gave the serve to the guys, to Stephen to be exact. His serve went over. Beth's return went wide.

"You ladies want to concede victory now and save us all some time?" Stephen called.

"Nah, want us to tell Joy the story of Valentine's Day when you were in eighth grade?"

"So that's the kind of game it is." His serve was hard, but Jane got it up. Susie got it over and Robert missed it.

"So tell me," Joy said as they regrouped.

"He photocopied a single valentine, complete with his signature, and gave a copy to each girl in the class," Jane said.

"And then couldn't understand why none of the girls would speak to him the rest of the year," Beth added.

"It was efficient and fair," Stephen called out.

"Watch out for his efficiency," Susie said and took her turn to serve.

In between rotations, Joy heard about the precise schedule Stephen had developed for his senior prom and how his sisters still wondered why his date hadn't killed him. They told her stories about the five pairs of identical blue corduroy pants he had his freshman year of high school and how he only agreed to buy a brown corduroy pair when some kids mocked him for having only one pair of pants. And about how he fixed the brakes on his bike so well one summer that he sped down a hill and into a neighbor's mailbox, needing fourteen stitches in his arm.

"Dad warned him that brakes were tricky," Jane said.

No one had to add that he hadn't listened. They all knew Stephen well enough.

The games ended when the scent of food distracted them all too much to notice the ball. By that time Joy had no idea who had won what, but she sure had a lot of dirt on Stephen.

"You must have been fun as a child," Joy said as they tackled the long climb back to the top of the bluff.

"I told you not to believe anything they told you," Stephen said. "My sisters are prone to gross exaggeration. Extreme to say the least."

"Oh, they never got gross," she said with a twitch to her lips. "They were very polite."

Supper was fried chicken, hot dogs, chips, potato salad and other appropriate picnic fare. People served themselves, scattering to eat at tables, on the ground or wherever suited them. It was all topped off with a dessert of homemade ice cream and cherry pie. Joy felt stuffed and, from the wide-eyed looks Katie and Robbie wore, her children were also.

While the kids were sent around with garbage bags to collect the paper plates and cups, a few of the adults gathered up the silverware and serving dishes. Joy carried a platter of a few pieces of fried chicken into the kitchen.

"What should I do with these?" she asked Jane.

Jane just waved her hand at them. "Hey, we'll take care of them. You're not supposed to be working. You're a guest."

"I don't mind helping."

"Next time," she said and shooed Joy out of the kitchen.

Joy left, but only because it seemed there were already more helpers in there than needed. Rather than go outside though, she wandered down the hall. The powder room was occupied.

"Let me show you where the bath is upstairs."

Joy turned to find Stephen's mother coming out of the living room. The woman's smile was warm and wide, making Joy wonder what she had been so worried about earlier.

"I'm so glad you could come," Trudy told Joy as she led her up the stairs.

"It was very nice of you to put up with me and my kids."

Trudy patted Joy's shoulder. "Thank you for putting up with my son."

"Oh, he's no trouble."

Stephen's mother just laughed. "Hey, now, remember I know Stephen."

"He's very nice."

"Oh, he can be." She wiped at her eyes. "But he very much needs someone to love. He needs a family with the humbling effect that only little children can give you. There's nothing like that wide-eyed innocence of childhood to bring a man down a peg or two."

Joy didn't know how to respond to that. She and Stephen were just friends. All right, more than friends, but they weren't really heading into a permanent type of relationship.

They reached the top of the stairs and Joy found herself unable to move. The wall ahead of her was covered with photographs, all sizes, all shapes and all ages, and some looked like formal shots from long ago.

"I call this my rogues' gallery," Trudy said. "Any house I move to has to have a wall big enough to handle all these."

Joy walked closer, staring at the photos. "What a wonderful way to preserve your family's history."

Trudy came to Joy's side. "No famous relatives, just the real ones. It sort of starts at this end. These are my parents on their wedding day."

There were few shots from long, long ago, and not quite so many of Stephen's parents as children, but there were loads of Stephen and his siblings. Baptisms, school days, graduations, weddings, all interspersed with candid pictures from picnics and parties. Joy saw Stephen grow from a serious little boy with a bossy look in his eye, to a serious young man with an authoritative strength to his jaw.

"He hasn't changed much, has he?" Joy asked with a laugh.

They moved slowly along the wall as Trudy recounted stories behind the pictures. Then the photos shifted from children to grandchildren—Jane's children and Robert's. Yet the arrangement of the frames seemed odd at one end.

"It almost looks like one's missing," Joy said, then scolded herself. Who was she to criticize the spacing of the photos?

"You think so?"

Trudy seemed to be staring at the wall as if trying to see what Joy meant, but Joy suddenly knew.

"It's for Stephen's child, isn't it?" she asked. "You've left a place on the wall for him."

The older woman turned to look at Joy, her eyes strangely penetrating even as they reflected a depth of sadness. "He told you?"

Joy nodded, unsure if she should have mentioned Michael. Of course, his grandparents knew about him, but it was such a personal thing. "He told me last weekend."

Trudy just shook her head. "He never talks about the boy. Sometimes, I had almost wondered if he'd forgotten."

"No, not hardly. It still tears at him a great deal."

"So, he hides it. That's Stephen, all right." She paused to make a minute adjustment to a frame. "You're the first one to notice the space here. The immediate family knows, of course. It was our way of remembering the grandchild we had never gotten to know. But no one else has ever noticed. We never talk about it though, not to Stephen. We don't want him to be hurt by the reminder. It has been our hope that he has been able to put things behind him."

"I don't think he has."

"Donna wasn't right for him. Locking yourself into a way of life that's not you never solves anything."

"No."

They'd reached the bathroom door, but before Joy went in, Trudy took her hand. "Help him get whole again, dear. He needs you so much."

"Come on, Katie," Robbie grumped. "Get down. Stephen doesn't have to carry you."

Stephen was carrying Katie across his parents' lawn to the car, while Joy and Robbie carried their shoes. Stephen tried to look at the girl's face, but she was facing away and had her head buried in his shoulder.

"She's not sleeping," Robbie said.

"I is too," Katie snapped. "My eyes is closed."

"That's because you're holding them closed," Robbie said.

"That's what you do when you sleeps," Katie replied. "You holds them closed up real tight."

"Mom."

A strong sense of injustice filled Robbie's voice and Stephen smiled. Bickering and arguing. Families had been doing that since man first stepped on this earth.

"That's okay," Stephen said. "She may not be asleep but I'm sure she's tired. Right, Katie?"

"Uh-huh," Katie answered.

"Mom," Robbie protested again.

"We're almost to the car," Joy said. "So it won't be much longer."

"Jeepers."

Stephen knew what Robbie was feeling, having gone through the same thing as the oldest in his family. The boy probably was just wishing he was small enough to get carried once in a while, too. Something they all wished at some time or another when things got tough. They had reached the car, and Stephen put Katie down so he could open the doors.

"Girls get away with everything," Robbie muttered.

"Little kids get away with everything," Stephen pointed out with a gentle smile. "I bet your dad carried you when you were Katie's age and tired after a picnic."

"We never went on any picnics." Robbie was glaring at Katie as she scampered over the seats, suddenly not so tired. "I'm not going to baby my kids when I grow up."

Stephen let a sad smile break across his face as he loaded a bag of leftovers his mother had packed into the trunk. "You're going to change the world when you grow up?"

"No. I'm just going to tell my kids they got to walk when they're tired."

Stephen just put his arm around Robbie's shoulders. "No, you'll carry them," Stephen said gently. "Because that's what parents do. Even if we're just as tired as they are, we carry them. That's what it means to be a parent—giving without thinking of the cost to ourselves."

Joy gave him a strange look as he got into the car, but he just concentrated on buckling his seat belt. He wasn't going to let her read anything extra into his words. Things had gone great today; his family had welcomed Joy and her kids just the way he'd known they would. Plus, there had been no talk about Michael or Laura or anything that had no relevance on today. And there would be none this evening.

Once they got back to Joy's place, all they had to do was get the kids cleaned up and into their pj's, let them watch a little TV, and work up a perfect ending between the two of them. Lots of pleasant activity and a minimum of talking. He pulled onto the road.

"Your feet are all sunburned," he said, nodding at Joy's bare feet.

She looked down at her feet as she rotated them. "They'll brown in a few days. Then everyone will know I'm just a small town girl who goes shoeless all summer."

He slowed down for a stop sign. "You'll fit right in with all the other small town girls around here, but then, I can't imagine a place where you wouldn't fit in."

Smiling, Joy took his right hand in her left. The kids were quiet in back, Katie was dozing and even Robbie looked like he was about ready to nod off.

Stephen suddenly remembered coming home from a picnic years ago. He'd been stuck in the back seat with Beth sleeping in his lap and Jane half-lying on his shoulders as she dozed.

"What's with everybody?" he'd asked his mother in a half whisper so as not to awaken either of the girls.

She had turned around to look over the top of the back seat at them all. Her eyes had gotten all soft with love. "They just feel safe, that's all. They're surrounded by their family and know nothing can happen to them."

Stephen gave the Lincoln a tad more gas. Katie and Robbie were sleepy because they'd had a busy day, not because they were surrounded by family. Because they weren't. He was a friend, but that was all. Nothing to them but a friend.

He turned down Joy's street and noticed that Robbie stirred in back. Stephen scolded himself for taking the turn a bit sharply and disturbing the boy. He'd make a smoother entrance into the alley.

"Mom," Robbie said as they drove past their house and slowed at the alley. "I think the window in our door is broken."

Both Joy and Stephen turned, but the doorway was blocked from their view by bushes.

"It can't be, honey," Joy said. "I'm sure you're mistaken."

"I don't think so."

A touch of worry nagged at Stephen as he pulled the car into the parking place off the alley. "You guys stay here," he said. "Let me check it out."

"It's probably just the angle of the sun," Joy said.

"Better safe than sorry," Stephen said.

He walked quickly around to the front and then just as quickly slowed his steps. Damn. Robbie was right. Up close he could see it as plain as day. The window in the front door was all smashed out. He tentatively pushed the door open.

"Oh, Lord."

Some punks had trashed the place. Pictures had been ripped off the walls and display cases broken into. The food scraps scattered over the floor and furniture were responsible for the garbagey smell that choked him. All that Joy had worked so hard for, trashed in a single afternoon.

After listening carefully for a moment and hearing only silence, he hurried across the rubble to Joy's office, side-stepping broken glass and debris. There was less trashing done in here, though papers seemed strewn all over. It was just as well he hadn't found Joy a used computer just yet.

He picked up the phone and dialed 9-1-1. Why would some stupid punks break into the gallery? How senseless. He tapped his fingers impatiently on Joy's desk as he waited through one ring, then another before it was answered. He had to get back outside before Joy and the kids came up to the house.

It must have taken all of two minutes to give the details and Joy's address, but it seemed like hours. He slammed down the phone and raced around into the showroom. He was too late.

Joy and the kids were standing at the door, horror filling their eyes to overflowing. He couldn't stand seeing their pain and fear and went forward, gathering them all in his arms.

"It'll be all right," he promised them. He would take care of them and make sure that it was.

Chapter Eleven

Joy just kept staring at the gallery, her eyes taking in the mess, but her mind refusing to believe it. This had to be a bad dream. Or somebody's idea of a bad joke. It couldn't really be happening. Not to her, not after all she'd come through to get here.

"Joy, are you okay?"

Stephen's voice sounded distant, as if from the bottom of a deep well, but Joy forced herself to turn toward it. His anxious face penetrated her fog.

"I'm fine." The words had come out rather squeaky and took more of an effort than they should have. "We should call the police."

"I did," he told her. "They'll be here soon."

"Are the bad guys still around?" Robbie asked.

Katie took a step closer and Joy picked her up, holding her close. The girl's warm little body gave her strength.

"We'll stay out here just to be on the safe side," she told Robbie.

"Your mom's right," Stephen said. "And even if nobody's there, we don't want to mess up any evidence."

Evidence. That's what her beautiful little gallery had been reduced to. She closed her eyes to ward off the pain and fear, breathing in the warm, lake-water smell of Katie. What mattered most in her life was right here and safe. As long as Katie and Robbie were fine, she could cope with anything else. She opened her eyes, staring down the street for the police cars.

"Did it look like much was taken?" she finally got up the courage to ask.

Stephen shrugged. "I couldn't tell. Offhand, I'd say no. Just a lot of trashing."

She could clean stuff up; she was good at that. She'd cleaned up Paul's financial mess. She could clean this up, too.

Two police cars turned into the street. The K-9 unit station wagon stopped in front while the regular sedan went around to the alley in back. A policewoman got out of the station wagon along with a large German shepherd. She came up the walk and glanced into the store, before turning to Joy and the others.

"They're probably gone by now, but I'd like you folks to stay down by the street." She waited while they moved away, then spoke into her hand radio. "We're going in now."

People trickled out of their houses, moths attracted to the flashing red lights. Marlene came over to Joy's side.

"You have a break-in?" she asked.

"Yeah." Joy gave Marlene a brief glance, but her eyes went back to the broken window in the door. That same gnawing was in the pit of her stomach that had been there when her dad had his heart attack. That suddenly, without warning, fate could swoop in and wreck the best of plans. The pain and fear began to be edged aside by anger. This wasn't the work of fate; it was people. People who gave no thought to anyone else.

Some of Joy's feelings must have flashed across her face for Marlene reached over and took Katie from Joy's arms. "Why don't I take the kids over to my place?"

For a split second, Joy felt lost without Katie to be strong for, but then she took a deep breath and nodded. "Thanks."

"Mom." Robbie wrapped the word in a thick blanket of pleading.

"We're just going to wait around, fill out papers and answer a lot of questions," Stephen told him. "You might as well go with Marlene and watch some television. It's going to be real boring around here."

"All right." It was obvious that Robbie didn't fully believe Stephen but at least he didn't argue.

"You guys can even stay overnight with me if you want," Marlene told the kids.

Joy looked at them. Katie's eyes were still wide with worry, Robbie was trying to look brave, but his eyes were shadowed, too. They didn't need to be here, even if she wanted them close to know they were safe.

"That's a good idea," Stephen said before Joy could summon the strength to send them away. "We'll bring their pajamas over later."

Whoa, fella! Joy wanted to protest his usurpation of her powers, but didn't.

"Now you guys be good." She gave each of the kids a hug and watched as Marlene led the kids around the block.

Stephen put his arm around her shoulder, sheltering her. "I thought it was a good idea," he said, sounding half apologetic, half explaining. "Katie looked pretty scared."

"I know," Joy said. "I feel almost violated myself."

The arm around her shoulder was joined by his other arm so that she was totally safe within his embrace. She laid her hand on his chest.

"Go ahead and cry if you want."

"I don't want. I'm more mad than anything."

"Okay." He kissed the top of her head. "You can punch me if it'll help, but not hard."

Joy chuckled and they parted to sit on the edge of a large cement planter filled with late-blooming tulips. After a few more minutes, the policewoman joined them.

"The house is all clear," she told them. "Officer Sheehan will be around to write out the report." Then she and the dog left in the station wagon.

"Everything all right?"

Joy turned to find an elderly woman who was her neighbor on the east side of her. "Just fine," she said.

"If there's anything I can do..."

Joy just nodded. "Thanks."

Another neighbor came over. "Seems no place is safe anymore," he said, shaking her hand before wandering back to his house.

What was safe? Joy wondered. Was this what her father had tried to protect her from when she was a child? But how did you protect yourself or your children from such random crime? Hiding away didn't work; they'd been sheltered from all life's realities by Paul, yet in the end he couldn't protect them from the consequences of himself.

"Who's the proprietor?"

Joy looked up to find a uniformed officer in front of them, pad in his hand.

"I can answer your questions," Stephen said.

Irritation fueled Joy. "I'm the owner." She slipped out of Stephen's protective grasp to stand up.

"I need some information for the report," the officer told her.

The questions were simple and Joy answered them without much intervention from Stephen. Her spike of aggravation had been over nothing. He wasn't trying to take over. He was just filling a gap that she'd left by not responding immediately to the officer.

"Call us with a list of anything missing after you've had a chance to take inventory," the officer said, handing Joy a copy of the report. "Although it just looks like a case of vandalism. We've had a problem with that around here lately. We have some extra patrols on and we'll catch them one of these days."

Joy carefully folded the report, almost dreading going into the house. She wanted to see the damage, but was afraid to in another sense. "Thank you," she told the officer.

"No problem, ma'am. Call us if anything else comes up."

Joy made a face as they watched the patrol car pull away. "I'd prefer not to have to talk to him again," she said. "Not professionally, I mean."

Stephen put his arm around her shoulders and together they walked back up to the store. The neighbors had all drifted away and the birds were calling out their goodnights as darkness began to creep forward. It was like any warm, spring evening, except for the chill in her stomach.

She stepped inside and looked around. Paintings on the floor, their frames cracked and broken. Glass from the display case doors lay sprinkled over handwoven tablecloths. A shiver dashed through her. She didn't want to sleep here alone and certainly didn't want to bring the kids back tonight.

"Why don't you give things a look-over?" Stephen said, releasing her. "I'll call someone to get this window covered tonight."

Joy nodded absently and picked up a wall hanging with shells woven into the pattern. It seemed fine. None of the shells looked cracked. Two of her paintings lay under the front window. The frame was broken on one, but the painting itself seemed undamaged.

"He'll be here in about half an hour," Stephen said, and helped her right a toppled-over display case.

"It doesn't seem as though much of anything was taken," she said. "Maybe it was just vandalism, like the officer said."

Stephen's desk was littered with the remains of a fast-food feast, but furniture polish would take care of that damage.

"I checked upstairs after I called," he said. "The door to the apartment is still locked. It doesn't look like they got in up there."

Joy nodded and looked around the store. Then she'd hide away upstairs for tonight and pretend that her dreams hadn't been threatened. She'd clean up tomorrow.

"Want to stay at my place tonight?" Stephen asked.

Joy shook her head. "No. I don't suppose they'll come back, but—" She shrugged. "I don't want to leave the house empty."

"Then I'll stay here."

She'd like that. In fact, she wanted that, but a little snippy voice said that he should have asked, instead of telling. How petty she was being, she scolded herself. She needed him here and he wanted to stay. There was nothing else to discuss.

"Let's go upstairs," she said and put her arm around his waist. There was a difference between being bossy and being supportive, she thought. Tomorrow she'd reassert herself.

* * *

"Shouldn't you be getting on to your office?" Joy asked. "I'm going to be pretty busy here today."

Stephen just looked at her. She had on jeans, an old work shirt, and her hair was tied up in a bandanna, and she looked beautiful. There was only the slightest trace of shadow in her eyes, but even that was hard to find because she was too strong to let it show. He wanted to take her into his arms and keep her safe there forever. Knowing she'd never agree to that, he settled for a quick kiss before getting gently pushed away.

"Don't you have any clients to see?" she asked.

"I'm with a client." He ripped the lid off a box of garbage bags and pulled one out, snapping it in the air to open it.

"Giving all your time to just one firm can't be very profitable, unless it's a Fortune 500 corporation, and I have a ways to go before I reach that size."

Stephen picked up some empty French fries cartons from the desk he'd refinished and dumped them into the bag. Her jeans certainly weren't a power business suit, but Joy sure had her power attitude on. She'd put it on as soon as she stepped out of the shower this morning.

"My business is in good shape," he said. "And this is an emergency." He picked up two hamburger boxes and about eight packets of catsup, all open and dripping ooze out.

"The emergency is over," Joy said. "I can take care of everything just fine from here on in." She put on a pair of heavy work gloves and picked up a plastic wastebasket before kneeling down near the broken glass.

"For God's sake, Joy, let me do that," he snapped. She was going to cut herself.

"No." She sat back on her heels. "I can do this. I am capable."

"I never said you weren't."

But she just glared at him a moment, then pointed toward her door. "Go and take care of your other clients."

Why was she being so stubborn? She needed his help and knew it. Why were they back to this silly game?

The door opened to let in a white-haired man in a shirt and tie. A referee. "Hi, Bob," Stephen said. "You handling Joy's claim?"

"Yep," the man replied. "She a client of yours?"

"Yep."

"I've got some forms that we need to fill out. Nothing too major. Maybe we could—"

Suddenly an earsplitting whistle pierced the air. "Excuse me, guys," Joy said, her hands resting on her hips. "But shouldn't you be including the owner—namely me—in your discussions?"

"The insurance forms are just paperwork," Stephen said. "And that's one of the things I do for my clients—take care of the paperwork."

"That's right, ma'am," Bob said. "And I might add that he's damn good at it."

Joy's eyes flickered from one to the other. Stephen wanted to tell her to relax, to take the kids and go to the beach while he cleaned the place up and got all the insurance work done. But he knew she'd never agree to that, so it had to be the next best thing.

"Bob and I can work on the forms while you call all the artists whose works were damaged," Stephen said. "You're the only one who has the personal relationships with those people. They certainly wouldn't want to hear from me."

Uncertainty flickered across Joy's face.

"This paperwork is just routine stuff."

"Absolutely," Bob added. "It would bore you to death in a minute. I don't really find it all that interesting myself."

"Fine." Joy's smile was rather tight, but she was giving in. "Why don't you use my office?"

"Thank you, ma'am," Bob replied.

Stephen led Bob to the little room at the back of the store.

"Lady's a little testy this morning," Bob said as he closed the door behind them. "Taking the break-in hard?"

"Yeah, I guess."

"Maybe she's aggravated by your pushing in and trying to run everything," Bob said.

"I'm just helping out."

"She looks like a tough little lady." The insurance agent pulled a stack of papers out of his briefcase. "You best ease up a bit or you're going to find yourself outside, flat on your butt."

Why did every salesman have to be a psychologist? "Shouldn't we be getting down to business?" Stephen asked. "I'm sure you have other clients to take care of this morning."

Bob shook his head. "Actually the morning is real light. Just this one."

"May I see Joy's contract, please?" Stephen snatched the bulky contract from Bob's hand and forced himself to concentrate on the gibberish before him.

"It's all pretty standard," Bob said as Stephen perused the words. "Deductible on her stuff. Hundred percent coverage for the consigned items."

Stephen nodded. "Things turned out lucky for everyone. There wasn't much damage at all. Place was mostly dirtied up, broken glass and damage to some of the picture frames."

The insurance agent made a face and squirmed in his chair. "Actually we may not be totally home free."

"What do you mean?"

"The lady was supposed to have installed a burglar alarm system. The police report says she doesn't have one."

Stephen frowned.

"Section three, paragraph five," Bob said quietly.

Flipping through the pages, Stephen quickly read the paragraph. There it was in black and white. No alarm, no payout. He flipped over to the last page. There was Joy's signature. Filled with the loops and waves that were her trademark. Damn. The damage wasn't all that much but given Joy's precarious financial position it would be enough to break her.

"She just got this policy last month?" Stephen asked, staring at the date.

"That's when she got her permanent policy. She had a temporary one before that."

Stephen looked up. "Why did it take that long?"

Bob shrugged. "The agent who handled her before wasn't too swift. I don't know what he was doing. Most likely he didn't either. Fortunately, he's not with us any longer."

Stephen paged back through the contract to the burglar alarm clause again. It hadn't changed. Damn. He had to do something. There was no way Joy could stand the loss.

"Was this clause in the temporary policy?" Stephen asked.

"No, it was added in the permanent."

Bingo. "She didn't initial this copy."

The insurance agent tightened his smile. "She signed the contract."

"Come on, Bob. How many people read this junk word for word? They depend on their agent to take care of them."

The smile slowly slid off Bob's face.

"Especially an independent agency like your own," Stephen said softly. "People really expect that you'll take care of them."

Stephen hated to put the muscle on Bob; he'd known him for years and Bob's father had taken care of Stephen's father's insurance needs. But, dammit. Joy was in trouble, deep trouble.

"Okay," Bob said slowly. "We'll cover the lady's losses."

"Thanks, Bob."

"But she has a week to meet the conditions of her contract."

"Two," Stephen said.

"Two or she gets dropped."

Stephen nodded and indicated Bob's forms. "Let's get those things filled out. The damages are under three thousand."

"Like you said." Bob smiled tightly. "We all came out lucky."

Keeping his own smile in place while trying to ignore the churning in his stomach, Stephen watched Bob fill out the claim forms. Joy was lucky; she could have been down and out. But the problem now was Joy's burglar alarm. Bob would give her a pass for two weeks, but that was it. Then she'd better have the equipment in place or no insurance. No insurance and no one would leave anything with her on consignment. No goods to sell and there would be no business for Joy. He doubted that she'd want to become a full-time pizza delivery person, or could afford to.

"Let's get the lady to sign these and then I'll be on my way," Bob said. "Have the check in her hands by early this afternoon."

"Thanks," Stephen murmured.

He'd be more than happy to take care of the alarm for her. It wouldn't cost more than six or seven thousand, eight at most. The problem was that Joy wasn't into accepting that kind of assistance from him, or anyone else.

Stephen watched Bob gather up the forms. Hell. He'd take care of the alarm and do it in a way that wouldn't bother Joy. A challenge like this was just what he needed, something to take his mind off the past and stir up his old take-charge drive again. Something to make him quit moping around like some kid with a lost puppy. He'd take care of Joy and she'd be home free.

Joy turned to pick up the dustpan as her office door opened. She turned slowly. Both Stephen and Bob were smiling, images of businessmen concluding a mutually satisfying meeting.

She breathed a sigh of relief. She'd paid her premiums and things should have been okay, but one never knew.

"I'll have the check to you soon after lunch," the insurance agent told her. "Doesn't look like there was much damage at all."

"Not really," Joy agreed. "Things are more dirty than damaged."

The man smiled at her, then turned to shake hands with Stephen. "See you around," he said. "And get that little item taken care of."

Stephen shook hands with the agent and nodded.

What little item? "How did things go?" Joy asked once Bob was gone.

"Fine."

"Are my premiums going to go up?"

"I don't think so." He looked sharply at her. "Did your other agent talk to you about a burglar alarm system?"

Joy nodded. "A little bit, but I said I couldn't afford it. He said to get one installed whenever I get enough money together."

Stephen came over and took her in his arms.

"Why?"

He kissed her.

"Stephen."

He kissed her again.

"Stephen." She raised her voice and pushed against his chest. "Get serious. We're talking business now."

His smile didn't take even the smallest step toward serious. "There's all kinds of business."

"And this is monkey business." She squirmed out of his arms. "Do I have a problem?"

"Nah. Not at all."

She relaxed, her guard came down, and she was in his arms again.

"You just have to get an alarm system installed."

She sagged against his chest. "I still can't afford it."

"I'll take a look at it."

Joy felt trapped. "But they're really expensive, especially for a big old place like this building."

"Hey." He reached down and kissed her. "Relax."

"Stephen."

"I'm your business adviser. My job is to figure these kinds of things out and I'm very good at that."

"Yes, but you're just an accountant, not God. You can't make something out of nothing."

"You don't have nothing. You have a lot going for you."

She looked skeptically at him.

"All you have to do is consider your assets," he said with a devilish grin.

"I'm not in the mood for your so-called humor."

"I mean your business assets," Stephen said, indicating the room and its contents with a wave of his hand.

"The building is mortgaged to the roof and the merchandise is all on consignment. Remember? That means I don't own any of it."

He hugged her tighter. "You have a lot of potential."

"Stephen. I'm serious," she said, pushing herself back.

Sighing, he dropped his hands to her waist and lifted her up on the counter, obviously so he could look her straight in the eyes. Boy, is he strong! a part of her mind exclaimed. So am I, another part answered.

"Look, I said I'd take care of things and I will."

"But how?"

"Trust me."

She felt a growing irritation. "Stephen, I'm not a child."

"I'll look things over and I'll develop a financial plan, then I'll get a bank to carry you. I'll also look for the best deal available."

The tightness stayed. "I should be doing that. This is my business, not yours."

"You can't do everything yourself. That's why businessmen hire lawyers, accountants and consultants. You're not superwoman. There's nothing wrong with hiring help." He stepped forward to take her into his arms again. "Especially such competent help like myself."

"I doubt that you're making much money off me."

"Things are slow in the beginning for most people," Stephen said. "This isn't the first time I've gone through a situation like this, but I always make out like a bandit down the road."

"Oh, yeah?" Suspicion hung heavy on her words.

"Yeah." His arms tightened around her. "Then you'll be wondering how come I'm making all that money for the little that I do."

She put her own arms around his neck and stared deep into those baby blues. They radiated honesty, integrity, strength. They said, I'll take care of you.

A little twinge of concern waved its flag but Joy squashed it down. Stephen was right. A good business person hired experts whenever they were needed. She'd just have to stay in charge.

"I intend to stay on top of things," she said.

Joy could feel the warmth climb in her cheeks even before Stephen's grin widened across his face.

"That's okay by me," he replied. "I'm flexible."

"Not that I've noticed," she sighed. She was going to repay him for all his help. And she knew just the way to do it. She would help him become whole again.

Chapter Twelve

"I don't see any problem, Mr. Sullivan," Joy said, try-ing to soothe the little gray-haired wildlife painter. "You can't see the damage unless you're looking for it. And once it's framed, you can't see it at all."

The artist folded his left arm across his stomach, using it to brace his right so that he could rest his chin in his hand. Standing perfectly still, he stared long and hard at his pic-ture of a mother fox and two gamboling baby foxes.

He was the last of her artists to come in to check the damage from the break-in. She'd kept his paintings in the back room, where they were waiting to be reframed upon his go-ahead. It was hard to believe it was only four days since they'd come home to find such mess.

"I suppose you're right," the artist finally mumbled.

Brendan Sullivan was a mumbler and a bit of a grouch, but his paintings were beautiful.

"I bet that'll be the first picture I sell for you," Joy said. "The animals are just so full of life and vigor. They look almost ready to spring out at you."

"Umm," Mr. Sullivan replied.

"All your pictures are beautiful," Joy said lamely.

The artist dropped his arms and turned toward Joy. "I hope that we won't have any more problems."

"I hope not, either." Joy shrugged. "The police said it was just a random occurrence. Kids out on a spree."

"The police always make light of things," Mr. Sullivan grumbled.

"My insurance covers all your works at full retail value," Joy said. "And I'm having an alarm system installed."

Joy turned around when the front door announced a visitor. She hoped she was having an alarm system installed, she thought when she saw her visitor was Stephen.

"Well," the artist said gruffly. "I must be hurrying along." He brushed by Stephen as he hurried out.

"Friendly little fellow," Stephen said, staring out after the artist as he let the door slam behind him.

"That's Brendan Sullivan."

Stephen appeared stunned and moved over to look out one of the front windows. "That's Brendan Sullivan? He doesn't look like a wildlife painter."

"What's a wildlife painter supposed to look like?"

"I don't know. He sure as hell shouldn't be wearing sandals and a New Kids on the Block T-shirt."

"Can't tell a book by its cover."

"Yeah, I know," Stephen grumbled. "But you'd think he'd at least wear a plaid flannel shirt. I mean all outdoorsy guys wear them."

"How are you coming on my alarm system?" There couldn't be a problem. If there was, she'd be able to tell.

"Maybe even a pair of hiking boots. Or at least moccasins." Stephen took one last look out the front windows. "Are you sure he's Brendan Sullivan?"

"I haven't run a fingerprint check with the FBI, but he did show me his driver's license."

"He looks like such a little wuss."

"I didn't do any strength tests on him, either." She moved forward and put her arms around Stephen's waist. "I just put my accountants through that sort of thing. My profits are going to get so big that they'll need a ton of muscles to handle all the figures."

He smiled down at her. Their lips parted as they touched and they kissed with their souls. The world could drift away and she wouldn't care as long as his arms would hold her and his lips would sing such sweet love songs to her heart. He slowly pulled away.

"How about the alarm system?" Joy asked, feeling that she needed one herself. One that would sound an alarm when fever was due to hit. That way she could not fall into distractions during working hours.

"How about another kiss?"

"No." She pushed herself out of his embrace. "You told me that as an accountant you work for your clients. So start working, buddy. Or else."

"Or else what?"

"Stephen."

"Okay. Okay." He put his briefcase on the counter and took a folder of papers out. "I got three estimates for your alarm system. They're all pretty close."

She took the papers and paged quickly through them. Seventy-eight hundred, seventy-nine hundred; and eighty-one hundred. They were all close all right. Close to impossible.

"Wow," was all she could say.

"That includes your backdoor upstairs and the windows off your porch," Stephen said.

"It's still a wow," she said.

"They're within your budget."

She gave him her best *aw, come on* look.

"Based on your projected sales," he hastened to add.

"Projected as in what you think is going to happen in the future but you're not really sure."

"I'm reasonably sure."

"Reasonable to whom?" she asked. "One of Santa Claus's elves?"

"Come on," he protested. "Have a little faith in your accountant."

"I have faith," she said. "And I have an awful lot of hope."

"How about some charity?" he asked, grinning.

"When appropriate. Like maybe after you explain these projected sales, profits and whatevers to me."

"Look." He came forward and put his arms lightly around her waist. "Trust me. I do these kinds of things for my clients all the time. I do a little number crunching and look out into the future. Most creditors demand it."

"I don't have eight thousand dollars lying around," Joy said.

"The security companies will carry you."

"Based on your projections."

"Yep."

Sighing, Joy pushed herself out of his arms. "I hate adding that much to my debt load."

"It'll work out." He put his hands on her shoulders. "Trust me."

Joy looked into his baby blues. They echoed Stephen's words, shouting *trust me* to the high heavens.

"Should I just pick the lowest bid?" she asked.

"Actually the middle guy would be better," Stephen replied. "He can start installing Monday."

"Are we in that much of a hurry?" She leaned into his chest, putting her arms around Stephen's waist. It would be all right; she would trust him. And she would also repay him for all of this.

"It's best to get it done quick." He kissed her. Alarm systems and projections of every sort went slipping off into oblivion. "You probably won't be hit again, but one can never tell."

"Hmm," she grunted, settling comfortably into his chest.

The front door chimes blared and screeched throughout the room, causing both of them to start. They separated from their clinch as a young woman with a small boy came in through the door.

"You get the woman," Stephen whispered out of the side of his mouth. "I'll get the kid. We'll toss them both out onto the street."

"Thank you for stopping by, Mr. Van Horne," Joy said in her coolest, businesslike voice. "And please see that the system is installed posthaste."

Stephen quietly walked to the counter and put the papers back into his briefcase before closing it. As he turned to leave, he paused with his back to the woman and stuck his tongue out at Joy, making a horrible face. She was facing the woman so she could only smile sweetly at him, hoping that he saw the promise of retribution in her eyes.

A half hour later though, all thoughts of retribution were forgotten as excitement took its place. Joy had sold Stephen's desk! It wasn't part of her repayment plan, but it was a nice prelude.

"I'm sorry it took so long," Joy said, handing the woman's credit card back to her. The approval cycle had taken longer than Joy expected.

"No problem," the woman said, laughing. "I wouldn't let anybody walk off with a two thousand dollar desk just on their say-so, either."

Joy smiled as she filled out the rest of the charge slip. Stephen was going to be so happy. This was the first one of his refinished furniture pieces that she had sold. "Sign here, please."

"I suppose I should have asked beforehand, but do you deliver?" the woman asked. "We have a summer home just up north on the shore, in Grand Haven."

"We sure do." Joy took the form apart and gave the woman her copy. "When do you want it?"

The woman blinked. "You don't have a regular schedule?"

"Sure," Joy replied. "Whenever you want it."

Her customer shook her head and laughed. "We just moved out here from L.A. I'm not used to this whenever-you-want-it stuff."

"No reason to inconvenience you," Joy said. "You're the one paying."

"How about late Monday morning?"

"Fine, I'll tell Judd and Willis," Joy said.

Joy bid her farewell, sighing with relief after the little boy had given his third goodbye. The woman and her family had given up the glitz and glamour of the West coast for the down-home style of the eastern shore. Joy hoped that they would find it a good trade. Joy knew that she had.

She held the charge slip out in front of her face and smiled. Of course, she'd found some extra benefits here that most people didn't. A little thing that made the laid-back life-style even easier to take.

Actually, he wasn't such a little thing at all.

Laughing out loud, the sound echoing throughout the now-empty store, Joy kissed the charge slip before looking at it again. Two thousand dollars, a reasonable chunk of which was hers for selling the piece. Super neato keeno. She could hardly wait to tell Stephen.

"Hi, Mom," her children chorused over the sound of the door chimes. Marlene was with them.

"Hi, guys, Marlene. Did you two have a nice time at the day camp?" Joy gave each of the kids a big hug.

"Super," Katie answered.

"I'm hungry," Robbie announced and hurried up the stairs with Katie close behind.

Marlene gave Joy a weak sort of smile. "I'm afraid I've a problem sitting for the kids tomorrow," she said. "Mom's going stir-crazy, so we're going down to see her over the weekend."

"How's she coming along?"

"Well enough to get grumpy. That's why we have to go to her place this weekend. The house isn't up to her standards and she's driving Dad nuts with her fussing. Sorry to leave you in a lurch though."

"No problem," Joy replied. "I'll find someone else or the kids can just ride with me."

"Let me know if you can't find a sitter," Marlene said as she went to the door. "I'll give my contacts a call."

"Don't worry," Joy said, giving her friend a smile and a wave.

"Marlene ain't sitting with us tomorrow night?" Robbie was sitting on the stairs, eating a blueberry muffin.

"No, she isn't," Joy said. "You may have to ride with me during my deliveries."

"That's boring," Robbie mumbled.

"How about if I play a banjo while I drive?"

"Uncle Stevie can stay with us," Katie said as she licked chocolate off her fingers.

"Yeah," Robbie agreed. "He's cool."

Joy wasn't sure if cool was a good word to describe Stephen. She certainly wasn't cool when he was around. Not that he had to be near for her temperature to rise, all she had to do was think about him.

"He's nice, too," Katie added.

"Go ahead, Mom. Call him," Robbie encouraged her. "He can watch us while you deliver pizzas, then when you come home, you guys can sit around and talk and stuff."

"Stuff?" Joy could feel her cheeks blazing. "What kind of stuff?"

"I don't know." He glared at her in that confused look of a smart-alecky, ten-year-old, trying hard to be a know-it-all. "Lying around and watching TV. You know, stuff."

Joy could feel her cheeks cool but in no way felt in control. She reached under the counter and pulled out two dust rags. "Why don't you and Katie go clean the picnic furniture?"

"That stuff's outside, Mom," Robbie said. "It'll just get dirty again."

"Humor me," Joy said.

Shaking his head, Robbie took the rags and handed one to Katie as the two of them headed out to the backyard. "Don't forget to call Stevie to baby-sit with us," he called back over his shoulder.

Joy waved him off and wandered back into her office. She put her hand on the phone but couldn't quite pick it up to dial. Should she or shouldn't she? The kids wanted Stephen and it really wasn't right to haul them all over the town while she delivered pizzas, but she didn't think it was right to impose on Stephen, either.

He was already doing so much for her. Helping her with the business, watching the kids, bringing light and love into her life.

Yep, it was true, her stunned heart realized. He had brought love into her life, for she had fallen in love with him. For all her speeches of independence and being on her own, she had fallen head over heels in love with one Stephen Van Horne.

She wasn't sure if she was happy or depressed about it, but she did know one thing for certain. He wasn't going to be her knight in shining armor rescuing her from life. She wasn't going to ask him for one more favor until she started giving back to him. And not just little ways like making him smile or keeping him company.

She'd found this number yesterday, but had stewed back and forth. Should she call it or should she just give it to Stephen? He wouldn't call though; she knew him well enough to know that. No, if he was going to start on the road to healing, she was going to have to put him there. She picked up the phone and dialed the phone number she'd written on the edge of her calendar.

"Adoption Identity Movement," a voice said.

Stephen looked around the gallery as he stepped through the door, his experienced business eye taking in the crowd. Joy should get herself some help, at least for the weekends. She could be losing business because of the long wait.

Joy flashed him a quick smile.

"Robbie called," Stephen said over the murmur of the crowd as he held up his baseball glove. "He wanted to do some batting practice."

She nodded but Stephen didn't think she really latched onto his words. He'd do a little practicing with Robbie, then come in and see if he could lend Joy a hand. Once outside, Stephen scanned the small backyard for Robbie, not seeing him anyplace.

"Up here."

His eyes went up to the lower branches of the big cherry tree. "Hey," Stephen said. "What do you want to be, a baseball player or Tarzan?"

"I dunno." Robbie balanced across a branch on his belly. "Which pays better?"

"They probably both pay about the same," Stephen replied.

Robbie dropped out of the tree. "I'm tired of climbing," he said, picking up his glove. "How about we do baseball?"

"Fine with me," Stephen replied. They took up places at opposite ends of the small yard.

"Marlene can't baby-sit with us tonight," the boy said.

"Oh." Stephen bounced the ball off the ground in front of Robbie. "So you have to go deliver pizzas with your mom?"

"Nah." He threw one fast and low. Not bad for a kid. "Mom went and hired a baby-sitter."

"Oh." Stephen threw a high ball.

"We wanted you to sit with us." Robbie paused to adjust his cap. "But Mom hired Becky Newbill instead."

"That's nice." Why'd she do that? He would have been more than happy to stay with the kids. Stephen caught Robbie's throw. "Want to practice some batting?"

"I guess." Robbie threw his glove onto the ground and picked up his bat. "She's a real geek."

"Who?"

"Becky Newbill." Robbie gave him a disgusted look. "She's got these really big glasses and she wears T-shirts that come down past her knees."

"That's probably the *style du jour*," Stephen replied.

"Huh?" Robbie missed the ball and trudged over to retrieve it.

"Choke up a little higher on the bat," Stephen told him. He caught Robbie's toss and pitched it back to him. Robbie hit that one and Stephen caught it on a bounce near his feet.

Joy was doing a good job with her kids. She was doing a good job in all parts of her life actually. Her business was coming along quite well.

He threw a slow ball that Robbie hit over Stephen's head. And with his help, Joy was going to do even better. This alarm thing worked out just fine, so now she'd let him handle more and more business matters without question.

Robbie hit the next few pitches, then missed about a zillion. Stephen could see the boy's shoulders sink with each miss, feeling his own stomach sink in response.

"Maybe you're getting tired," Stephen suggested.

"Maybe I'm just no good," Robbie muttered and threw the bat down.

Robbie trudged over to the picnic bench and sat down. Stephen joined him.

"Hey, it's okay not to be the best ball player around," Stephen said. "Your timing's just a little off, that's all. No big deal. You'll get it one of these days."

Robbie just stared at his sneakers, kicking at the patio stones as if he could wear them away. "I hate baseball anyway. I wish soccer was still on. Soccer doesn't have stupid stuff like father-son games."

Was that what was bothering the boy? "You got one coming up?"

Robbie just shrugged.

"Look, Rob," Stephen said. "I know I'm not your dad, but if you're looking for someone to go with you, I'd be glad to. I'm sure we wouldn't be the only non-father/son combo there."

Robbie shrugged again. The extent of his repertoire of movements, or did it mean something?

"Whatcha doin'?" A boy about Robbie's age appeared on the edge of the yard.

"Batting practice," Robbie replied.

"That a friend of yours, Robbie?"

"Sort of." Robbie reached up to adjust his hat. "That's Matt."

"I got a radio-controlled car for my birthday," Matt said.

"Yeah?" Interest and excitement were obvious in Robbie's voice even as he tried to maintain a cool demeanor.

"It's a police car. Want to see it?"

Robbie looked at Stephen and got to his feet. "Nah. I gotta practice batting with Stevie."

"It's got a real siren."

"You can go see his car," Stephen assured him. "My arm's getting a little tired anyway."

"Okay." Robbie hustled over toward Matt. "Why don't you go in and see if Mom needs any help?"

"Right." Stephen laughed as he watched the boys walk down the alley.

Surprisingly, there was only a single customer in the store and Joy was putting something into a bag for her. He hung back while she gave the woman her thanks and told her to come by again soon.

"When I first came in, it looked like the whole town was here," Stephen said.

Joy smiled, looking a bit weary. "This is my first break the whole day. Business has been good today."

"Probably exceeding my projections."

She came over and put her arms around his waist. "I'm glad you came back in. I've been wanting to talk to you."

He bent down to kiss her, pausing to smell the clean in her hair before straightening up again. "The guys are coming in Monday morning to install your alarm system," he told her.

"Hmm." She was leaning on his chest. "Don't I have to sign some papers?"

"No. I just told them you were accepting their bid."

"I meant for the loan. Isn't some bank lending me the money?"

"They're extending the credit themselves," Stephen said.

She looked up at him and blinked, looking somewhat confused. "Don't the installers want me to sign something?"

Stephen shook his head.

"They just trust me?"

"They're just small town sort of guys," Stephen replied with a shrug.

He thought he could see a tightening around the corners of her eyes but just then the front door chimes called for attention. Stephen breathed a sigh of relief as a large contingent of people, probably off some tourist bus, stepped into the shop.

Joy went to the door to greet the customers while Stephen drifted back toward the paintings, ready to help if anyone asked.

Boy, he was going to be glad when that damn system was finally installed. If Joy ever found out he was paying for it, she'd skin him alive. She was so damn touchy about accepting help.

But no bank in the world would advance her the cash. Hell, she had no track record and was in debt up to her eyeballs. She was going to make it tough. Stephen knew that. She was a lady with grit, but bankers tended not to look at that sort of thing, especially these days.

"That's a real man's picture."

Stephen surfaced from his own thoughts to focus on an elderly couple standing in front of him. The short, slight man looked even smaller next to the tall, husky woman.

"You know this here Brendan Sullivan?" the man asked Stephen as he nodded toward a painting of a wolf glaring out from the canvas.

"Kind of."

"What sort of man is he?"

"Man?"

"Yes." An impatient edge crept into the old man's voice. "Is he short or tall? Husky, lanky, or what?"

Stephen didn't think the truth—that Brendan was a short, skinny fussbudget kind of guy—would sell the painting, but he didn't want to lie, either. He just shrugged and waved his hands in front of him. "Yeah, sort of."

"Sort of?" the man snapped. "How can a man be short and tall, husky and lanky, and everything all at the same time?"

"Ah, he's a guy who blends in real well. It's hard to remember what he really looks like."

The man stared at him.

"That's why he can catch these animals in such beautiful poses," Stephen hastened to explain. "He just blends in with his surroundings and the animals don't even notice him."

They stared at each other a long moment and Stephen had to wet his lips.

"Do you like the picture, Henry?" The woman had a surprisingly thin voice for her husky body.

"Yes, I do, Irma."

"Then buy the damn thing." She wandered over to look at some furniture while Stephen wrapped the purchase.

"That's a real man's picture," the buyer said, as he counted out six crisp fifty dollar bills.

"It certainly is," Stephen agreed as he gave the man his receipt.

The tourists stayed for another half hour or so and Stephen serviced a few other smaller purchases. It would be interesting to see the numbers at the end of the month. The store could turn out to be reasonably profitable. The problem was that Joy needed to make a year's profits all in the summer because tourists were an endangered species around here in winter.

"Thanks for the help," Joy said when the store was quiet again.

"No problem."

"Brendan's going to be happy to see a picture of his sold. How did you do it?"

"I'm just one hell of a salesman." He took her in his arms, glad to see that no defenses stood in his way. He lingered on his kiss. She was so delicious.

"Think your baby-sitter would be willing to stay late tonight?" he asked, when they came up for air.

"I think she'd be more than happy to. She's into buying clothes, lots of clothes."

"Good."

"Why?"

"Well." He kissed her again, but didn't linger as long. "I thought, that is if you didn't have anything else planned, we could go out tonight. A nice meal, a little dancing. That kind of thing."

"You mean stuff?"

"I guess."

"I think I can work it into my schedule."

Chapter Thirteen

This time the deliveries went perfectly and Joy arrived at Stephen's house a little after nine o'clock. When he answered her knock though, he stood a moment in his doorway, looking her up and down.

She twirled before him. "No. I didn't spill anything on myself this time," she said.

"I didn't say anything," he protested.

"I know." She leaned forward to kiss him, a soft promise of what the evening would hold. "But you were thinking it, so I thought I'd put you in line before you started anything."

He stepped aside to let her in. "Boy, you're mean."

"Comes with the mommy license. If you're not mean enough, they make you take lessons." Joy held both hands out, one had a skirt, the other a blouse. "I want to change into these."

He waved her inside and toward the powder room. "I could have come by your house to pick you up."

"That's okay, this'll be quicker."

Besides which, she didn't want to pull this quick change under the watchful eyes of the kids. She wasn't up to another discussion of "stuff" with Robbie. This wasn't exactly brave knight riding in on his white horse to pick up fair maiden, but it felt a little more date-like than her other evenings with Stephen.

Joy touched up her makeup, fluffed her hair and made her exit to Stephen's waiting eyes. She twirled around before him. "Okay?"

He shook his head.

Her heart fell slightly. "Not okay?"

"Okay doesn't do you justice," he replied.

She took time to linger in his arms, resting her head on his chest as she relished the sweetness of the moment, the sense of rightness being in his arms brought. She felt his heart beat beneath her. Tonight she would tell him about the adoption-search organization; she would help him see that finding Michael would be finding a piece of himself that had been lost.

She pulled away from him and smoothed down her skirt, as if smoothing away her nervousness. "You, sir, are a scholar and a gentleman."

"I'd appreciate it if you kept that under your hat."

"My Bruno's pizza hat?"

"That'll be fine." He kissed her and little fingers of flame shot out around her heart.

There was no need to worry. Stephen would be glad she called.

"Your carriage awaits, fair lady."

"I put my truck over by your garage," she said, taking his arm.

"I'm sure it'll be comfortable there." Stephen opened the door and stood back for Joy in a gentlemanly fashion. They walked across the lawn, holding hands like high schoolers.

"I made us reservations at Alfie's," Stephen said, as he pulled out from his drive. "It's a roadhouse out east of town over toward Vriesland. Food is on the plain side, but they have a great little band on weekends."

"Sounds wonderful."

They were quickly out of the city, leaving behind the glow of streetlights and the murmur of traffic. Sleepy farmyards, lights twinkling from the widely spaced houses like some distant stars, silently watched them pass. Stephen had the window open and Joy breathed in the fresh air. She couldn't tell him now. She had no idea when they'd be getting to the restaurant and it wasn't a discussion to be interrupted.

"Strawberries will be ripe in a week or so," Stephen said. "Lots of pick-your-own places around here."

"Could the kids come?" Joy asked.

"I'm sure Robbie could but I think Katie might be too young."

Joy laughed. "Too bad. Katie'd love to come. I doubt Robbie would." She leaned against his shoulder and let the scenery speed past them.

The roadhouse sprang out of the dark woods crowding alongside the road, its red sign sending a welcome like a campfire in the wilderness. The parking lot stretched out into the surrounding trees, stones crunching beneath the tires as they turned into the drive.

It was fairly crowded; the deep murmur of voices greeted them as they opened the door, along with a young man in slacks and golf shirt.

"Hi, Stephen."

"Hi, Al," Stephen replied. "Crowd looks good tonight."

"Yeah." Al pulled two menus from the *maître d'* stand. "We're hanging in there." He led them to a table in a far corner, dark but with a full view of the band.

Joy stared at the menu. Maybe after they ordered she'd tell him. Work slowly into the subject of Michael and then tell him about the search organizations. But soon after their waitress came by to take their orders, she was back with salads. Then some friends of Stephen's dropped by.

She wasn't really scared to tell him, Joy assured herself, but the timing had to be right. She called the search group late yesterday, and they said they'd send some information out within a few days. She probably had until the middle of next week before he got anything. She could afford to wait for the right moment.

The band started playing while they were eating and it made conversation difficult. The rhythm was too infectious for Joy to care, though. She was glad once they were finished eating and could get out on the dance floor.

As if the band knew when that would happen, they switched to soft ballads just as she stepped into Stephen's arms. The dance floor was dark and dreamy and Stephen's embrace became her whole world. She lay against his chest, marveling how far they'd come since that evening a month ago when she'd tried to deliver him a pizza. He had helped her keep her independence and she would help him put the past truly behind him.

"This is a great place," she told Stephen.

"One of the better ways to spend a Saturday evening," he agreed.

He was a marvelous dancer and Joy found herself relearning steps that she didn't even remember she knew. Rock and roll, waltz, samba, fox-trot and that old favorite—clinging and swaying. By the end of their evening she'd discarded her heels, burying herself deep into Stephen's chest and dancing barefoot on top of his shoes.

On the ride back, she sat in a silent limbo between sleep and desire, breathing in the country air. It made her feel at one with the earth, ready to nurture.

"Tired?" Stephen asked.

"In a way." Relaxed, content, whole. She let the night speed past them for a long moment, knowing that time for her talk was running out. "Do you think men or women are more sentimental?"

"Depends on the person," he said. "Why? Did I miss our anniversary?"

"No, silly. I was just wondering."

"That story that Jane and Beth told you about Valentine's Day in eighth grade wasn't a true reading of my character, you know."

"No? What was Valentine's Day like in ninth grade?"

"I didn't give any valentines out."

"The girls still weren't talking to you, eh?"

"What a low blow," he scoffed and slipped his arm around her shoulders. The mood shifted from softness to sultriness. "Nothing can beat the pure magic of a spring night, can it?"

She thought of the sweetness of his arms and the heavens they could reach together. "Oh, a few things come close."

He glanced at her, darting a look before his eyes went back to the highway. "Yes, you're right."

The moment to talk was gone, but she didn't mind. She'd find another one. Maybe it was better to wait anyway, let the bonds between them grow closer.

When they reached her home, they walked hand in hand to the door. The coolness of the earth and wooden porch both soothed and excited her.

While Stephen took the baby-sitter home, Joy checked out her sleeping children and changed into a light summer robe. She poured some Chablis for the two of them and wondered if she could find the words if they sat out on the porch under the cover of the night.

But when Stephen came back, the night turned out not to be a time for talking. He opened his arms and she practically ran into them. His lips opened the floodgates of passion. Thought was not only hard, it was impossible.

They took their wine out onto the porch and cuddled on the swing. The air was cool but it didn't lessen the fever in her blood. She lay in Stephen's arms, his hands running lightly over her shoulder and arm, and thought of how much stronger she felt because of his faith in her.

She looked up at the star-filled sky, diamonds there for her plucking. "Ever make wishes on stars?" she asked him.

"I thought it was supposed to be on the first star."

"You're avoiding an answer."

He turned so that his lips could take hers. Their hunger was voracious, pulling at her soul and she met his desire with an answering passion. His hand slipped inside her robe to touch her breast; the roughness of his skin brought fire to her heart. His mouth pulled away slowly.

"I always thought wishing was dumb," he said, his voice a hoarse whisper. "Go for what you want or let it be. What good is wishing?"

It was the perfect opening she'd been waiting for all night, but she let it slip by. The needs of the night were more urgent, her body too hungry for his to have a philosophical discussion. He took her hand and pulled her to her feet.

"Want to shock the neighbors or go inside?"

"Shocking the neighbors sounds like fun, but I'm not sure it would help your political career."

"What sacrifices you're willing to make for me."

He swept her up into his arms and carried her back into the house. The bedroom welcomed them, the privacy a heady aphrodisiac so that they wasted little time in words.

In the shadowy darkness, they swept each other away into a timeless whirlpool of passion, then lay together letting the silence of the night soothe them to sleep.

Joy was humming as she rearranged pictures on the display walls, inserting new additions in among the old to give everybody a whole new look. It had been a wonderful weekend. Dancing Saturday night and then a busy Sunday in the store.

All right, she hadn't had the talk with Stephen she'd wanted, but that was her own fault. She'd been waiting for the time to be right, rather than to make the time right. She'd do that today, over lunch. She had invited Stephen here and, over hot dogs and chips, she'd tell him about the search organization.

Knowing the rightness of her plan, she'd been so relaxed that she'd almost overslept this morning. Good thing their neighbor's dog had his daily welcome-the-sun barking fit. If it weren't for the noisy little terrier, Joy was sure that she would have slept right through lunch. The kids would have missed their day-care trip to the zoo in Grand Rapids and there would have been no one around to let in the alarm system installers.

The chimes signaled a visitor and Joy hurried to the front of the store. "Hi, Bob," she said.

"Hi, Joy," the insurance agent said. "Just came by to see that your alarm system was going in as scheduled."

Joy nodded. "Yep. They were here bright and early this morning. A lot brighter than I was and a lot earlier than I wanted."

Smiling, he went off to check the installers. Joy yawned and went back to her picture hanging. Stephen would be checking out their progress when he came by for lunch, she was sure. Probably her luncheon invitation was the only reason he wasn't here already. His other clients should be grateful to her. It was about time he gave them some of his attention.

"They're doing a good job," Bob said as he came back into the room. "They should be done by Wednesday morning."

"Do you always check on these installations?" Joy asked.

"You betcha," he replied. "We consider security systems a necessity."

Joy straightened a picture. "Well I'm glad that things worked out so I could have one installed."

"You very well should be," he said. "You're lucky."

"Lucky?"

"If you weren't installing your system by this week, you wouldn't have any insurance."

Joy turned and stared in surprise. "I wouldn't?"

"That's the deal I made with Stephen."

Deal? With Stephen? She could feel a warmth creep up her neck and into her cheeks even as a chill crept into her heart.

"You were supposed to have the alarm system installed close to two months ago."

"I couldn't afford it at that time," Joy said.

Bob shrugged. "Well, it's a good thing that your business improved."

The chill grew and she clenched her fingers as if to will warmth into them. Her business hadn't really improved. It was better, but that was because of the summer tourist season. It would be another year or so before she knew whether or not she was successful.

"Your other agent was supposed to have explained all that to you," Bob said. "But as Stephen pointed out, there were certain things that weren't done quite right. So we carried you another couple of weeks without the alarm system."

"Oh," was all that Joy could say. Why hadn't Stephen told her that? He'd never even hinted at the urgency of getting the system in.

"Without insurance I would guess you'd be dead in the water," Bob said. "I doubt that your consignees would be willing to risk leaving their works here if you had no insurance."

"That's true." She knew that and so had Stephen. Was that behind his selective silence?

"Well, everything's in order now." Bob gave her a wave as he pulled open the door. "Good luck for the summer. The chamber's forecasting an increased number of tourists for this year."

The chimes seemed to mock her. Everything's in order now? Indeed. She hurried out to find the foreman of the installation crew.

"Larry, may I speak with you a moment?"

"Yeah, sure." He put down his tools and came over to her, a quizzical expression on his face.

"I was just wondering how I go about paying for all this," Joy said.

Quizzical turned into a frown. "Ma'am?"

"Well." She felt like an absolute fool. "I didn't get any papers to sign or anything and no one talked about a payment plan."

"Oh." The installer laughed. "I just do the installing and maintenance. They don't let me handle the money end. Probably afraid I'd just spend it all on whiskey and wild women."

"I see," Joy said. "Well, who should I talk to?"

"Call the office and talk to Boomer."

"Boomer?"

"Yeah, he owns the place. The big mugwa. What he says goes."

"Well, thank you." Joy hurried down to the phone in her office. She had no idea what was going on, but her suspicions had to be wrong. They had to be.

"Boomer, please," she told the woman who had answered the phone.

"Sorry, he's not here at the moment. Can I take a message?"

"Yes, this is Joy Chapin. Your people are installing an alarm system at my store."

"Uh-huh," the woman said cheerfully. "The art store over near the edge of downtown."

"Yes. Well, please tell Boomer I'd like to discuss my payment plan."

"Payment plan? We don't have payment plans."

"Mr. Van Horne said that you did."

"Mr. Van Horne? Just a moment please."

Joy waited with her silence, thankful that at least she wasn't being subjected to canned music.

"Mrs. Chapin. I just checked our records and your account is paid in full."

"Paid in full?" Joy could feel her heart sink down to the bottoms of her shoes.

"That's right, ma'am. Paid in full by Mr. Van Horne."

Joy leaned against the wall near to tears. She hoped that she had thanked the woman but she didn't even remember hanging up.

She wasn't being financed by the security company, and she'd bet her last cent no bank had forwarded the money, not without asking for her signature on a million papers. There was no payment plan, no financing based on projected earnings. Maybe there weren't even any projected earnings. It was just Sir Stephen jumping in and taking care of things as if she was some little girl.

Her eyelids stung, ready to pour out a torrent of acid tears, but she couldn't cry, not yet. There were things she had to do. She hurried off to find the installers.

"Larry," she called out when she found the foreman.

"Ma'am."

"There's . . . there's been a change of plans." Joy felt tongue-tied and unable to speak coherently. "You— Would you please pack up your equipment? I . . . I can't use the system right at the moment."

He stared at her for the shortest moment, but thankfully didn't press the issue. He just nodded and gathered up his men and equipment. Joy wanted to thank the man for his understanding but was afraid that such words would just unleash her pending flood of tears.

Stephen sat at his desk and stared at the form. Adoption Identity Movement. At first, he had thought it was just a standard, direct mail solicitation for funds.

But the letter didn't ask for donations. It just told him what the fee for registering with the group was. A fee for helping him find his biological child who had been given up for adoption almost eighteen years ago. It went on to further point out that there were no guarantees, although they had a high degree of success and worked with a national organization headquartered in Carson City, Nevada, in case his biological issue had himself registered.

Who could have talked to this outfit about him and Michael? Stephen felt a whole slew of emotions run through his body. None of them were good. Actually he could think of only one person who would do this. One person, to whom he'd recently spilled his—

Suddenly his door burst open and Joy stood there, with hands on her hips and red in her face. "We need to talk."

"I'm sorry, Mr. Van Horne," his secretary said, hurrying in behind Joy. "I tried to—"

"I'll take care of this, Mrs. Dehmers. Thank you."

Reluctantly, like a child afraid she was going to miss out on something really interesting, Mrs. Dehmers backed out the door and quietly closed it behind herself.

"Have a seat," Stephen said.

"I don't need one, thank you," Joy said. "I'm not going to be long."

"Oh?"

"I just came to prostrate myself at the feet of my benefactor," Joy said.

Stephen bit back a sigh. She had found out about him paying for the system. Just what he needed this morning, on top of this adoption search group staring him in the face. Anger, impatience and fear churned inside him. He felt spied on, pried into, that his secrets were laid open for the world to peck at. He hurt and his store of patience and understanding were precariously low.

"Sit down, Joy, and tell me what the problem is." His voice was hardly gentle and reassuring, but it was the best he could do.

"You weren't being honest with me."

"Joy, I'm not—"

"There is no payment plan," she said. "No loan based on projected earnings. Just Big Daddy and his big wallet."

"You needed that security system," Stephen said. "You were going to lose your insurance coverage without it."

"You never told me that."

Just as she'd never told him about that adoption search organization? Or that she had turned his name in to them?

"You lied to me," she said.

"No, I didn't."

"You twisted the words around so that I'd see what you wanted me to see and not what was real."

At least, he hadn't gone sneaking around behind her back. "Joy, you need that security system to stay in business."

"To install or not to install a security system was my decision to make," Joy said.

"Damn it," he exploded. "There was no decision to make. If you didn't install it, your dream was dead."

She turned away a moment and brushed at her eyes with the back of her hand. Stephen looked away, his stomach a churning cauldron of emotions. Yesterday he would have just gathered Joy into his arms, made sure that pain never touched her again. Now? Now, he didn't know what the hell to do. He felt betrayed, not just by Joy but by himself, by those stupid emotions that he should have known better than to trust.

"Don't you understand?" she cried. "This is more than a business to me. I've put all of myself into it. It's nothing unless I run it myself and make it on my own."

"I wasn't paying for it. I was just financing it."

She stared at him.

"I'm just advancing you the money. I'm not giving it to you. There's a big difference."

"That's what a bank is supposed to do."

"The banks have different criteria than I do."

"Right." The bitterness was returning to her voice. "I'm a poor credit risk and they won't touch me with a ten-foot pole."

"You're not a poor risk, you're just new to the business world and don't have a track record."

Joy stared at him, green eyes large, reflecting hurt like a wounded deer, but Stephen turned away. He'd taught himself well not to feel, not to get close, but those green eyes had been his downfall. Never again.

"Look," he said. "I've backed any number of new, start-up type businesses. My clients find themselves in a

tough spot and I help them out. That's my job. I've alway
considered myself a full-service type of guy.''

One side of her lips curled upward but the other staye
down. ''You've certainly given me a wide range of yor
services,'' she said quietly.

''I have a close relationship with all my clients.''

''How nice.'' Her face turned cold as her lips twisted int
a sneer. ''And does that mean you mess around in all you
clients' personal lives?''

''Mess around in my clients' personal lives?'' Stephe
could feel himself slip over the edge of control. ''You ob
viously don't know the difference between business an
personal.''

''Oh, yeah? Well—''

''Now this—'' He tossed the Adoption Identity Move
ment packet in front of her. ''This is messing around i
someone's personal life. Poking in where you aren
needed, aren't wanted.''

She stared at him. Her anger was gone from her eyes
leaving just pain and fear. ''I was going to tell you abou
them over lunch today,'' she said.

''Why? It was so much nicer as a surprise.'' His voice wa
pain scraped raw.

''You aren't the only man going through this,'' she said
''Or the only one afraid to look for your child. They tol
me—''

''I'm not afraid,'' Stephen snapped. ''I just don't wan
to.''

''Losing a child to adoption isn't something you ever ge
over,'' she said. ''Lots of men and women who gave up
child have the same problems you do in maintaining rela
tionships, in relating to kids.''

''Look, I've been carrying this monkey on my back fo
almost eighteen years.'' The words clogged up his throat
having to be forced out. ''But I've been getting it unde

control. I don't need anybody's help in digging up my ghosts. I don't want to dig them up. I want to keep them dead and buried.''

"That's not healthy.''

"When did you get your degree in psychology?''

"The AIM people were very knowledgeable. They have group counseling sessions to help you deal with all these emotions—''

"So now I'm supposed to bare my soul in front of strangers," he said with a bitter laugh. "But why should that bother me? The only person I trusted with my secret has already blurted it out to the world.''

"Stephen, I—''

"No, Joy. I think you've said enough. Do what you want about the security system, but right now I'd like to be left alone.''

Joy stared at him for a long moment; her eyes were deep pools overflowing into rivers running down her cheeks. She turned and ran from his office.

Stephen slumped down in his desk, staring blindly at the door. What a loser he was. He'd only really cared for two women in his life. Laura and now Joy. And he'd sent both of them running.

"Mr. Van Horne.''

He forced his eyes to focus on the figure in the doorway. "Yes, Mrs. Dehmers?''

"Is there anything I can do for you?''

"No, Mrs. Dehmers," he said wearily. "It's something I have to take care of myself.''

He had to close the door, come back to his desk, put his face in his hands and scream out his pain. Scream until he hurt no more. He'd probably lose his voice first.

Chapter Fourteen

"Boomer here."

The gruff voice barking in her ear caused Joy to jump so that she almost dropped the phone. "Ah, Mr.—"

"Ain't no mister, ma'am," he interrupted jovially. "Just Boomer."

Joy swallowed hard, hoping to send her nervousness down to some bottomless pit. "Boomer, this is Joy Chapin. I own Holland Arts over on the edge of downtown."

"Yes, ma'am." Boomer's voice boomed and echoed in her ear. "You threw my boys out yesterday."

"I didn't throw them out," Joy protested. "I just asked them to leave."

"Uh-huh."

"They were very nice about it," Joy assured him.

"Weren't they doing the job?"

"Oh, their work was fine." Joy took a deep breath. This was stupid. "I'm concerned about financing the installation and I had to get things straightened out before I let them continue.''

"We have you marked as paid in full," Boomer said.

"That was something Mr. Van Horne had arranged with his own funds," Joy explained. "I was, ah—"

"Looking around to see if you got the best deal," Boomer said, jumping in to finish her sentence.

"Yes, yes. That's it."

"That's what you got to do. Don't know if you can get something better unless you look."

"My sentiments exactly," Joy replied. "The business-like way. That's why I'm calling."

"Uh-huh."

Joy cleared her throat. "Ah, what kind of terms do you offer?"

"Cash only," Boomer replied. "In God we trust, everyone else pays cash."

"I see," Joy said slowly.

"I'm too small a guy to get involved in extending credit," Boomer explained. "I'd have to do credit checks, set aside an allowance for bad debts and that kind of thing. I got enough trouble just doing the basics, selling and servicing."

"Okay." Joy paused a moment. "Well, thank you for your time."

"I can give you a couple of banker names," Boomer said.

"I'll check with my own banker first," Joy replied.

"Let me know how things work out," Boomer said. "I sure do want to keep your business."

"I'll be back to you within a couple of days," Joy promised.

She stared a long time at the wall after she'd hung up. Should she really bother calling her banker? She had bought her building on a land contract and had another eighteen months of payments before she could even apply for a mortgage.

She'd borrowed to the hilt for the few counters and shelves she had in the store. Her banker had told her at that time that they were stretching things for her, extending themselves to help a businesswoman get started in the community. Probably wouldn't be a good idea to let them know that she needed more money.

So where did that leave her? What else did she have for collateral? At best, her furniture would bring her a few hundred at a garage sale and her truck was existing on a hope and a prayer. Plus she still owed Lou for his repair work.

Repairs from the night she'd broken down in front of Stephen's house. Her lip quivered, but Joy quickly got it under control with a sharp clamping down of her teeth. This wasn't the time to give her emotions free rein. She'd gambled and she'd lost.

She left her office, walking to the windows at the front of the store to stare out at the languid street, a small town slouching along under the heat of an unseasonably hot noonday sun.

She wasn't wrong in her belief that Stephen was hurting; everything the people at Adoption Identity Movement had said confirmed that. But she hadn't expected that in trying to find the key to Stephen's healing, she would lose him.

She wrapped her arms around her body and took a deep breath. Well, maybe losing him was the price that had to be paid for him to reconcile the past. He might not ever forgive her for her prying, but maybe he'd give more thought to AIM and how they could help him. The woman Joy had talked to said sometimes it takes months for a birth parent to take that first step. Joy'd given Stephen a little nudge, the only thing she could do, and now it was time to move on.

As wounded as her heart might be, she had the kids and a livelihood to think of.

Was she going to be able to keep her gallery open without asking someone for help?

Her parents would cut their vacation short if she called them, but they'd want to rush her and the kids back to Chicago. Her parents would devote their lives to taking care of the three of them, trying to protect them from "the slings and arrows of outrageous fortune." It was a way to survive, but only as an absolute last resort.

It had taken Joy long enough to grow up. She had no desire to return to the dependency of her childhood. It wouldn't do her kids or her parents any good.

Besides, she was really starting to enjoy Holland, Michigan. A little bit of unease fluttered in the pit of her stomach. Of course, now that relations had soured between her and Stephen things might not be that pleasant. But even with the problems, it was starting to feel like home.

So where did all this leave her? Joy sighed. That was very easy to see. She, Joy Chapin, was between the proverbial rock and a hard place.

Without Stephen's money, there would be no security system installed, which meant she would have no insurance. Which meant no more Holland Arts. At least, a Holland Arts as owned by Joy Chapin.

To keep her business, she would have to accept money from Stephen Van Horne. Stephen of the baby blues. Stephen whom she had loved and lost. Joy sighed and forced all personal feelings out of her mind.

She had to concentrate on the survival of her business, which in turn would determine the survival of herself and her family. This was no time to play a high school queen whose heart went pitter-patter because the captain of the football team walked by. Would she accept Mr. Van Horne's financial largess?

She paced her store for several minutes, grateful for the moment that no customers were present. Her mind twisted and turned, examining alternatives from every angle but everything led to one option. It was like it said in the Bible, that all paths of righteousness led to the same destination of truth. She really had no choice.

Joy put both hands to her face and wiped her eyes. The real question now was, did Stephen Van Horne's offer still stand?

The gray-haired secretary glared at Joy, frown lines saying she obviously remembered yesterday's turmoil.

"I just need to see Mr. Van Horne for a few minutes," Joy said. "And I promise not to become violent."

"One moment, please." The woman reached for the phone and buzzed Stephen's office. "Mrs. Chapin is here to see you. I told her you were quite busy and—"

For just the slightest moment, the secretary's lips squeezed into a thin line of disapproval, but her face quickly relaxed. "Very good, sir." She hung up the phone but didn't look up at Joy. "You may go in."

Joy paused a moment. She wasn't sure whether that was good news or bad, but then she straightened her shoulders and marched to Stephen's door. It would have been ridiculous to come all this way, then turn and run. Besides, running really wasn't an option in her old kit bag.

Stephen was standing behind his desk, waiting for her. His face was solemn while her stomach was tight and her mouth was dry. If she'd had any hope that this would blow over, it died at that moment. There was nothing in his eyes, not anger, not impatience. Nothing. This was a total mistake. Maybe running was an option she should consider.

"Good afternoon," he said.

Just a few short days ago, they had been high up in the blue skies of happiness and now they were circling each other warily like jungle cats. Joy blinked, close to tears.

But she wasn't a little girl anymore. There was no room of her own, paid for by Daddy, where she could fall into bed and cry crocodile tears of anguish. And there was no mommy to bake her brownies, telling her everything was going to be all right and nothing was her fault.

"Hello, Stephen," Joy replied.

"Won't you sit down, please?" His voice was soft and comfortable, like it would be when talking to any business associate. "Would you like anything to drink?"

Joy shook her head. They bounced the silence between themselves, each avoiding looking directly at the other.

Stephen broke first. "I'm sorry about what happened." He took a deep breath and slowly let it out. "I should have told you what I was doing. I was going to tell you everything but I was waiting for the right time. Things sort of got away from me."

"I'm sorry too," she said. "I'm sorry I got so upset about the system and I'm sorry I didn't talk to you about the Adoption Identity Movement before I gave them your name."

She wanted to say more, wanted to explain why she had done it, but the words wouldn't come. Her throat was tight and the tears kept trying to surface. Joy held all the gates tightly closed.

"It's all right," he said, but his words were politely dismissive, not lover-like. "That was my fault. I shouldn't have told you. I shouldn't have talked about Laura and me and the child, and all that stuff from the past. I should have left it buried."

"People talk about such things only when they feel a need to," she said softly.

Stephen shrugged. "Sometimes. Other times there is no need."

Joy's lips turned in a half smile. To a woman there was always a need. At the very least, it was just to get something off your chest, that in itself made a person feel better.

"Especially in a case like this," Stephen continued. "What's done is done and no amount of talking will change the facts."

He glanced down, shuffling some papers on his desk, but he hadn't moved quickly enough to hide the coldness in his eyes.

Joy knew then and there that she was grown-up. It was over between her and Stephen. The loving relationship they'd shared was through. But for her children's sake, for the sake of her dreams and hopes, she had to fight to continue their business relationship.

She was a survivor. She didn't need anybody to take care of her. She could take care of herself and those dependent on her.

"I didn't come here just to apologize," Joy said slowly. "I came to ask you something."

"Oh?" He looked at her, his baby blues placid and unblinking.

"I was hoping you would continue helping me."

"As your financial adviser," he said and nodded. "I'd be happy to."

Joy took a deep breath as if about to plunge into the icy torrent, then jumped in. "I want to keep my business. I think I can really make a go of it, but I need that security system. I don't know if you are still willing to lend me that money, but if you would, I would like to borrow it."

"Okay."

"I want this to be very businesslike. You know, with a regular payment plan. I'm sorry to bother you for it. But

he bank won't lend me any more money. And Boomer says
ie doesn't extend credit."

"Joy. I said, okay. I'm more than happy to lend you the
noney."

She felt relief wash over her. Not happiness, but relief.
The business at least was safe. "I want to pay it back."

"Fine."

"And at a fair rate of interest," she said.

He bobbed his head. "I'll take care of it."

"I'm not sure what kind of payment plan I should
have," Joy said. "Things are a little tight right now, but as
the business develops things should be better."

He nodded. "I'm sure they will be, but I'll take care of
it."

"Maybe something where my payments increase every six
months."

"I'll take care of it," Stephen said.

"I don't want you taking care of everything," she
snapped. "Then we'll have an argument again."

"Joy. I have to look at things. See what your cash flow
is. I'll figure things out, then present the facts to you. You'll
make the decisions."

She stared at him a moment. His hair had fallen over
onto his forehead, just begging to be brushed back, but she
kept her hands tightly clenched together. "Okay."

"Okay," he echoed.

Again the silence came to hang over them, heavy like the
dark blanket of a storm-threatening night. Joy wished there
were some way to right things. To set them back to the way
things were before they each started to meddle in the other's life.

"Well, thanks for all your help." She stood up. "I need
to get back to the shop. The kids will be getting back from
day camp soon."

He stood up and nodded.

"Not to mention a stray customer or two," she said.

"Right," he replied softly.

Joy waved tentatively, then hurried out of his office, past the hard-eyed secretary and out into the parking lot. Only when she was in the safe confines of the truck did she let the tears flow.

Stephen stared at the door a long, long time, stared at it until the whole wall blurred into a beige haze.

Joy hadn't worn any perfume today. She rarely did during working hours, but the scent of her freshness hung in the air. Clinging to each molecule of oxygen so that with every breath he brought her to life. Set her green eyes to dancing about the room, filled his eyes with the brightness of her smile and heard her soft laughter sing to him.

"Damn." His fist slammed his desk, giving him the unique pleasure of pain. "Mrs. Dehmers," he snapped into the intercom. "Bring me the Caulfield file, please."

What the hell was wrong with him? He was a professional, not some sissy poet. Most likely that was what was wrong with him. He was acting like someone he wasn't.

Businessmen learned from their experiences, good or bad. Then they put the past behind themselves. Poets kept the past in front and moped about it.

There was a light tap on the door, after which his secretary stepped into the office. She carried a stack of files in her hand.

"The Caulfield file, Mr. Van Horne." She put the stack on his desk. "Actually, I should say files. There's been a lot of activity with his real estate venture."

Stephen nodded and looked grimly at the pile of papers. "Does this include the data on the Dutch Village development?"

"No," she said, shaking her head. "That's registered as a separate corporation, so we have a separate file for it."

"You'd better get that for me also," Stephen said. "I've got a good bit of work to do on all of it." Mrs. Dehmers was barely able to suppress the sour face she wanted to make. "Don't worry, there won't be any weekend work for you."

"Oh, I don't mind usually," she said. "It's just that this Sunday is Father's Day and all the kids are coming this year for a picnic."

"Just get me the other papers," Stephen said. "This is all paperwork I need to do myself."

Once the door had closed behind Mrs. Dehmers's back, a dark, heavy gloom fell into Stephen's office, filling every corner and crack. The pall was so heavy that he almost had trouble breathing.

Father's Day. A stupid commercial gimmick to perk up the slow retail months of summer. Stephen dropped his face into his hands.

Oh, hell. They'd have a get-together for his father. They always did. All his siblings would descend on the Grand Haven cottage, bringing their gifts and their kids. He didn't want to go.

There was a movement at the door and he quickly looked up. Mrs. Dehmers stood there, one arm full of files and the other holding the door.

"You have a guest, Mr. Van Horne."

"Hello, Stephen," his mother said as she strode into his office.

"Hi, Mom."

Mrs. Dehmers followed close behind, dropped the files she was carrying on the corner of his desk and then quickly exited, closing the door.

His mother sat down, took a moment to gaze at the piles of paper scattered about his desk and made a face. "What are you doing?" she asked. "Building a wall around yourself?"

Stephen found himself unable to look her in the eye. His mother was an expert at the sharp phrase, the one that cut to the heart of things. "I have a lot of work to do."

He knew the words came out in a mumble but there wasn't anything he could do about it. Besides, from the look in her eye, it was obvious that his mother had things to say to him.

"How has Joy been?" she asked.

So that was it. Stephen swallowed hard. "Fine."

"Hmm."

"I've been busy." He shrugged. "She's been busy."

His mother let the silence drag out before she spoke. "I understand you two have had words."

Damn town. Stephen kept a smile glued to his face. Always someone around to report to your parents, no matter how old you were.

"Yeah. I advanced her some money to put in a security system at her store. She didn't think I discussed it properly with her."

Those blue eyes stared at him, peering deep into his soul, scratching at the doors, looking for the truth. Everyone told him that he got his eyes from his mother, but Stephen knew that he could never freeze his as deeply as she could hers.

"You told her about Michael," his mother said.

How did she know? Anyone could have told her. Everyone in town knew about it. That's the way it was in a small town.

"So it slipped out," he said offhandedly. "No big deal."

"Michael is almost a man now." His mother's words came out gently, like a soft summer's rain. "Maybe now is the time."

"Right." A painful laugh escaped Stephen's throat. "He should be big enough by now to spit in my eye."

His mother's expression stayed calm but Stephen felt his own gut twist in pain. He was shocked at the words that had slipped out of his mouth. All these years he'd been telling himself that he didn't want to just drop in on Michael, upset what was probably a well-ordered life. But maybe he was just a coward. Maybe what he was really afraid of was rejection, the rejection of his own son.

"Well, anyway, I just came by to give you your gift assignment," his mother said. "I know I usually call, but I was in town to visit Mabel Fulmer in the hospital so I thought I might as well drop by."

"Gift assignment?"

"Sunday is Father's Day." Those blue eyes seized Stephen's and held them tight. "You are coming, aren't you?"

Stephen tugged but he could not pull himself loose from those eyes.

He couldn't go. He just wasn't good with this family personal relationships crap. Every time he tried he screwed it up. Laura, Donna, Joy. Everybody.

He was good at his job and that was where he should stay. Sure, it was lonely sometimes, but at least he didn't hurt anybody. And with his civic activities he actually helped people. Maybe not directly, but he put the infrastructures and systems in place for others to do it. He was a back-room type of guy.

"I'm sorry, Mom. But I have a lot of work."

"I see." His mother stood up.

"I'll call Dad."

"All right."

His mother walked to the door. One didn't have to be too sensitive to read her body language. She wasn't pleased with him at all.

"Oh, Mom."

She partially turned to face him. "Yes?"

"What am I supposed to buy Dad?"

She just stared at him.

"You know," Stephen said. "What gift am I assigned?"

"That's okay," she replied. "He really has more than he needs."

The door closed quietly behind his mother and Stephen grabbed at the Caulfield files. The words were blurred on the paper. Damn it. Big boys didn't cry.

By Friday morning, Joy was handling things better. She'd resigned herself to being without Stephen in her personal life, while still seeing him on business matters. When his secretary had called yesterday, Joy's heart hadn't even raced. She had known it was just business.

"I have an appointment with Mr. Van Horne," Joy told Mrs. Dehmers when she got to his office.

"Go right in. He's expecting you."

"Joy." Stephen nodded toward a chair. "Why don't you have a seat?" He gave her a quick smile, then turned his attention to the papers before him. "I could have mailed these to you. You didn't have to come all the way downtown."

No, she didn't have to. She could just stay completely away from Stephen. They could be strictly consultant/client, communicating by mail and telephone, messages through Mrs. Dehmers. But she couldn't do that, not quite yet.

"I just thought this would be easier, in case I had any questions," she said. Like, why don't we go out to dinner with a little dancing tonight?

"It's quite straightforward," Stephen replied, as he pushed the papers across the desk toward her. "But that doesn't mean we can't change something, if you have a problem with it."

Joy picked up the loan agreement and tried to focus her eyes on the words and numbers. If she had a problem with anything, they could fix it. She had a problem with their staying apart. Could they fix that?

But nothing happened. Stephen stayed on his side of the desk and she on hers. Disappointment sharpened her eyesight. She started reading the agreement as Stephen sat— silent.

"My payments don't start until October 1," Joy said.

"Right." Stephen's voice was brisk and businesslike. "You need all the cash you have right now to keep your business going. Plus by October, we should have a better idea of how your operation is going. If we have to, we can make adjustments to your payment schedule then."

Joy nodded and glanced through the rest of the pages. "You've never sent me a bill for all the work you've done for me," she said.

"That's okay," he said, waving a hand dismissively.

A little spark of irritation flared within Joy and she took a moment to push it to the background. If it was going to be all business between them, then it should be all business. "I don't need charity," she said quietly.

"We all need help when we're starting out," Stephen replied.

"I know, but I'm not expecting a free ride."

"It's not a free ride," Stephen said. "It's just someone who's established, giving you a helping hand."

"I just don't want our arrangement to be a one-way street."

"Don't worry about it."

She put on her brightest smile. "It seems that I owe you at least a lunch or two."

"I said you were going to make it," Stephen said, laughing. "That doesn't mean that you're flush at the moment. You still have to watch your pennies."

"How about a home-cooked meal instead?"

Joy held her breath. The words had just popped out. Sure, she'd been thinking about asking him, stewing about it, in fact. But now the invitation was out, lying at his feet, and her heart felt in danger of being broken all over again.

"That's okay," Stephen answered and gathered up some papers. "I think it best we stay away from all that."

She let her breath out slowly, her smile wanting to fall off her face, her heart wanting to curl up and die. It took all of Joy's strength to keep a mask of utter calm on her face.

"You're probably right." She stood up and held her hand out. "Thanks for the security system and the payment plan."

Stephen stood up, his smile equaling her joviality. "Glad to do it."

They shook hands and Joy strode out of the office, head high and shoulders back. She even gave the dour Mrs. Dehmers a hearty farewell.

Once in her truck though, Joy slumped against the steering wheel a long moment, but she didn't cry. It was over. She was beyond tears, beyond any easy fixes. It was time to get on with her life.

It was close to noon so instead of going to the store, she drove by the park to pick the kids up from day camp. This was what mattered; this was a treasure that she would never put in jeopardy.

Katie dashed over when she caught sight of Joy. Robbie dragged along in the rear. He seemed to be doing a lot of that lately, Joy thought as she hugged Katie.

"How is it going, sport?" she called over to Robbie.

"Okay," he mumbled as he opened the door for Katie, then climbed in himself.

"Feeling okay?" Joy asked.

"Yeah," Robbie replied.

"You've seemed down in the mouth lately," Joy said.

"I said I was okay," Robbie snapped. "Okay?"

Joy started the truck as the kids got their seat belts buckled. Why shouldn't kids have the right to be down? She probably hadn't been a bundle of brightness herself lately.

"We was making Father's Day presents," Katie announced, holding up a plastic coffee mug. It had a crayon drawing, obviously made by Katie, applied to the surface.

Father's Day. Great. "That's really nice, honey." Joy prayed her voice didn't echo the hopelessness she felt.

"They made us make a stupid old belt," Robbie said, every word touched with sour.

And who was he to give it to? Joy understood all too well.

"I'm giving my present to Stevie," Katie said.

"How? He ain't been around lately," Robbie pointed out. "I'll see if Grandpa wants a stupid old belt or else I'll just throw it away."

"I bet Grandpa will love a new belt," Joy said brightly, but nobody bothered to answer.

Chapter Fifteen

"Oh, this will be perfect," the woman cried, catching sight of the playful puppy sculpture. "I'm so glad you're open on Father's Day."

Joy just smiled as the woman oohed and ahed over the sculpture and the store itself. She was staying open on Father's Day for economic reasons, but also emotional ones. The kids were there helping her put out some new merchandise. Seeing as how she didn't have them help very often, it was turning out to be an adventure.

They had talked about Paul this morning and thought up gifts to give him—Katie was going to brush her teeth better because he'd want her to and Robbie was going to take out the garbage without being told—the day wasn't as mopey and gloomy as she had feared. No one mentioned Stephen.

"I can't imagine a better gift for Harvey to give," the woman said, carrying the statue over to the counter. "I'll take it."

Joy pulled out some tissue paper and carefully wrapped the sculpture. "Is Harvey your son?"

"Goodness, no. Our puppy." She pulled her wallet out. "I don't suppose you have gift cards, do you?"

"Mommy." Katie climbed onto the stool next to Joy, tugging at her mother's sleeve. "Mommy, Grandpa's on the phone."

Joy put the sculpture into a box as the customer perused the little gift enclosures Joy had in a stand on the counter. "I'll be there in a minute, sweetie. You and Robbie talk to him. Thank him for the packages they keep sending us."

Katie made a face. "I'm tired of jelly."

"Thank him anyway."

Katie climbed down and went around the corner to Joy's office, mumbling all the way. This was the first Father's Day Joy hadn't spent with her own father. She was glad he called.

"I'll take this one." The woman handed Joy the card along with her charge plate. "This is such a quaint little place. I'm going to have to come back here when I have more time to browse."

"Please do."

In a few minutes, the woman and Harvey's gift had departed and Joy was alone. She pushed the hair off the back of her neck and sighed. It had been a long few days, a long week. She walked back to her office, wondering what Stephen was doing. Probably at his folks' place, but would his mind be there or on his son?

"Yeah, it was really neat," Robbie was saying as she got to the door of her office. "They had this police dog that checked everything out first, just like on TV."

Oh, no! She hadn't planned on telling her parents about that little episode.

"Yeah, she's here," Robbie said handing the phone to Joy. "Grandpa wants to talk to you."

She bet he did. "Hi, Dad. Happy Father's Day."

"What's this about a break-in?" her father asked, his voice booming across the lines as if he was next door. "Why didn't you call us?"

"We called the police, Dad. They were closer."

"Joy, you know what I mean."

"It was just vandalism, nothing was taken. And I've got a security system installed now."

"Well, thank God for that."

"Yeah." God and Stephen. "So how's the vacation so far? We've really enjoyed your little packages."

They talked for a few more minutes, thankfully never returning to the subject of the break-in. Could it be that her parents were enjoying their independence as much as she was hers? When she got off the phone, the silence seemed oppressive.

"Well, want to get back to that unpacking?" she asked, trying to force enthusiasm into her voice.

"Okay." Katie was out the door in a flash.

"Jeez, it's boring, Mom," Robbie moaned and struggled to his feet. "Can I go outside for a while?"

"Sure."

She watched from the back window as he shuffled out to the yard and kicked at the dirt for an eternity. Finally he climbed up into the cherry tree, sitting against the trunk and staring off into space. Poor kid. She felt his misery, echoed it in her heart, but didn't know how to solve it. Stephen didn't want their love; he didn't seem to want anyone's love.

"Mommy, come on," Katie said. "You said I could put out the little horses."

"So I did, partner, so I did." She put on a big smile for Katie and let herself be led over to the display cases.

Katie lifted a carved horse from the box and put it on the bottom shelf. "Mommy, how come Stevie don't come over no more?"

"I don't know, honey. I guess he's busy."

"Does he have the chicken pox? Maybe we should be his knight and rescue him."

Joy had tried. Some people just don't want rescuing though. "He's just an important businessman," Joy said. "He really helped us out for a while, but now he's got to help other people out."

"He got to bring other little girls movies?"

Joy shook her head. "No, I don't think so. I think he did that just for you." She wished he did have other people, other families he was close to. He wouldn't be hurting so much if he did.

"When can I give him his mug? Can we go to his house today?"

"I've got to keep the store open, honey. We can't go anywhere now."

Katie just looked at her for a long moment as if she could read something in Joy's words. Finally she looked away, busying herself with some more of the horse carvings. Why did Joy feel like the girl had read the truth in her heart, that Stephen was never coming back here?

"Yeah, well, you have a good Father's Day, Dad," Stephen said heartily. "And I'm real sorry I wasn't able to make it up there. Like I said, things are hectic around here."

"Good thing you're young enough to handle it," his father joked.

"Maybe next week I can take you and Mom out to dinner."

"Whatever," his father said. "Look, you take care of yourself. Don't work so hard that you neglect that nice little Joy you brought up here. The ladies don't like to be ignored."

"Won't do that, Dad. Gotta go."

Stephen hung the phone up, feeling like he had been through a war. He closed his eyes and let the silence surround him. What was the matter with him? He should be up there with his family. He'd been up there every Father's Day for years, missing only one when he was married and they went to see Donna's folks. So why this year couldn't he manage it?

Joy. That was the reason, pure and simple. She'd awoken something in him that, like the dragons in fairy tales, should have been left sleeping.

He closed his eyes and saw her before him. Joy. His father had been right, her name suited her! She carried so much exuberance, so much sunshine around with her that it almost hurt. She had come into his life and turned everything topsy-turvy. Which is exactly why he needed to buckle down and put everything back in place.

He'd finished with the Caulfield projects and pulled over a stack of Jaycee newsletters. Lord, but he'd gotten behind in everything once Joy had come into his life.

The first newsletter dealt with some upcoming elections, the next one with the sports programs the Jaycees were running. The soccer program concluded a couple of weeks ago; baseball and softball were in full swing, with both programs holding their annual father/child game on Father's Day.

Damn. Stephen put the newsletters down. He'd promised Robbie he'd go with him to the game. Why hadn't Robbie called to tell him when it was?

Because Stephen had been moping around like a spoiled little kid, that was why.

He hurried upstairs and changed into shorts and a T-shirt, grabbed his mitt and raced out to the car. He'd never meant for the kids to suffer just because he'd lost control of things. This little example showed just how lousy he was at relationships.

He pulled up in front of the store and, noticing the Open sign in the window, went inside through the front door. Joy and Katie were working in front of a display case.

"Stevie!" Katie cried and flew over to hug his knees.

"Hi, kid." His gaze fell on Joy. She looked as beautiful as ever, her eyes deep green pools that he longed to lose himself in. "I was supposed to take Robbie to a father/son game. Am I too late?"

Joy just shook her head. "I have no idea. He didn't say a word to me."

She walked over to the window to call Robbie inside, her body moving with a fluid grace that tugged at his soul. Lord, how he missed her! Yet what had he given her but pain? A security system and some proper business procedures. The extent of the good he could offer anyone.

Robbie came dragging inside, his gloomy face bursting into a smile when he saw Stephen. That hurt just as much as Katie's delight at seeing him, but Stephen just buried the pain he felt.

"Hey, what time's our game?" Stephen asked him.

"One-thirty," Robbie said.

"Looks like we've just got time to get there then."

Robbie nodded, looking like he'd won the lottery, and raced off, presumably to change his shoes and get his mitt. That left Stephen with Katie and Joy.

"You ain't been around," Katie said accusingly.

"I know, kid. I'm really busy." He smiled down at the little girl, but his eyes kept straying back to Joy.

"You didn't have to come for Robbie," she said slowly. "It means a lot to him, but it wasn't necessary."

"Yeah, it was. I made a promise."

He wanted to say all sorts of other things, wanted to make her understand that he never meant to hurt any of them, that he just wasn't good with relationships. But it sounded like such a lame excuse, a weakness that he should have identified years ago and protected others from.

"I'm all set," Robbie said, flying down the stairs. He carried a small duffel bag in one hand, his baseball cap in the other. "This is gonna be great."

Joy walked them to the front door. "Why don't you come back after the game and have dinner with us?"

Stephen just shrugged, looking away at something safer. "I've got a lot of work waiting for me at home."

"Right. I forgot." Her voice was even, carefully controlled. "Have fun."

That wasn't necessarily on his agenda, not anymore, not without her. But he managed to find some sort of a smile to put on his face by the time he climbed into the car.

"So which park are we at?"

"Prospect." Robbie was busy putting his seat belt on, then settled back in the seat with a grin. "Boy, this is great. We're gonna win, I bet."

"Oh, yeah? How do you figure that?"

He wanted to ask the boy why he hadn't called, especially if it meant as much to him as it apparently did. But the answer seemed obvious. Stephen wasn't around. It didn't matter what he had promised; he wasn't around to prove that he'd meant it.

"The dads have to run their bases backward," Robbie said. "And the kids don't get any strikes called on them. It's gonna be great."

"Sounds like it."

But Stephen actually had a good time. The boys did clobber the dads and Robbie got two hits, walking the other times he was at bat. Better than that, he caught Stephen's one hit to make him out. The boy's face just glowed as the boys crowded around him in congratulations. Afterward, Stephen bought each of them a hot dog at the concession stand and they sat in some shade, eating.

"My dad never came to any of my games when I played before," Robbie said suddenly.

"I guess he was a pretty busy guy."

"He used to say he'd come, but he never did."

Was that the reason why Robbie hadn't really expected Stephen to show up? "Your mom said he was trying real hard to make money to buy you guys all sorts of things. Some dads think that's most important."

"I wish he had come just once. Even if he didn't have time to coach or be there all the time like some of the dads, I wish he had come at least once."

"I bet he's sorry he didn't," Stephen said. Robbie looked confused. "If he'd known what little time he was going to have with you guys, I bet he would have done things differently. He probably thought he could get all caught up on those things later, but then there didn't turn out to be a later."

Robbie lay back in the grass, digesting that for about a split second. "Do you think I'm ever going to be really good?"

"You had a great game today."

"But that was with different rules. If I don't get to be real good, who's going to take care of Mom?"

"How about your mom? She's doing just fine now, isn't she?"

"Grandpa told me that I was the man of the family now and that I had to take care of her."

Stephen just stared ahead of him for long moments, the breeze carrying the laughter from another game over toward him. What did "man of the family" mean? He had wanted to be the man of his little family, but had lost the chance. The only good things he had given Joy were as a result of his business expertise, not his role in their relationship. How could he advise a ten-year-old when he had failed so miserably himself?

"I don't think your grandfather meant you had to support her financially," Stephen said. "She can do that herself just fine. I think he meant to take care of her in other ways, like offering to help when she seems tired, making her smile when she seems unhappy."

"Like being her friend."

"Yeah. Exactly."

"I could even do that now."

"Right. No waiting until you sign a major league contract."

Robbie got to his feet. "Maybe we ought to get back then. She's been kind of sad lately. Maybe I should be there to cheer her up."

"Okay."

Stephen said no more though he felt the burden of his guilt increase. They walked to the car and were soon back at the store. Stephen pulled up in front.

"Thanks a lot," Robbie said. He undid his seat belt but seemed in no hurry to get out of the car. He reached into his duffel bag. "I made this in day camp. I was gonna give it to my grandpa, but if you want it, you can have it." He handed Stephen a belt.

Stephen just looked at it, at the star design hand-pounded into the leather and felt a burning behind his eyes, a tightness in his throat. "It's great. Thank you," he managed to say somehow.

Robbie opened the door. "You know, when I get older I hope I can be a friend just like you. Helping my mom and Katie and me."

The burning threatened to get out of control. "Right." Stephen looked straight ahead, concentrating on the stop sign up at the corner, on keeping the letters firm and un-hazy.

"You coming in?" Robbie asked.

"Sorry, no," Stephen said. "Got a lot to do."

"Okay." Robbie closed the door. "See ya." He waved and then raced up to the house.

A friend just like you. The words echoed in Stephen's mind, mocking even as they seared a hole into his consciousness. What kind of a friend had he been to Joy? One she was better off staying away from.

Joy dumped the pot into the soapy dishwater. "Sounds like you had a great time," she told Robbie.

"Yeah, we did. It was great." He put the stack of plates on the counter by the dishwasher and went back to the table for their glasses.

Joy just smiled after him. He must have said it was great about a hundred times since he got home, along with the fact that he'd given Stephen the belt he'd made.

"When am I going to get to give Stevie my present?" Katie asked.

"I don't know, honey. I wished we'd thought of it while he was here."

While Katie and Robbie loaded the dishwasher, Joy washed the pots, scrubbing at the dried edges of potatoes that had stuck to the pan. She wished she could scrub away at Stephen's pain as easily. Was what she had done so bad that he couldn't forgive her? They'd been growing close, very close, and she could have sworn that she wasn't the only one to have deeper feelings. Yet in the end, he'd been willing to throw them away.

Or was he?

Everything she knew about Stephen said he had to be in control. How did he feel about not being in control? Or wasn't that pretty obvious? He didn't know how not to be in control.

"Mom, can we play out back?" Robbie asked.

She turned to find the two kids staring at her, their jobs all done. "Sure, guys."

She paused as they ran out, her breath catching as she strained to hear the even rhythm of their feet on the stairs. The way they raced down them, she was sure someday they would fall. Maybe it was just a mother's job to worry every time her kids left her side. How did Stephen handle not knowing if his son was all right?

Joy walked to the window and stared down at the kids. They were planes or birds or something, flying around the yard in happy abandonment.

It wasn't parenthood that brought the worries; it was love. When you loved someone as much as she loved the kids—or Stephen—your happiness was totally in their hands. If they hurt, she hurt. If they were happy, so was she. She had no control over anything. She was a puppet and Stephen pulled the strings. His smile brought sunshine into her life; his silence despair.

And what was he feeling? If he was hiding from her, from his son, it was because he felt out of control. Did that mean he loved her?

Joy turned from the window, biting at her lower lip. Was that a reasonable deduction? Was that sane logic? She wished she trusted her own instincts more. She closed her eyes and took a deep breath. If she did nothing, Stephen would stay locked in his safe little business world. If she took a chance, she might break him free of it. The worst she could do would be embarrassed and, hell, she'd been there before. Maybe not to this extent, but then as a free and independent woman, she had the right to all sorts of new experiences like being a knight in shining armor herself.

A half hour later, she was pulling up to Stephen's house. The kids were at Marlene's and she was ready to fight for what she wanted. No more sitting around and waiting for someone to give it to her.

A deep breath gave her the strength to walk up the long sidewalk. The doorbell seemed outrageously loud, loud enough to alert the neighborhood that something was happening here. She clutched the two boxes in her hands.

Stephen pulled open the door. Surprise rode his eyes briefly, mixing with a flash of something she hoped was pleasure, before wariness took over.

"Joy. Hello." He frowned. "Nothing's wrong, is there?"

"Nope. Not like you mean, anyway."

He had the door open wide enough for her to enter, so she did. Best to humiliate herself in private. He was just staring at her, waiting, so she waved the hand holding the videotapes in the air.

"I've brought you a present. *Pinocchio* and *The Velveteen Rabbit*. Katie highly recommends them. Actually, I do, too. Best things in the world for when you're feeling blue."

"Joy."

She knew what he was going to say. She could read it in his eyes, hear it in his voice, but she wouldn't let him send her away. Not yet.

"Hey, look, we've both apologized, so there shouldn't be problems, right? Except we both know there are and that it's my fault."

"No, it's not. It's mine. I never should have—"

She put her hand over his lips to keep him from speaking. The touch jolted her. She wanted so much to be in his arms, to feel the wonder of his embrace. She pulled slightly away.

"You see, I was sitting 'round today watching these movies and I realized that I was just like Pinocchio, not really alive until you came along. I was just like the rabbit,

not alive until I was loved. See, I became a whole new per
son because of you. Strong—''

"You always were strong."

"Capable—"

"You always were capable."

"Bossy."

"You always were . . . wonderful."

The tiniest of smiles was in his eyes and she took hop
enough to step closer. "Stephen, I love you, but you don'
have to love me. It's okay. I've never been in control of m'
life before, so I can manage without control now. But
don't want to feel that I lost you because you didn't know
what was in my heart."

There was the longest silence as he stared into her eyes
She heard the clock ticking in the living room, the fa
whirring in the kitchen and the world spinning outside
Then Stephen turned away. He leaned against the doorwa'
to the living room, his forehead against his forearm. He
heart sank.

"You know," Stephen said, "today Robbie told me he'
supposed to be the man of the house. I tried to help him se
what that meant, and discovered I didn't have any bette
idea than he did. The man of the house takes care of hi
family. He supports them, brings home his paycheck. Cut
the grass and drives the car when they go out."

He turned to face her, his eyes deep and dark with som
unreadable emotion. "Pitiful, isn't it? It reads like som
sitcom from the fifties."

He took a step closer to her and she began to hope tha
that emotion would end in laughter and sunshine.

"Then I started thinking about being the man of you
house and all sorts of other images came to mind. Making
you eat when you're dead tired, giving you my shoulder to
lean on when you're scared, and loving you late at nigh
when the day is over."

"Stephen."

He shook his head. "I'm the one that came alive because of you and I'm scared to death that I'll fail again. I let Laura down. I let my son down. I never really gave all of myself to Donna, but I just can't risk you."

She just smiled and stepped into his arms. They closed about her as if they had no choice. "There's absolutely no risk involved. You see, I have it from the most respected of authorities that I'm going to be very successful."

"I don't want to hurt you, Joy. I love you too much."

She kissed his lips, a tender brief touch that was all she dared. "You won't because you've never hurt anybody. Not Laura, who made her own choices. Not your son, who was given a good solid set of parents. Not Donna, even if it didn't work out. Someday you'll see that, too."

He looked down at her, his eyes so filled with love that she wanted to cry. She didn't though, just reached up to meet his lips with a hunger all her own.

The touch was electric, stirring a passion that was new, wild and strong. Broken free of its bonds, it celebrated their newly found love with a strength that left her shaking when Stephen pulled slightly away.

"After we get married, we'll live here," he said. "I've got lots of room and a better backyard for the kids to play in."

"Stephen."

"You can still have your store, of course, but—"

"Stephen." She put a little more force into her voice.

He stopped and frowned at her. She just waited, smiling ever so sweetly at him until he caught on.

His grin was a kid's with a new toy. "Will you marry me?" he asked carefully.

"You bet."

"And think it would be a good idea to live here?"

"Sounds great."

He kissed her, slowly and very thoroughly, before h
spoke again. His arms stayed tightly around her. "Are yo
going to be patient with me when I get bossy?"

"Maybe."

"Are you going to be mad at me when I try to help you?"

"Maybe."

His look changed, a tentative edge crept in. "Are yo
going to come with me tomorrow to Grand Rapids?"

"What's in Grand Rapids?"

"My first counseling session."

"Oh, Stephen." Her love for him was never stronger. H
was on the way. He'd taken that first step and was closer t
being whole. She loved him so much. "Of course, I'll com
if you want me to."

He held her then, and she held him. Supporting eac
other, rescuing each other. She felt safe, she felt needed
She closed her eyes and lay against his chest. Her swee
knight.

"What do you say we tell the kids?" Stephen suggested

"I'd like that."

He let her go slowly, though his hands still held hers
"Maybe after that, we could all go up to the cottage and se
my folks."

"Sounds perfect."

Epilogue

The Christmas turkey was in the oven, filling the house with the wonderful aromas of the holiday. The kids were playing board games in the living room with their two grandfathers, while the rest of them filled up the kitchen.

"We always put vanilla ice cream inside the Yule log cake," Stephen argued.

"We use chocolate," Beth told him, then glanced accusingly over at Joy. "I thought marriage was supposed to mellow him."

Joy just laughed as she set the dinner rolls on the cookie sheet. "Not in regards to old family recipes."

"Frankly, I don't remember ever making a Yule log cake before," Trudy pointed out.

"Mom!" The protest came jointly from Beth and Stephen, which sent both Joy and her mother into gales of laughter.

Joy was still chuckling as she went through to the front of the house to answer the door a few minutes later. She never thought she'd be so happy. Everything was perfect, well, almost everything. And she had decorated the house to show that. The huge Christmas tree seemed to fill up the living room with its glittering. Pine garlands hung from the banister, held in place by bright red bows. But best of all was the laughter that always seemed present.

She pulled open the front door, the ribbon of sleigh bells jangling with the motion. A young man in an army uniform stood there. He took his hat off as he greeted her.

"Sorry to bother you, ma'am," he said hesitantly. "My name is Micky Burnette and I'm looking for a Mr. Stephen Van Horne." The young man's bright, blue eyes reflected uncertainty. His hair was clipped short, but as blond as any little Dutch boy's.

Joy just stared at him for a long moment, unbelievable excitement welling up in her. There was no doubt in her mind who this stranger was—he was a younger Stephen with Beth's slight build. What a wonderful Christmas this would be!

"Come in," she said. The warm sound of family laughter drifted out to welcome him.

"If this is a bad time..."

"Not at all. Let me take your coat."

He slipped out of his long overcoat and waited uneasily as Joy hung it in the closet. "I would have called, but we've got leave for the day and some of the guys were driving up this way..."

"No, this is great. Stephen will be so glad to meet you."

The young man followed her through Stephen's office and into the small back parlor. She could hear Stephen and Beth's bickering continuing.

"Are you an ice-cream lover, too?" Joy asked.

The young man grinned, turning into a little boy. "How'd you know? My dad always said—" He stopped, confused and embarrassed.

"Your dad," Joy agreed.

The boy relaxed and his grin came back. "My dad always said I must have ice cream in my blood the way I always eat it."

Joy waved him into a chair. "The old ancestors strike again. I'll go get Stephen."

She left him in the small back parlor and hurried off to get Stephen. He and Beth were still arguing over the cake filling.

"'Fraid you're going to have to let Beth handle that," Joy said, taking Stephen's hand. "You've got somebody here to see you."

"Now? Who is it? Stan Herman. I can't believe that man would come on Christmas."

"It's not Stan." She opened the parlor door. Michael had been standing in front of a shelf of framed photos and turned to face them.

Stephen stopped just inside the doorway, as if recognizing the boy. She could feel a tidal wave of emotions race through him and squeezed his hand in reassurance.

"You two have two hours before dinner's going to be ready," she said. "Take your time." She brushed away moisture from her eyes as she softly closed the door and went back to the kitchen.

"Looks like we'll have another place to set," she said.

Beth looked up from the thin sheet of cake she had coated with vanilla ice cream. She was in the middle of a second coat, this time chocolate. "He'd better like ice cream as much as we all do."

"I'm sure he'll fit in just fine."

* * * * *

COMING NEXT MONTH

AVAILABLE THIS MONTH:

Silhouette Special Edition®

Commencing in May . . .

The stories of the men and women who ride
the range, keep the home fires burning and
live to love.

Cowboy Country

by Myrna Temte

For Pete's Sake (#739) - May
Silent Sam's Salvation (#745) - June
Heartbreak Hank (#751) - July

Where the soul is free and the heart
unbound . . . and the good guys still win.
Don't miss *For Pete's Sake*, #739, the first
of three stories rustled up with love from
Silhouette Special Edition.

SEDAW-1R

FREE GIFT OFFER

To receive your free gift, send us the specified number of proofs-of-purchase from any specially marked Free Gift Offer Harlequin or Silhouette book with the Free Gift Certificate properly completed, plus a check or money order (do not send cash) to cover postage and handling payable to Harlequin/Silhouette Free Gift Promotion Offer. We will send you the specified gift.

FREE GIFT CERTIFICATE

ITEM	A. GOLD TONE EARRINGS	B. GOLD TONE BRACELET	C. GOLD TONE NECKLACE
# of proofs-of-purchase required	3	6	9
Postage and Handling	$1.75	$2.25	$2.75
Check one	☐	☐	☐

Name: _____

Address: _____

City: _____ State: _____ Zip Code: _____

Mail this certificate, specified number of proofs-of-purchase and a check or money order for postage and handling to: HARLEQUIN/SILHOUETTE FREE GIFT OFFER 1992, P.O. Box 9057, Buffalo, NY 14269-9057. Requests must be received by July 31, 1992.

PLUS—Every time you submit a completed certificate with the correct number of proofs-of-purchase, you are automatically entered in our MILLION DOLLAR SWEEPSTAKES! No purchase or obligation necessary to enter. See below for alternate means of entry and how to obtain complete sweepstakes rules.

✂ SS2U

ONE PROOF-OF-PURCHASE
To collect your fabulous FREE GIFT you must include the necessary FREE GIFT proofs-of-purchase with a properly completed offer certificate.

(See inside back cover for offer details)